IN DARKNESS

NICK LAKE was born in Britain but grew up in Luxembourg, where his father worked for the European Parliament. Nick works in publishing by day and writes in every spare moment he can find. In 2012, his powerful and moving novel *In Darkness*, about the Haitian earthquake, was published for adults and older teenagers, receiving huge acclaim. *Hostage Three* is his very different but equally powerful new novel for teenagers.

Nick lives near Oxford with his wife and family. His long commute to work gives his imagination time to explore places he's never visited.

IN DARKNESS

Nick Lake

BLOOMSBURY

LONDON · NEW DELHI · NEW YORK · SYDNEY

Bloomsbury Publishing, London, New Delhi, New York and Sydney

First published in Great Britain in January 2012 by Bloomsbury Publishing Plc
This paperback edition published 2013

50 Bedford Square, London, WC1B 3DP

Pages 15–18 include dialogue that is based on original
speeches by Jean-Bertrand Aristide

A CIP catalogue record for this book is available from the British Library

ISBN 978 1 4088 3034 5

1 3 5 7 9 10 8 6 4 2

Typeset by Hewer Text UK Ltd, Edinburgh
Printed and Bound in Great Britain by CPI (UK) Ltd, Croydon CR0 4YY

www.in-darkness.org
www.bloomsbury.com

For the people of Site Solèy

At the beginning of the troubles in Haiti, I felt that I was destined to great things. When I received this divine intimation I was four-and-fifty years of age; I could neither read nor write.

Toussaint l'Ouverture in a letter to Napoléon Bonaparte

Though fallen thyself, never to rise again,
Live, and take comfort. Thou hast left behind
Powers that will work for thee; air, earth, and skies;
There's not a breathing of the common wind
That will forget thee; thou hast great allies;
Thy friends are exultations, agonies,
And love, and man's unconquerable mind.

William Wordsworth, To Toussaint l'Ouverture

NOW

I am the voice in the dark, calling out for your help.

I am the quiet voice that you hope will not turn to silence, the voice you want to keep hearing cos it means someone is still alive. I am the voice calling for you to come and dig me out. I am the voice in the dark, asking you to unbury me, to bring me from the grave out into the light, like a zombi.

I am a killer and I have been killed, too, over and over; I am constantly being born. I have lost more things than I have found; I have destroyed more things than I have built. I have seen babies abandoned in the trash and I have seen the dead come back to life.

I first shot a man when I was twelve years old.

I have no name. There are no names in the darkness cos there is no one else, only me, and I already know who I am (I am the voice in the dark, calling out for your help), and I have no questions for myself and no need to call upon myself for anything, except to remember.

I am alone.

I am dying.

In darkness, I count my blessings like Manman taught me.

One: I am alive.

Two: there is no two.

I see nothing and I hear nothing. This darkness, it's like something solid. It's like it's inside me.

I used to shout for help, but then after a while I couldn't tell if I was speaking through my mouth or just in my head, and that scared me. Anyway, shouting makes me thirsty.

So I don't shout anymore. I only touch and smell. This is how I know what is in here with me, in the darkness.

There is a light, except it doesn't work. But I can tell it's a light cos I feel the smooth glass of the lamp, and I remember how it used to sit on the little table by my bed. That is another thing – there is a bed in here. It was my bed before the walls fell down. I can feel its soft mattress and its broken slats.

I smell blood. There is anpil blood in this place, on me and all around me. I can tell it's blood cos it smells of iron and death. And cos I've smelled blood before. I grew up in the bidonville – it's a smell you get used to.

Not all of the blood is mine, but some of it is.

I used to touch the bodies, but I don't do that anymore. They smell, too.

*

I don't know what happened. I was in bed minding my own zafè, then everything shook and I fell and the darkness started. Or maybe everything else fell.

I'm in Canapé-Vert Hospital, this I know. It's a private hospital, so I figure the blancs must be paying for it. I don't know why they brought me here after they killed Biggie and put this bullet in my arm. Maybe they felt bad about it.

Yesterday – or possibly it was longer ago than that – Tintin came to see me. It was before the world fell down. Tintin must have used his pass – the one that Stéphanie got him – to get out of Site Solèy through the checkpoints. I wonder how Stéphanie is feeling now that Biggie is dead, cos she's UN and she shouldn't have been sleeping with a gangster. She must have really loved him.

Tintin signed my bandage. I told him it's only plaster casts that people sign, not bandages, but he didn't know the difference. Tintin doesn't know much about anyen.

Example: you're thinking that he signed his name on my bandage, but he didn't. He signed *Route 9*, like he writes everywhere. Tintin doesn't just tag. He likes to shout, Route 9, when we're rolling in the streets, too – Route 9 till I die, dumb stuff like that. I would look at the people we were driving past and say to him:

— You don't know who these people are. They might be from Boston. They might cap you.

— That's the point, he would say. I'm not afraid of them. I'm Route 9.

I thought Tintin was a cretin, but I didn't say so. Old people

3

like my manman say Route 9 and Boston used to mean something back in the day. Like, Route 9 was for Aristide and Boston was for the rebels. Now they don't mean anything at all. I was in Route 9 with Tintin, but I didn't write it anywhere and I didn't shout it out, either. If anyone was going to kill me, I wanted it to be for a good reason. Not cos I said the wrong name.

Anyway, when I was rolling with the Route 9 crew, I didn't want the Boston thugs to know me. I didn't want them to know me till I had them at the end of my gun, and they would have to give my sister back. I tried that in the end. It didn't work out how I wanted it to.

In the hospital, after Tintin wrote *Route 9* on my bandage, he shook my hand. It hurt, but he didn't notice.

— How are you? he asked me.

— I got shot, I said. How do you think I am?

Tintin shrugged. He got shot a couple of years ago, and Biggie and Stéphanie arranged for him to come here to get sewn up. For him, it obviously wasn't a big deal. But that's Tintin. He's, like, so full of holes, so easy to hurt, that he stops the world from hurting him by hurting it first. If he found a puppy, he'd strangle it to stop himself liking it. He knows I got shot, too, before, when I was young. But I don't remember that so well.

— Everyone in the hood be giving you props, blud, Tintin said in English. Tintin was one of those gangsters who talk all the time in English, like they're from the hood or something, the real hood, like in New York or Baltimore. You was *cold* out there. Vre chimère.

4

I didn't know what to say, so I just said:

— Word.

This is what American gangsters say when they want to agree with something. I said it so that I would still sound like a player even though I couldn't care less about that thug shit anymore, for reasons which you will learn for your ownselves. But that seemed to be OK, cos Tintin nodded like I had said something profound.

— Leave here, you'll get a block, gen pwoblem. Maybe be a boss one day your ownself, Tintin said. You killed those Boston motherfuckers stone dead.

Now I shrugged. I didn't want a block. I wanted all the dead people to not be dead anymore, but that's a lot to ask, even in Haiti, where dead people are never really dead.

Vre chimère.

A real ghost.

Chimère is for *gangster* in the Site. Chimère cos we melt out of nothing and we go back to nothing after. Chimère cos we die so young we may as well be ghosts already. You're thinking, strange thing to call yourselves; strange thing to have a name that means you're gonna die young. And yeah, it's a name that the rich people came up with, the people who live outside the Site, but we took that name and we made it our own. Same as *thug*. Same as *bandi*.

You wanna name me a chimère? Too late. I already named my ownself.

5

Anyway, now I think it's kind of a good name. Now, I think, maybe I *am* a real ghost. Not a gangster, but a dead person.

Sometime today or another day, I heard people shouting from far, far away in the darkness. It sounded like:

— . . . survived?

— . . . alive . . . in there?

— . . . wounded?

I shouted back. You can guess what I shouted. I shouted, yes. I shouted, help. I shouted those words in French and English. I shouted in Kreyòl to tell them there was an accident and I was hurt. Then I thought that was a dumb-ass thing to shout, cos this is a hospital, so of course I was hurt, and it must have been anpil obvious there had been an accident, with everything fallen down.

But nobody answered and the voices went away. I don't know when that was. I don't know when it's night and when it's day, or even if night and day exist anymore.

If I can hear people shouting, but they can't hear me, does that make me a ghost? I think, maybe yes. I can't see myself. I can't prove that I exist.

But then I think, no, I can't be a ghost. A ghost does not get thirsty, and as I'm lying here in the broken hospital it's like my mouth is bigger than me, bigger than the darkness. Like my mouth contains the world, not the other way round. It's dry and sore and I can't think of anything else. My thinking, cos of my thirst, is like this:

. . . WATER, WATER, WATER, WATER, WATER, WATER. Am I dead? WATER, WATER, WATER, WATER. What

6

happened? WATER, WATER, WATER, WATER. Is this the end of the world? WATER, WATER, WATER, WATER, WATER, WATER ...

That is how my mouth swallows everything else. Maybe my mouth will swallow me, and then this will be over.

I decide to crawl, to measure the space of my prison. I know the rubble and the hand on my left – I don't need to go there again. I don't want to touch that clammy skin. In front of me, and to my right and behind me, is just darkness, though maybe I should stop calling it that cos there's no light at all; it's more blackness. I shift forward on my hands and knees, and I scream when my wrist bends a little and the wound opens. The scream echoes off the concrete all around me.

I shuffle, and I feel like I'm not a person anymore, like I've turned into some animal. I move maybe one body length and then I hit a wall of blocks. I reach up with my hands and stand up, and I feel that it goes up to the ceiling. Only the ceiling is lower than I remember, so that's not great, either. To my right, the same thing – a broken bed, then a wall of rubble. And behind me. I'm in a space maybe one body length in each direction.

I'm in a coffin.

I hold my half of the necklace, and it's sharp in my hand where the heart is cracked in two. I think of my sister, who had the other half of the heart and who I lost when I was a piti-piti boy.

I try to say the invocation, the words to the Marassa, cos

7

they might be able to bring my sister back to me, but I'm too thirsty and I don't remember them.

Listen.

Listen.

You're the voices in the dark, so the world can't all be gone. There must be people left.

You're the voices in the dark, so listen, mwen apè parlay. I'm going to speak to you.

I'm going to tell you how I got here, and how I got this bullet in my arm. I'm going to tell you about my sister, who was taken from me by the gangsters, by the chimères. This was 2,531 days ago, when my papa was killed. At least, I think it was. I used to know how many days cos I marked them in my head. Now I don't know if it's two or three days I've been in the darkness, so I don't know how long ago my papa was chopped to piti-piti pieces and my sister was taken. But I know this: it hurts every day as much as the last, as much as the first.

It hurts now, even, and you would think I have other things to worry about, what with being trapped with no water and no food, and no way out.

Maybe, maybe, if I tell you my story, then you'll understand me better and the things I've done. Maybe you'll, I don't know, maybe you'll . . . forgive me. Maybe she will.

My sister, she was my twin. She was one half of me. You have to understand: a twin in Haiti, that's a serious maji; it's

8

something powerful. We were Marassa, man. You know Marassa? They're lwa, gods, the gods of twins – super-strong, super-hardcore, even though they look like three little kids. They're some of the oldest gods from Africa. Even now in vodou, the Marassa come right after Papa Legba in the ceremony. Marassa can heal you, can bring you good luck, can make people fall in love with you. Marassa can see your future, double your money, double your life. People from where I come from, they believe human twins can do the same and can talk to each other in silence, too, cos they share the same soul.

So you see? Me and my sister, we were magic. We were meant to be born. We were special. We shared the same soul. People gave us presents, man – total strangers, you know. People would stop us in the street, want us to give them our blessing.

We shared the same soul, so when she was gone I became half a person. I would like you to remember this, so that you don't judge me later. Remember: even now, as I lie in this ruined hospital, I am only one half of a life, one half of a soul. I know this. That is why I have done the things I have done.

But you don't know them yet, of course – the things I've done, the reasons why I am half a person, the reason why I was in this hospital when everything fell down. You don't know the hurt I've caused.

So I'm going to tell you everything.

First, I must explain the blood.

Some of it is mine. My bandage got all torn up when I was

9

crawling around, looking for my half of the necklace, and I cut myself on some broken glass, I think. I already got shot, you know that, and there's blood coming from there, too. The way the hospital fell down, it hasn't been so convenient for my healing.

I can't explain all of the blood, though. I think some of it comes from the dead bodies. This was a public ward before the ceiling and the walls fell down. There was a curtain around my bed that the nurses could pull if I wanted to use the toilet, but that was it for privacy. Those bodies are the other people who were in here. When the walls fell down, they fell down on them. I can tell cos there's a hand near me, and I reached out and touched it, and followed it to the wrist and then the arm, feeling to see if it was a man or a woman. I don't know why. And I couldn't tell, anyway, cos after the arm there was no shoulder, just rubble.

Me, I was lucky. I was on the far end of the ward and the walls didn't come down here.

Though maybe I'm not so lucky, cos I'm still trapped.

Maybe I'll just die more slowly.

After I've thought about dying for a long time, I stop, and I eat the blood from the floor.

I figure it's food and WATER, WATER, WATER, WATER, WATER, WATER, WATER at the same time. I mop it up with my fingers and lick them. It's disgusting but, like I said, some of it's mine, and it makes the hunger in my stomach cool

10

down a bit, and my mouth gets a bit smaller, like maybe the size of a city. Only now that I've eaten the blood I'm not thinking so much about my mouth; I'm thinking more about how hungry I am.

In Site Solèy when you're hungry, you say you got battery acid in your stomach, that's how bad it burns. In Site Solèy you can buy a cake made from mud and water, baked in the sun with fat. Right now, I think, in Site Solèy they know nothing about hunger. If you gave me a mud cake, I would kiss you.

But then I get to thinking. If I'm hungry, that means I can't be dead. Does a ghost eat blood? I don't think so. A zombi, maybe.

I hope I'm not a zombi. I hope I'm not . . .

No.

I dig my fingernails into my palm. I don't believe in zombis and the darkness can't make me. Zombis scare me. And cos I'm scared, I say some words from a song to myself. They're from *MVP Kompa* by Wyclef Jean, which was the song that was playing in Biggie's car when I first met him.

Wyclef Jean was from Haiti, but now he's a high roller in the US – big rapper, producer, businessman. Biggie was always listening to his music. Wyclef was a hero to him – a kid from Haiti who had made it in the music world. I guess Biggie thought that might happen to his ownself one day, which shows you how stupid Biggie could be.

Anyway, there's this bit in the song where Wyclef Jean says that his friend Lil' Joe has come back as a zombi. It's midnight

11

and Lil' Joe is supposed to be dead, but he's not. He's back and he's a zombi, and he has all his zombi friends with him. Wyclef sings this chorus where he tells everyone to catch the zombis, to grab them. And it's good in the song cos you can catch zombis, you can hurt them and they can't hurt you.

I like that idea, with the dead hand next to me.

So in the darkness I shout out to any zombis that I'm gonna catch them. I shout it till my throat hurts even more with dryness and thirst. And yeah, it makes me feel a bit better.

Yeah.

I don't believe in zombis. I don't believe in all that vodou shit. That's kind of a lie, though, cos I saw a houngan turn into Papa Legba right before my eyes. So, yeah, maybe I do believe in vodou. But that doesn't mean I have to believe in zombis, does it?

No.

Anyway, I think, what did vodou ever do to help me?

Vodou, it's the old religion of Haiti. The slaves brought it over from Africa. In vodou, you got lwa, who are like gods, but sometimes they can be ancestors, too. Haitians, they believe that the lwa can come down and possess their bodies during ceremonies, talk through them. We call it *mounting* – the lwa mounts you and uses your body. See? It's not like in the Kretyen religion. We talk to our gods; our gods talk through us. Manman talked to our gods, I should say. Me, I didn't have a lot to do with them, apart from when me and my sister used to pretend in the ceremonies Manman organized. They didn't seem very interested in me, either.

Manman, though, she loved all of it, and she believed in it all, even if she knew me and my sister were frauds, were bullshit. She had a houngan she went to. That's a kind of priest who knows all the songs to bring down the lwa, and the foods they like to eat, and the veves – the symbols to paint on the ground to draw them to you. Like, if you want to be possessed by Baron Samedi, the lwa of death, you got to give him whiskey and cigars, stuff like that.

Right now, I'd be happy if Baron Samedi came for me and took me away from this place to the land under the sea where the dead go. At least then I wouldn't be thirsty and hungry anymore.

But Baron Samedi is not coming.

Manman used to go to the houngan, but none of that stopped us losing the farm and ending up in Site Solèy. None of that stopped my papa being chopped up with machetes, my sister Marguerite being stolen.

Biggie said his houngan took a bone from Dread Wilmè after Dread was shot by the UN soldiers. He said the houngan ground that bone up and sprinkled it on Biggie, and that meant bullets couldn't touch him, cos Dread died for Haiti, like Toussaint. So Biggie was proof against bullets, immortal, cos he had Dread's bone powder on him. That's what he thought, anyway. I even saw the bone dust in a jar when Biggie took me to see the houngan. Sure, I saw Biggie live through shit that no person should be able to. But I also saw Biggie take a full clip from a machine gun and those bullets tore him to dog food in the end, bone powder or no bone powder.

I don't see what I got to thank vodou for. Anyway, Dread Wilmè didn't die for Haiti. He died cos they shot him. I don't think he wanted to die at all.

I don't want to die, either.

I was born in blood and darkness. That's how Manman told it, when I joined Route 9, when I started to roll with Biggie.

— He was born in blood and darkness, and that's how he'll die, the houngan told her.

Maybe she was right. Maybe I will die in blood and darkness. Maybe she would be happy if she saw me here.

Probably not.

The year I was born, it was when Manman had just moved to Port-au-Prince. They told her there'd be jobs there, electricity, running water. Well, she got the electricity from a line someone hooked onto the public cable, but the only running water was the sewer in the middle of the road and there were no jobs, not for anyone. Me, I was brought into the world as a symbol; I was marked from the beginning. There were some, even before the world fell down, who believed I was meant to do something special. It started right from the time I was born.

This was 1995. That makes me 15 now. See? I can do math, just like I can read. My papa taught me both, before he was killed. After that, Dread Wilmè put me in school, gave us a home to live in, too, cos Manman was Lavalas to the bone. Sometimes, I think, if it wasn't for Dread Wilmè, none of this shit would have happened. But then I say to myself, no. Dread

14

Wilmè was not there when your papa died and they took your sister away. He tried to help.

Anyway, Manman was at a Lavalas rally. She had a great big belly and in that belly was us. She said she could hardly stand up she was so big. She was frightened by what might come out. But she went to the rally anyway cos she thought Lavalas would change everything in Haiti.

This was Aristide's new party, the ones who were going to keep him in power. Manman loved Aristide – he was a communist and that meant he believed everyone should have ègal money, ègal houses and jobs. At that time, Aristide had been in power for about five years and no one in the Site had any jobs, but Manman said that was cos it was hard for Aristide. The Americans and the French had made such a mess of the country it was going to take him a long time to sort it out. Me, I think maybe Aristide was just a liar, but I didn't say that to Manman – she would have been anpil upset to hear me say so, even later, when everything had gone to shit and it was obvious to everyone Aristide was not such a great guy.

Papa was somewhere else, working, I think. So Manman went to the rally alone, even though she was eight months pregnant and big-bellied like a swollen, starving donkey. That's what she said, not me.

Aristide was standing on a chair at the back of this little meeting hall. He used to be a preacher, so he was accustomed to shouting at people. He was saying:

— Ever since it was discovered by Christopher Columbus, this nation has been enslaved. Columbus was a slave-driver. The

French and then the Americans are his successors – and they more than equal him in cruelty and injustice. But we do not bear their yoke lightly! For five hundred years they have robbed us, but for five hundred years we have defied them!

He said:

— The Americans would like the people of Haiti to vote in a new government. They would like to get rid of me, as I have become inconvenient for them. They would like to control our companies and make us slaves again for their own profit.

People cheered. My manman cheered. She had worked in an American company and they had paid her piti-piti money, and then they fired her when she missed a day cos she was sick. I know what you're thinking. You're thinking, how can I know this? How can my manman have remembered Aristide's words? And I answer you – she didn't. But Aristide wrote them down in a book, and I have that book still. Manman threw it away, and I picked it up out of the trash cos I thought it might have some power. Aristide signed it for my manman, you see. He put his name in it, and that's serious vodou.

I used to look at his signature and think how sad it was that a man with such good ideas turned into such a monster. Biggie was like that, too, I think. And me. I had a big idea to get my sister back, but all I did in the end was get a lot of people killed, get a bullet in my arm.

But I'm telling you about the day I was born – I'm sorry, I keep getting distracted. It's crazy – it's not like there's anything here to distract me.

So on his chair at the back of the church, Aristide said:

— Put Lavalas in power and we will throw the Americans into the sea. We will invoice France and America for all that they have stolen from us. They took our freedom, our labor, the fruits of our land. They must be held to account! Two hundred years ago, our coffee beans and sugar cane turned to gold in the coffers of merchants from Paris, while the French slave masters here in Haiti turned our people into animals, trammeled with chains, lashed by whips.

The people shouted:

— Yes! Yes! They made us animals.

Aristide laughed. He always knew how to make people shout and chant, though toward the end they were chanting for him to go away, to leave the country alone, to stop his chimères killing his enemies.

— And what happened when we had our independence?

— Tell us! Tell us!

— Once we had set aside their chains, once we had stayed their whips and stood up on our own two legs, beasts of burden no more, the French sent an invoice to *us*, demanding that we pay for our freedom in taxes and in trees. We were forced to cut down our forests to provide France with wood for building, and the rains that followed washed away our farming land. Everything that was left is being taken from us even now.

Aristide touched the cheap wooden table that served as an altar.

— The colonial powers have been enjoying a banquet at our expense, he said. They sit at the table, which is dressed with indigo cloth exported from Haiti, set with bowls of

17

sugar taken from Haiti, and cups of coffee robbed from Haiti. And where are the Haitians?

— Where are they? Where are they? called the people in the church.

— The Haitians are under the table, eating the crumbs like mice! The rules of the UN, of the IMF, are devised to keep the mice under the table, to stop them from joining the banquet. But we must not be made into animals again. We must upset the table! We must rise up!

At this, Aristide put his palms under it and threw over the wooden table.

— We must overturn the table! he shouted, as it clattered to the ground.

Everyone cheered, cos all the people in the Site loved Lavalas and Aristide. They loved the idea of receiving money and land from the rich. Later, of course, they just started to take it. And that's when all the trouble began.

But this was before all that. So, everyone was cheering, when suddenly there was a shaking and the power went out and the lights stopped. This happened a lot in Port-au-Prince – it still does. On that night in 1995 there was no moon and it was very dark. People started to scream. Manman knew it was an earth-quake and, like the others, she panicked a bit at first, turning to run out into the street, but then the trembling stopped and she heard Aristide call out:

— It's OK! Nen inquiet!

He took a lighter from his pocket and lit a small candle. Then he showed the congregation where there were more candles in the church. Soon people began to calm down.

But Manman was not feeling so good. She stood there in the darkness, with only the candlelight flickering, and she felt a great pain in her stomach. She had a sick feeling in her spirit. She knew something bad was happening. When she had been to the houngan some months before, when she knew she was pregnant, he drew a veve in the ground and called up Papa Gede, and Papa Gede said the baby in her belly had a fierce soul and would begin and end in darkness and blood, but it would live forever, too.

At that moment, the earth shook again – an aftershock – and Manman was afraid the beginning and the end of her baby would come at the same time. She screamed. She looked down and her legs were wet; she thought her waters had broken. But when she touched her fingers to her thighs she found them sticky with blood. She felt faint and she sank downward to the ground – which was just earth, the church built right over it.

— Souplè, she called. Souplè, mwen ansent.

Please. Please, I'm pregnant.

Someone caught her. Someone else said something about a doctor. But then there was a commotion and Aristide was suddenly there, standing over her, in his glasses and his western suit. He smiled down at her, and he knelt on the ground. With gentle hands, he helped her to lie on her back.

— In my time as a priest, he said, I did this many times. In rural places.

Manman stared up at the roof of the church, and she saw that there was a hole in it. Through it, the stars shone out of the blackness, as if to say that darkness is never complete, that there is always hope.

She felt a tearing and she screamed again and again, and soon the screaming was a symphony, higher pitches joining her voice. She hauled herself up on her elbows to see first the big flaque of blood between her legs, and then Jean-Bertrand Aristide, the Prime Minister of Haiti, holding two babies, one in each arm.

He had delivered her children.

— A girl and a boy, he said. Twins! The Marassa Jumeaux made flesh. This is a sign. These are the first babies born in a free Haiti. They will never be slaves. They're like a new Adam and Eve.

Everyone cheered, even my manman, though at the back of her mind she was thinking of the houngan. He'd said I – we – would be born in blood and darkness, and that had turned out true. But he'd said we would die in blood and darkness, too.

Years later, when Manman told the story, I said to her:

— Manman, everyone dies in darkness. Most people, anyway. And in the Site, a lot of people die in blood, too.

She said:

— I know.

But it didn't make her any less sad.

It's so hot in here, it's like I'm in an oven, like someone is baking me. Some giant, maybe, so I can be his dinner.

Me, I'm trying not to think about food and drink, but have you ever tried to not think about something? It's a joke. The more you don't think about it the more you do think about it.

So, I'm making a meal in my imagination. I lay it out in front of me, and in the absolute blackness it's easy, cos you don't even have to close your eyes to picture anything you want. Actually, that's half the problem, cos that's how you stop knowing what's real anymore and go shit-crazy. But, yeah, there's a steak in front of me and chips and a big glass of Coke.

I've only ever had steak once. My papa brought it home one day. I never knew how he got it. He just came home all proud and smiling – he had a good smile, my papa, a bright one – and he laid this bag of steaks on the table. They were sweating blood; it was coming right through the plastic of the bag.

— For dinner, he said to my manman.

She gave him this look, like, what, are you serious? Where did you get them? She could say a lot with one look, my manman. He just laughed.

— Only the best for my lady and my twins, he said.

Before we ate the steaks, he took me outside and we threw a ball back and forth, back and forth. It was lame really, but it was fun, too.

Now I take a bite of my steak. In my imagination I have overcooked it a little, but it's all good – it gives a little crust to the meat. I have put anpil salt on my chips, so I drink a

21

great gulp of my Coke, and that's good, too. Then I stop, cos I hear something. It's a scrabbling sound, but it's too small to be people digging, too delicate.

I turn toward it very slowly.

Skish, skish, skish. Tatatatatatata. Skish, skish, skish.

My hand snaps out toward the sound and I feel the smooth swish of a tail, hear something fast and skitterish disappear into the darkness.

Rats.

I take a long, slow breath. I can hear a gnawing sound now, or maybe I'm just imagining it. I need to get out of here. For a moment I'm on the verge of real panic. I start praying, like, get me out of this fucking place right now; there are rats eating the dead people, there are rats eating the dead people. Suddenly I can't breathe, but then I think about Marguerite, my sister. I force myself to think about Marguerite.

Marguerite had curly hair and a smile as big as the moon, and she was my best friend. We were twins, but we didn't look the same. I was big and strong, and she was a small thing, like a ghost already.

Marguerite, she had this necklace. I am holding half of it in my hand now. I should explain – it was a silver necklace with a heart pendant. The heart you could pull in half, and it would go into two jagged pieces. Papa got it for her from some mystery place. As soon as she got it she broke the heart in two and gave one half to me.

— Maybe you should keep it, give it to a boy one day, I said to her.

— We are twins, she said. We are the same person broken in half. So you have half my heart.

So I kept it and always carry it with me, even now, as I lie trapped in the darkness.

Marguerite was my twin, but she wasn't like me, not at all. I was into machines; anything that had an engine, or electrics, or gears, I wanted to take it apart and see what made it go. I collected stuff from the street, from the garbage, from everywhere. My papa said I would be an engineer one day, but I don't think even he really believed it.

Marguerite, she was different. She looked different, too. She had this tiny constellation of freckles on her nose, these enormous gray eyes. She was something too beautiful for the Site, everyone could see it. Looking at her, you felt like someone should come along and put her in a bulletproof case and just keep her safe, keep her happy. But then, you'd think, well, being in a case wouldn't make her happy. Cos she loved *everything*, man. She wasn't like me, with my bikes and my radios and my wires. She would walk around and it was like everything was fresh to her and new-made and wonderful, even the rats.

Yeah, even the rats. She loved those things, just like she loved the sky, and the sun, and bits of rubbish floating down the street when they made pretty patterns in the air. She saw some beauty in those filthy creatures that the rest of us could not recognize. Once, Manman found a nest of baby rats in one of the walls. This was when we were seven or something, I guess. Before Marguerite could stop her she killed the

23

mother rat, whacked it dead with a broom. She wanted to kill the babies, too, but Marguerite would not let her.

— No, Manman, she said. I want them.

No one ever refused Marguerite anything. There was anyen that the people of the Site would not do for her, especially the older ones. It was this glow that she had inside, this way of lighting up like a lamp when she saw something that made her happy. So Manman let her gather up the nest, carefully, and take it to a place in the corner of our dirt yard, where she made a wooden box and filled it with newspaper, and that made her happy. She would just lie on the ground, right in the dirt, on her front with her elbows propped up, and I would watch her as she watched the rats. She brought them food; I don't know where she found it, we never even had food for ourselves, not really. But the stuff Marguerite found was not food a person would eat – it was always moldy stuff, old, perished. The rats didn't care; they loved it.

One day, though, the box was gone.

— The rats, are they OK? I asked.

— Yeah, she said. It was time for them to go and explore.

— Oh, I said. OK.

And she looked at me with those eyes like the ocean at dusk.

— I'm going to explore one day, too, she said. I'm going to get out of this place, and I'll take you and Manman and Papa with me.

You know what? I believed her. You get me? I believed that shit. Cos when Marguerite said something, you listened. She was that beautiful, see, and that special, you just knew that whatever she wanted to be, she could be. She was like . . . like someone who had lived many times before, and knew how to be grateful. That sounds stupid, but it's true. It's like she had a soul that was much too big for her; it filled her to the brim till there was no more space, so then it flowed out through her eyes. It made her care for people, for animals, too.

Tintin was also like that – sort of, anyway. But with Tintin, what was inside was rotten, and it made him crazy, made him hurt other people.

But I'm talking to you about Marguerite. It wasn't always rats with her, you have to understand.

This other time, not so long afterward, I was with her and we were walking to the sea to try to find Papa, see if he would take us out on his boat. He did that a couple of times; he would let us drop lines into the water, and we would wait for the fish to bite, and as we did we would look back at Site Solèy, rising up squalid from the ocean, and it would seem smaller and like a place you *could* escape from.

Papa would say:

— The sea, it's a kind of freedom. But you two must do your schoolwork, OK? Then maybe you can have a better freedom.

Marguerite would say:

— Yes. See those big houses on the hill, for the rich? I'll have one of those one day. I'll have a swimming pool and a car, and you'll all live with me.

And we believed her. We believed in her dream. Of course we did. When Marguerite said something, it was real.

So, that day, we were walking to the sea. We were on one of the wider streets; there was more room to avoid the sewage, and there were even a couple of carts with colorful umbrellas, selling fruit, but we weren't the kind of people who could afford fruit. The sun was high above us and it was brutal hot, like a hammer on the skin. We saw this old guy who had a monkey on a chain – it leaped at us and screamed as we went past. Marguerite squealed and grabbed my hand, and the old guy cursed and pulled the monkey back – but not before we'd seen its big white eyes, the teeth in its wide-open mouth.

— I bet you wouldn't feed that monkey if you found it, I said.

— The monkey's OK, she said. It just doesn't enjoy being chained like that.

Marguerite was famous for that kindness. She'd take a pigeon that had broken its wing and she'd make it better, no matter that Manman said pigeons were rats with wings.

That was Marguerite. You could stab her and beat her and steal her money, and she'd say that she understood, that you were hungry, that you didn't know any better. Not that anyone would do such things to her – she was like an angel in the Site. Grandmothers would touch her for luck, I'm not fucking kidding. Really, we both should have been lucky. We were Marassa – I was just as much a twin as her, just as much maji. But ain't no one ever touched me and looked happy about it, I'm telling you.

After the monkey, we walked for another block. Then we

26

heard a sound. It was a crying sound, low and miserable. We both looked around. Marguerite spotted it before me and she walked over to this trash heap that was right at the side of the street. I followed her and suddenly we were looking down at a baby.

— Wow, I said.

This baby, it was just lying in the trash, crying, but in a kind of weak way. It was moving its limbs, too, but sluggishly, slowly. It had an enormous head, all swollen and sore-looking.

— It's alive, said Marguerite.

That sounds a kind of stupid thing to say, but the way she said it had all this wonder in it. You have to imagine her saying it in this hushed voice and that there are, like, angels flying around and violins playing.

Course, this baby being alive *was* a big deal. Truth is, it wasn't that uncommon to see babies in the trash in the Site, but mostly they were dead when you saw them. You'd clock them sometimes, from the corner of your eye when you were walking by, or when you were throwing something in the trash, and you'd try not to look. You didn't blame the mothers. I didn't blame the mothers anyway, though I think Marguerite did. Me, I know it's hard enough to feed yourself if you live in the Site. Gen surprise that not many women want to feed a baby, too.

It was a crazy thing, those dead babies. Sometimes you'd go back the next day, or whatever, and they would be gone. Just disappeared. No moun knew what happened to them. Some people said that Dread Wilmè stole those babies away and ground them down in a big pestle and mortar, used them to

27

make a dust that protected him. They said that that was why he was always coming up alive, always indemne, no matter how much the UN and the other gangs tried to kill him. They said Dread Wilmè used some serious black maji, and there wasn't anyen that could give as much power and protection as a ground-up baby.

I should explain something here. Thing is, people like to say bad stuff about vodou. The Kretyens, they have often made out that vodou is violent and dangerous and evil, when really it's a religion like any other and it can be beautiful. So when I say this about the babies, I don't want you to get the wrong idea. It's not like it's normal in vodou to grind babies up into powder. It's pretty far from normal, in fact. It's fucked up. But where I come from, it's the same as anywhere else: there are always some people who are ignorant and superstitious. Those people, they thought the babies could be used for black maji, and that was why the babies would disappear.

Anyway. This baby. No one had made it disappear. This baby was alive.

— What's wrong with it? I said.

— Her, said my sister.

— What?

— It's a her.

I looked at the baby. I couldn't see how she knew what it was. All I could see was it was ugly, with that big head like a great boil full of pus. Noisy, too. It was still crying. I turned to her, like, huh?

— Pink clothes, said Marguerite. Dumb-ass.

28

— Oh. Yeah.

Marguerite bent toward the baby and I grabbed her arm, asked her what she thought she was doing.

— She's sick, said Marguerite. Hy— hydro— something. Her head is full of water.

— Serious? How do you know that?

Marguerite shrugged.

— From Manman, I think. She touched the baby's face. I'm going to find someone to help her. Someone from outside the Site.

I stared at her.

— You're kidding?

But Marguerite wasn't the type for kidding. She picked up the baby and, for a moment, it stopped crying. It looked up at her with its piggy eyes stuck deep in that fat head. Then it started to cry again.

— Hush, said Marguerite. Hush.

She carried the baby and I followed behind, of course I did. You didn't have any choice but to follow Marguerite. I don't know if I can really explain that without you seeing her. It was like . . . It was like her personality went in front of her, bright, like a reverse shadow. You felt the force of her from meters away.

So I followed her, and I guess we both knew where we were going. It was the only place we could go. At that time, the Site was not closed off. I mean, there were no checkpoints, no MINUSTAH troops to stop you leaving – those are the soldiers from the UN who came to bring peace to the Site by making

29

it into a prison. It was still closed off in a way, though, you understand, cos it wasn't like you could just walk out and get a job and not be a slum-rat anymore. There's no McDonald's in Haiti, there's no Burger King, nowhere that a person with no real education can get a job. Mostly, if you went out, you got picked up by the police, or a gang. The police would return you to the Site, but a gang might just kill you, or worse.

And yet . . .

If you did want to leave you could – if you were determined. You just walked to the end of the street and you kept on walking till you were past the shacks and the mud. So that's what we did, me and Marguerite, her carrying this little baby, its swollen head bobbing, crying all the way.

I said:

— I'll carry it. I mean, I'll carry her for a bit.

But Marguerite shook her head.

That walk, it must have taken a couple of hours. We didn't have any water with us, nothing, and it was hot. Even thinking about it is making me feel thirsty, and I have more than enough reason to feel thirsty already, what with being trapped underground in a baking oven.

Anyway, the sun was battering down on us, like a sledge-hammer. We were sweating, and anpil times we had to stop and sit down. But you know what? I never once said to Marguerite we should stop. She had this look in her eye, see. People didn't ask her to stop.

We passed the long wall with the painting on it. Everyone knew this wall. Someone did it years and years ago during the break-bones time, when Aristide was gone and the Lavalas were trying to bring him back and the attachés were shooting protesters in the streets of Site Solèy. It's of a load of kids playing, and underneath there are some slogans:

Aba lavichè. *Down with poverty.*

Pa fe vyolans. *Don't commit violence.*

Aba kidnaping. *Down with kidnapping.*

Nou vle lape. *We want peace.*

Nou gen dwa pou nou edike tout moun. *We want to educate everyone.*

These slogans are a big joke, cos there's only poverty in the Site, and violence is everywhere. Peace is the biggest joke of them all. The education thing is pretty funny, too – me and Marguerite, we were pretty rare cos we could actually read that wall.

The only thing on the wall that had actually happened was that the kidnappings had stopped. The kidnappings belonged to the break-bones time, when the attachés would come into the Site and take Lavalas supporters away. No one ever saw them again.

Eventually we saw the runway, and we knew we were close then. We turned onto the big road that led from the airport to the town. Marguerite looked around, then sat down in the dirt below a billboard with an advert for Coke on it, with these people on a beach, taking bottles from a cooler full of glistening ice. I thought that was unbelievable. Absolutely fucking unbelievable.

Cars were going past, some of them beat-up taxis, some of

them private vehicles. A few, coming from the airport, on our side of the road, were bringing people in – aid workers, adventurous travelers, diplomats, UN with blacked-out windows, air con.

Marguerite, she scooted till she was as close to the road as she dared. Then you know what she did; you know it already. She lifted that baby and she held it up. She fixed her eyes on those cars going past, the ones going to and from the airport, and she just sat there. After a while, I could see the muscles trembling in her arms.

— Hey, let me, I said.

Then she looked at me. She nodded, and I took the baby from her. I held it up so the people in those cars would see its head. I managed, like, ten minutes, man. Marguerite, she could hold it for an hour. She took it back, and that's just what she did. She didn't move for one minute, not to go pee, nothing. It was so hot, man, but she didn't move. Her skin was all honey in the sunlight, frizzy hair on her head like heat haze, so you didn't know where Marguerite ended and the light began. She just sat there, so beautiful, perfectly still, and she held up that baby.

And nothing, anyen at all, happened.

Nothing.

The cars, they just kept chugging by, clouds of dust with wheels, and the smell of diesel was a live creature in our nostrils, breathing black air. The sun kept beating down like a weapon, deadly. I was worried we were going to die out there, that we'd run out of water in our bodies and go like raisins, that someone would find us there with that big-headed baby and they'd have anyen idea what the hell had happened. I was so thirsty, I thought I was going to die.

I know what real thirst feels like now.

The sun began to go down, and we were handing the baby back and forth when I saw that Marguerite was crying. But I didn't say anything. I'm a boy – what do you want from me? I didn't touch her, either. She had holes in her; the world could get in. She wasn't protected enough to be touched – she would just melt down in tears, I knew it, and that would be it, the day would be over. So I just looked away and said I'd hold the baby for a moment.

I guess we were both looking down when the car stopped, so we heard it before we saw it, the crunch of the tires as it pulled off the road and onto the dirt, the clunk of the door opening. Then there was this woman coming toward us, quite old I thought then, but I guess she was kind of young, really. She had on a T-shirt, with *Médecins Sans Frontières* on it. She had blonde hair, too – I'd never seen women with blonde hair before. And blue eyes! She crouched down beside us and someone in the car shouted to her, but she waved back at them and said something short, something angry.

She peered at the baby. Me and Marguerite, we kind of averted our eyes, like we might ruin this if we said anything, like this woman was a wild animal who could be scared away.

— She has hydro-encephalitis, the woman said in French. By her accent, she was from somewhere else, though. She looked at Marguerite. Do you know what that is?

Marguerite shrugged.

— She's sick, she said. My sister's voice was kind of croaky and dry, cos she was thirsty. Will she die?

— That depends, said the woman. Not if she's treated. Is she yours?

Marguerite blinked. We were, like, seven.

— No!

— Your sister?

— No.

The woman ran her hand through her hair. It was loose, but some of it was tied in this clip that looked like a bird. I thought that was amazing, the most amazing thing I'd ever seen. There was a fine down of blonde hair on her ears; I loved her ears. Manman, she would talk about the lwa Erzili Danto and how she was the most beautiful woman, the most beautiful goddess, how anyone who looked at her would fall in love with her. I thought this woman must be Erzili Danto in that case, or possessed by her, or something.

— Then what . . . ? she said, hesitant.

— We found her in the trash, I said.

The woman stared at me, then put her head in her hands and kicked the dirt. Some of it went in my face, but I didn't say anything.

— Fuck, she said.

From the car behind her came this man's voice, pretty loud now. It sounded like he really wanted her to get in the car. The woman turned around and shouted something back, and she was doing this twisty thing with her hands.

— Fuck, she said again. Wait.

She went to the car, and for a moment we thought, yes, she's going to take the baby. But she came back with two little bottles of water. She handed them to us and we opened them straight away, drank them down.

Till then I didn't know water had a taste. I thought it was like air: flavorless. But this water that the woman gave us, after we had been walking and sitting in the sun all day, it tasted of a thousand things – sunshine, shadows, bananas, mangoes.

I finished my bottle and saw that Marguerite had, too. We put them down.

— Thank you, we said.

The woman nodded. I thought she was going to turn and leave, that she had given us water and that was all we could hope for. I think I would have cried if I wasn't such a boy.

Then the woman held out her hands.

— Give her to me, she said. Quickly.

Marguerite handed over the baby and the woman glanced all around, like someone was going to jump out and grab her, like anyone in Port-au-Prince cared about a sick baby, unless they were going to grind it up for vodou or something. She glanced back at us and made this funny expression that was halfway between a smile and a frown. She got in the car, closed the door, and it peeled off in a cloud of that diesel smell. Then it was gone. Just like that. We never even knew if the baby survived or not.

Marguerite stood up, brushed some dust from the seat of her pants, then staggered and swayed. I caught her just before she fell, before she fainted. She was like a thing made to resemble a person, but with all the bones taken out, just soft stuff put in instead, like a toy animal. I thought I'd better get her to the shade, to some water.

— OK, she said. OK, let's go find Papa.

That was Marguerite.

THEN

On the night that rebellion caught like a flame in Haiti, the slave named Toussaint swung down from his horse. It was a good horse – it had been a gift to him from his master, Bayou de Libertas, and despite its age it still served him well. It was, Toussaint reflected, a fitting horse for him to ride. He, like his horse, was old and had served his master well.

Soon, though, there would be no more masters, and no more slaves. Or so Boukman hoped.

As always, one or two people flinched when they saw Toussaint. He suffered the misfortune of having been born hideous, with a face so ugly that even his wife had called him the Ogre. His nose was both flattened and swollen, an unusual combination, whilst his eyes were small and deep-set. He carried this face around with him everywhere; it was like a calling card, a badge. He was known by it.

But, he reasoned, perhaps it was better to be known than not. Then no one could say that you had never existed; no one could turn you into a ghost. Since an early age, Toussaint had held the conviction that one day he would achieve something great, that one day everyone would know his name. Yet, until now, he had done nothing but heal the occasional sick person and tend his master's horses (which, for the most part, lived in conditions markedly superior to those of the sick people). He did not even know how to read and write, and it struck him as he stood in that marshy place, with the torchlight flickering through the trees, that it was too late. He was too old.

Toussaint looked over at Boukman. The man was nearly as aged as Toussaint himself – in his late forties, at least. His face was a criss-cross of incisions. His pride and his tribal belonging had been cut into his skin when he was a child, and now he was on the other side of the world, and was allowed no pride and no belongings.

The ground underfoot was spongy and wet. This was marshland, the Bois Caiman, and Toussaint could see in the darkness to the west, silently slithering, the alligators that had given the wooded depression its name. He shivered, although the air was warm and humid.

What are we doing? he thought. *This is madness.*

Toussaint had always felt out of place – he was too clever for his confrères, but too black to truly socialize with his master. His twin sister, born one minute after him, had died of diphtheria before she could walk, and he could only remember her now as an indiscriminately visaged ghost, a blur on little chubby limbs, giggling. He had never had friends. He had never considered himself as belonging to a society of slaves, only as an individual – and this ceremony was no different. He couldn't totally give himself up to this hysteria, but nor could he repudiate it. Africa was in his blood, even if he wasn't of the Dahomey race that had been primarily responsible for bringing vodou to Haiti.

He slowly made his way over to the assembly and Boukman greeted him warmly. They had first met many years ago, for Boukman was a close friend of Pierre-Baptiste, Toussaint's godfather, who had taught Boukman his smattering of Latin and theology. After Pierre-Baptiste had died, Boukman had continued to come to Toussaint's home, had drunk with him, played cards with him, talked with him. He was a great friend and confidant, even if his zeal was sometimes excessive.

— You should learn to read, Boukman always said, as I have. Then there'd be nothing to separate you from these whites. You are just as swift of mind.

— There's nothing to separate me from them anyway, Toussaint replied. And I have no use for reading.

He was Master of Horse, and was allowed the freedom to live in his own cottage in comfort; he had shared it with his wife until her death from consumption. Before that he had been a shepherd, and he had been granted the liberty to wander the hills unsupervised with the sheep. *Why should I read? What happiness could it bring me?*

Still, he had to admit that it would be pleasant to read the French books Boukman had told him about – Rousseau and Raynal and so on. Raynal, according to Boukman, said:

— Liberty is everyone's property.

Raynal, too, predicted the coming of a negro king, a man who would liberate the slaves and submit the fertile lands of the new world to his furious vengeance. Boukman thought himself that king, Toussaint could tell. *A dangerous idea*, he thought, but he kept his tongue. Boukman could be fierce when aroused to anger, as when he'd first seen the silver cross around Toussaint's neck.

— Why do you wear the Christ martyr on your person? he had asked. You, who have need only of the lwa of your people to protect you?

Toussaint had shrugged. His father had taught him to worship Christ and the one god, although he had told him that the lwa were real, too; Toussaint's father was Arrada, from the lands where many of the vodou lwa had been born, yet he had learned the Bible from his master. Toussaint knew that many of the slaves carried with them icons of Mary to stand in for the lwa Erzili Danto. It allowed them to worship her; at the same time it let them conceal their true beliefs and pretend, in the eyes of the master, to practice a species of ignorant Christianity. In this way were not the two faiths coming together?

Toussaint hadn't said any of this to Boukman, though. He had just shrugged and said that Christ was the one god, which he knew would irritate Boukman and put an end to the conversation.

In truth, he had inherited from his father a complicated attitude toward religion. He considered his father's view – that all gods should be given their due, as being representative of the qualities people wished to nurture in themselves – to be largely correct.

It was also his father who had taught him the use of simples, which many Christians considered tantamount to witchcraft, and how to draw them from the growing things all around: sarsaparilla to cleanse the blood, catnip to calm babies, quassia to stimulate the nerves and to expel worms. Toussaint had healed his master more than once, and his children, and he had been repaid kindly.

All of this meant that Toussaint was both a Christian and a believer in the old ways. He might not want to utterly reject the gods of his ancestors, but, by the same token, why should he reject the Catholic faith his master had taught him, so beautiful and mystical in its dedication to the notion of a single divinity, and of which Pierre-Baptiste had spoken so eloquently?

This ceremony then, tonight, in the boggy land of Bois Caiman, was all Boukman's doing. It was vodou superstition and Toussaint didn't believe in it, but he came despite his battle with the contradiction. He had been lucky, he knew. He had seen the whip-scars on the backs of his fellow slaves, had seen children plucked from their mother's breast and their necks broken. He had seen men killed for falling asleep on their feet. He himself was free, after a fashion, but he could see that his brethren were not. He believed in Boukman's cause, even if he didn't believe in the blessing Boukman insisted on applying to it.

41

— Tonight, Boukman shouted to the crowd that had gathered, we rise up! It is time for rebellion against the whites. The mulats demanded their freedom and the slavers repaid them with blood.

Two months earlier, the mulats had revolted against the whites. These mulats were the half-breeds; that is, the sons and daughters of white men and black women – for the opposite configuration was unthinkable. Mulats had more freedom than the blacks, but of a very limited kind. They weren't chattel, but they weren't citizens, either. They had tried to overthrow the whites, only to be brutally repressed. Their insurrection had been a crushing failure, but it had one lasting repercussion.

It had inspired the blacks.

— Now, shouted Boukman, the slavers will come to learn the real meaning of fear.

A general and wordless acclamation greeted this, people roaring and cheering.

— France declares the mulats, the bastard sons of slaver and slave, free! Yet what does France say of the negro slaves – mothers to those men of color – who grow her sugar, who prepare the indigo for her fine clothes? Nothing!

— Nothing!

Boukman gestured to the blind houngan beside him.

— Before we fight, we must join the spirits to our cause. We must be sure that the old gods are on our side, and the ancestors who, in turn, have become gods.

He gestured to the ground at his feet, and Toussaint looked

down to see that there was a patch of earth darker than that surrounding it, an oblong patch about the length of a man.

Boukman picked up a spade that had been lying on the ground. Toussaint wondered why he hadn't noticed it before, and was beginning to have a bad feeling.

— Two nights ago, said the houngan, one of our number bravely volunteered to be made a zombi.

Toussaint clenched his fists. He had heard about this practice; it was deep, dark vodou. A person would be given certain plants, the extract of a certain fish, and these would conspire to slow his heartbeat, his breathing, so that on cursory inspection he would appear dead. Toussaint could imagine what would happen when these ingredients were combined. Following this, the zombi would be buried and later exhumed to see the world anew. Toussaint had always thought the process a punishment. Why had the man – Toussaint shivered to acknowledge the possibility that there was a man buried under this dark patch of ground – chosen to be treated like this?

— The man under our feet is the first soldier in our war, said Boukman. He has died, and he will be reborn tonight. He has traveled to the land under the sea, where the dead live. He has been guided by Baron Samedi, the lwa of the cemetery, into death and he has caroused with our ancestors under the waves. He alone knows the disposition of the dead!

Ah, thought Toussaint. *So the man is a kind of ambassador to the spirits of the ancestors, to the lwa. What a ridiculous farce, and how unpleasant, too.*

Boukman bit down into the earth with the spade. It only took one scoop before he struck a wooden box. Quickly, he cleared the earth from it, then someone else stepped down to help him prise off the lid. Inside was a man who looked to be dead, only his skin didn't have the pallor, nor his lips the blue tinge, that Toussaint had learned to associate with the truly departed.

Boukman guided the houngan's blind fingers to find the man's face. On doing so, he took a vial from his coat, unstoppered it, and, pulling open the mouth, poured a liquid down the throat of the apparent corpse.

With a great shudder, the man sat up in the box, coughing.

Pure drama, pure theater, Toussaint thought.

But at that moment a cloud parted and the moon shone down, and he found himself trembling like any superstitious pagan.

Control yourself, he thought.

— Tell us, Boukman said to the reanimated zombi. Tell us what you have seen, you who have been reborn this night.

Do the others know about the drugs? Toussaint wondered. *I think not.* He thought they probably believed, really believed, that this man had died and had been reawakened by magic. He himself only knew the trick because his father had spoken of it, had warned of the power of the fish in question, warned him never to touch his store of its powder. No wonder the other spectators were staring, hanging on Boukman's every word.

The man looked right through Boukman, right through the swamp, too, and his lips twitched.

— I saw Baron Samedi, he said, all bones with a suit over them. He took me under the waves, and I saw the swimming creatures and the ocean floor. And oh! I saw la Sirene. She was so beautiful with her fish's tail, and she took me into her husband Agwe's house, and in that house that is a country I saw all our dead departed.

— You saw our ancestors, asked Boukman, the ancestors of the slaves?

— Yes, even unto those whose bodies were left in Africa.

A hush had descended; people were craning closer to see. The script – for Toussaint assumed there must be a script and he further presumed that Boukman had written it – was melodramatic, but it was having its desired effect.

— And what did the ancestors say to you? asked the houngan.

— They said they would help us. They promised they would lend us their strength.

Boukman smiled. He clapped the man on the back, and a fresh bout of coughing began. Toussaint guessed the zombi must have got some earth in his throat when he was buried.

— We have the support of our ancestors, the gede lwa, the men who became gods when they died! said Boukman. We have the support of Baron Samedi, who is lord and gate-keeper of death. We have the support of la Sirene, who owns the sea that surrounds us and the house of the dead.

He paused.

— But there is one whose support we still require.

Another hush.

— Who?

And:

— Who?

And:

— Who?

The questions echoed in the clearing.

Boukman grinned.

He owns them more completely than if he had seized their balls in his hands, Toussaint realized.

— We must call down Ogou Badagry, the lwa of war, said Boukman, and ask him into our met tet, into the seat of our souls. We must be possessed by war itself!

He looked around him, silent.

— YES!

Not an echo this time, but the whole crowd all together. Before he could stop himself, and to his shame, Toussaint answered, too.

— But Ogou will not possess us all! The man he chooses will be the one sent to free us.

More shouting from the assembly:

— You!

— We choose you!

— Lead us, Boukman! Command us to victory!

Boukman graciously waved their words away.

— No. The lwa will choose.

Toussaint sighed. Their cause was just. Hadn't Rousseau

himself said that man is born free, but everywhere is in chains? So Boukman had told him, anyway. The philosophers agreed that liberty was a right which could not be taken away, except as punishment for criminal acts. So could they not simply rise up, with justice in their hearts, and take their freedom by force? Was it necessary that they cement their alliance with this superstitious ceremony?

Toussaint glanced around at the gleaming, avid faces of his companions.

Yes, apparently it was.

Boukman raised a stone to his lips and kissed it. It was his pwen. In it was one of the gods the Dahomey had brought with them to this new world, a god of war called Ogou Ferro. Or so Boukman believed. After kissing the stone, he slipped it back into his pocket. Boukman believed the stone would protect him from those who wished to hurt him and would help him in times of need. Toussaint thought it was just a stone.

The ancient houngan stepped forward and, taking a stick, drew a symbol in the mud. Toussaint flinched at the man's eyeless sockets. His master had ordered them to be put out when the houngan – who was called Louis, even though that wasn't his true name – had dared to look upon his daughter in her underclothes. That the daughter had gone to the houngan to seduce him meant nothing to the master.

The old man's blindness hardly diminished his skill at drawing the veve in the mud. The image was complicated: a pair of swords; several symmetrical curlicues; a shepherd's crook.

Satisfied, the houngan raised the ason, a rattle filled with

47

the tail bones of snakes, and began to shake it. Then, slow on his rickety old legs, he danced the Rada dance, foot to the side, left then right, to a one-two-three-rest count, his shoulders rolling back and forth. He was wildly waving a machete in his other hand.

Toussaint also held a machete, although it didn't sit so easy in his hand. He hoped he would not have to use it. He had advised his master to quit the country when the mulats fell, as he had sensed – from Boukman, but also from the sullenness in the faces of all the slaves – that the negro uprising would swiftly follow. Yet Bayou had stayed, insisting that the commissioners would protect him, that even if the blacks obtained their freedom – which he believed, with certain caveats, that they one day should – the issue would be decided civilly, with no bloodshed. Toussaint believed the opposite. He believed that the slaves would have their freedom, but they would needs soak the land in the blood of the slavers to achieve it, and this was a prospect that filled Toussaint with sadness.

The houngan sang. He sang so that Legba of the crossroad might open the gate, and the lwa might flow down into him when he needed them:

— Attibon Legba, ouvri bayè pou moin!
Ago!
Ou wè, Attibon Legba, ouvri bayè pou moin, ouvri bayè!
M'apè rentrè quand ma tournè,
Ma salut lwa yo.

Boukman came to stand next to Toussaint.

— You doubt the necessity of this, he whispered.

— I doubt the wisdom of it, said Toussaint, not bothering to keep his voice down. The whites believe us to be superstitious and unschooled. We're proving them right.

Boukman waved his hand dismissively.

— We're proving ourselves African. If we take the whites' religion and their education, then we'll only ever be free on their terms.

Toussaint nodded slowly. He didn't agree, but he could appreciate Boukman's reasoning.

He was becoming distracted as the dancing of the houngan grew wilder. Toussaint told himself he was imagining it, but it seemed that the very trees were dancing, their broad leaves waving back and forth in a breeze that had just arisen, as if the land had awoken and were breathing. Shadows licked across the sluggish waters like dark flames.

— He's calling Ogou now, said Boukman. Do you feel it?

Toussaint shook his head. But he wasn't convinced he did not. Did it seem that the low long shapes of the alligators had drifted closer, that the trees were hemming them in? All of a sudden the moon seemed close over the water, fat and sickly pale, and there was a smell all around him of organic richness, of the dark soil where dead things rot, of freshly uprooted plants, of crawling things squirming in their roots.

— Ogou is the father of war, said Boukman. In the country

of our fathers they say, deye morne ga morne; deye feu ga feu. *Behind the mountain is another mountain; behind the fire is another fire.* Ogou is the mountain. Ogou is the fire. Do you understand?

— No, said Toussaint.

Boukman studied him a moment.

— You will.

The houngan, still dancing, scuffed out the veve of Legba, the lwa who opened the doors to the spirit world, and began to draw a new shape. This one showed a mountain, a fire, a sword.

He danced quicker and quicker, wailing:

— Papa Ogou qui gagn yun cheval!

Toute moune pas montè'l!

Papa Ogou qui gagn yun cheval!

Toute moune pas montè'l!

Toussaint, who had previously been present only at Rada rites, and never the fierce, secret Petwa ceremonies for the war gods, listened to the words of the houngan's new song. *Papa Ogou rides a horse. It's not just anyone who can ride him.* He knew that the vodou worshippers believed the lwa could take over a man's body by crossing from the land under the waters and possessing the man's master spirit, his met tet. He had seen a female slave become Papa Gede, the father of death. Her voice had deepened and she had drunk a bottle of moonshine, then breathed out fire.

50

It had been impressive, but was no less a pantomime for it.

Toussaint glanced at Boukman. *Does he truly believe in this?* he wondered. *Or does he merely intend to claim possession by Ogou himself, and so cement his leadership?*

He was still wondering this when something plucked his spine at both ends and pulled it taut as a piano string, causing his head to snap back and his teeth to clack together on his tongue. His mouth flooded with blood, but he couldn't taste it and there was no pain.

He was dimly aware of darkness rushing in, and of blood and spittle spraying from his lips.

As if through water, he heard the houngan singing more urgently now:

— Ogou Badagry, c'est neg politique, yo!
A la li la, oh, corde coupe corde, oh!
Ou maît allè, ou maît tourney
Ogou Badagry c'est la li ye!

Ogou is here, Toussaint understood. *The master is returned. Where?* he wondered. *Where is Ogou?*

Toussaint felt something hot on his arm. It could have been a match, or it could have been a burning tree, but he seemed to have a sense neither of the shape of things, nor of the extent of his own body anymore. His head was in the heavens and his feet were in the sea under the world. At the same time, he was the size of a cockroach, looking up at the world through refracted lenses, a creature in

51

miniature surrounded by giants. He tried to turn, but could only roll his eyes to the side.

Boukman was grinning at him, grinning and grinning, and Toussaint could see the skull under his skin.

Then something snapped, and he . . .

NOW

In the darkness I can't tell when I'm dreaming and when I'm just thinking. I hear the dead hand beside me scrabbling, scrabbling at the floor. For a moment, I'm scared. Then I think, well, at least I'm not alone.

But I realize it was probably just the rat, come back to gnaw on the dead people again.

I see people coming through the walls, pulling the concrete apart with their bare hands, coming to rescue me. I'm pretty sure they're not real cos I see them, and it's not possible to see anything real in here – it's too black. But they seem real, these people, with their strong hands and their smiling faces.

I'm hallucinating, I know this. Do I? I'm seeing shit that isn't there. I've taken drugs before – everyone does in the Site – so I know what it feels like. Maybe I even dreamed those people calling?

My mouth has grown enormous again. Hours or days ago I

had to pee and I collected the liquid in my hands, as much as I could, and I drank it.

Oh, Manman. Look at me now. You told me I would get what was coming to me.

At some point I close my eyes. Suddenly I'm drifting up, up through the half-fallen ceiling, the concrete flesh of the building skeletoned with rods of steel, and then further through floors upon floors of twisted metal and bodies, and then up into the sky. It's light out here. I can see the hospital below me. It's so broken that it doesn't look man-made at all; it's just a pile of random blocks.

I'm in the clouds. I think, maybe I am magical, maybe I am still Marassa, even if my sister is gone. In the Site, ever since we were born, people said we were special. They said we were Marassa, and that gave us powers to change the world. They said we had been given life by Aristide, and so the spirit of the people and the revolution was in us.

Even after Marguerite was taken from us, people said these things. They said that Dread Wilmè had died to protect my life, so all that rebellion had been made even stronger, like when you put carbon into iron and it makes it harder, makes it steel. Some even said that Dread Wilmè lived inside me, and they would look at me strangely as I walked down the street.

I thought that was stupid, but now I think, maybe it's not so stupid after all.

I can see the whole of Port-au-Prince – the palace, the

homes of the rich, the open-air prison of Site Solèy. It's all collapsed. The palace is just dust and rubble, the homes are destroyed. Only Site Solèy looks the same, and that's cos Site Solèy was a ruin to begin with.

There's a gull beside me in the clouds. It peers at me, and banks and screams. I can see planes circling above the airport, and helicopters flying back and forth above the city. There are people crawling over the wrecked hospital below me, like little ants in hard hats.

Earthquake, I think, cos it's the only thing that could smash everything up like this. When we were little, my sister and me, we would make cities out of the mud in the gutters of Site Solèy, and then we would say we were dinosaurs or earthquakes and stomp those cities to nothing.

The devastation I pictured in my head never got close to this, though. From above, Haiti looks like it's been wiped off the earth by an angry god. Maybe Dread Wilmè *was* made into a zombi, and he's come back to punish the land and has shaken everything to pieces in his anger.

I wonder if I can fly, and I try to bank toward the palace to get a better look. But I can't move where I want. Suddenly I'm rising again, up, up among the clouds and then bursting through them, and it's like the flattened city had never been there; I'm in clear blue sky above soft white clouds and it goes on forever.

Then I'm descending very fast. It's night-time now, which seems strange and at the same time not strange. I must have flown far over the clouds, cos I'm not above the city, either;

I'm looking down on marshland, dense with trees. There are no electric lights, though I can see a tentative, reddish light on the other side of the trees, flickering like bloody water, which must be torches or candles.

My speed increases. I'm breaking through the treetops now and I see that there are people below; they're standing in a circle and looking very intently at a man who's dancing and singing like a mad person. They turn from him and look at another man – he's big and tall and wildly ugly, his nose sort of squashed and swollen. He's leaning back, screaming, it seems to me, looking straight up at me as I hurtle downward. I just have time to see that he's foaming at the mouth – he's having some kind of fit – then his mouth is getting bigger and bigger, like mine did when I was so thirsty, and his mouth takes over the world, like mine did, contains it within its twisted and blackened teeth, its diseased gums, and I'm inside it and I'm sinking, sinking into the darkness.

THEN

Toussaint looked at Boukman's concerned features and tried to work out what was wrong. It took him a while to discern that the angle between his eyes and the man's face was awry – that he was, in fact, lying flat on his back. He raised a hand for help and Boukman seized it, pulling him to his feet.

— You were chosen, said Boukman.

— Pardon? said Toussaint.

He wasn't sure how he had ended up on the ground but, now that he was on his feet again, he found that he was looking around him with something like satisfaction and something like equanimity. He felt like he belonged in this place, like he would be comfortable speaking to any of these people, like this was his land and it would support his feet no matter what tried to upset his balance. *That's usual, isn't it?* He had the strange feeling that he had always been incomplete until this very moment.

He remembered, before now, feeling always on the outside of things. At the same time, it seemed to him that he remembered being young and angry, and hurting many people, and this was peculiar because he had never hurt anyone in his life. Terrifying images flashed across his vision: a curved thing of metal and glass on wheels rolling down a strangely smooth, black road between shacks, before exploding in a white-hot flash, people screaming, diving out of the way; young men in bizarre dress with objects in their hands which could have been guns if they weren't so compact and alien-looking; a great flying thing, hovering like an enormous insect, fire spitting from inside it, the whole contraption roaring.

As he saw this thing a foreign word echoed in the recesses of his mind, a word that matched nothing in his mental lexicon, meant nothing to him. *Helicopter*. He clutched his forehead.

He saw many people lying dead in a muddy street, burned and bleeding. He was looking at them and he knew it was his fault they were dead, and he was aware that in his hand was another of those unusual guns.

All this time, he was still in Bois Caiman.

He had a sudden and all-encompassing conviction, something which struck him with the force of lived experience, that revenge could only lead to pain. This, too, was odd, because he had never taken revenge on anyone in his life. But his mind felt . . . different now. He felt simultaneously wise and hopeful and vulnerable.

It hurt, but it was extraordinary.

Toussaint shook his head. He looked around him and saw

the gathered slaves observing him with awe. Previously he would have shrunk away, but now he understood – he was whole now, and he had to lead them.

Why? he asked himself. *Why you? You're more than fifty years old.*

Because, he answered himself, *they're rebelling only to hurt the whites. They're doing it for revenge, not freedom, and that will kill their revolution before it's even born, like a slave mother doing violence to herself to destroy her mulat baby in the womb, the fruit of rape killed on the branch before it can fall.*

He asked himself why *he* was rebelling, then, but he already knew the answer. He himself was free – as free as he needed to be, anyway. He enjoyed satisfying employment and lived with his son, Isaac, in a cottage with a vegetable garden behind it. But others were not free. Every day he saw them sold and exchanged and raped and murdered.

Now he would attempt to stop this ownership of people and the evils it engendered. Somehow – perhaps it was something Boukman had said, perhaps it was the ceremony – he knew that he could.

Boukman leaned in close and whispered to him:

— I told you. Now you are Ogou, and you will make us strong.

— No, said Toussaint. Not Ogou. Something else.

Boukman looked troubled.

— Are you sure?

Toussaint nodded. Boukman lowered his head in disappointment.

— I'm so –

Toussaint smiled.

— I didn't say I would not do this thing.

He turned to the blacks all around him, all of them armed with the best weapons they had been able to lay hands on – knives and machetes and spades.

— Tonight, we rise! he shouted.

For a moment he grasped for the right thing to say, but just for a moment – the only thing he could possibly say was at the forefront of his mind. It was a lie, but a truthful lie. Fifty faces, maybe more, gazed at him from out of the darkness.

— Ogou Badagry is inside me! he shouted. He tells me we will win this war! We *will* be free!

The assembled slaves and free blacks screamed their approbation, even as Boukman looked at him with a frown on his face. Toussaint ignored him – he would explain everything later, when the night was done.

Good god, this is what power feels like.

He stalked over to where a horse stood tethered to a tree. It wasn't his horse, but that didn't matter. He untied the horse and swung himself atop it, machete in hand.

— Kill anyone who resists, he shouted. But only them. If a white lays down his arms, give him safe passage. Let him go to Port-au-Prince and tell the people there that we're free now. Let him go to France and tell the king.

As he turned the horse ready to make for his plantation, he thought of something else.

— Destroy no property, he called out. This land will be ours soon, and we must needs live off it.

Then Toussaint whirled the horse round and kicked his heels into its flanks, heading for the trees. Their branches seemed to reach out at him, clutching. Wild shadows shifted, dancing in the wind, as the moon hung bloated above him. He was aware of people following, some on foot and some on horseback; he could hear the beating of their feet and hooves on the dense, loamy ground. Torchlight flickered. Forms rose up from the swamp on either side of the path. He hoped they were just logs and not alligators.

Gritting his teeth, he spurred the horse on further, leaving the sound of his followers behind.

Once on the road to the Libertas plantation he began to pass small, huddled groups of people. Boukman had already assembled those most capable of influencing the masses, but all of the slaves knew something important was happening at Bois Caiman tonight, and they were gathering, excited.

Toussaint noted one group cutting down a black man who had been hanged from a tree. He rode the horse into a lather.

I'm not a leader like Boukman said, he thought. *Not yet.*

He was deathly afraid. It was a distance of only a few miles between Bois Caiman and his home, but he was a black man on a horse at night. If there were any slave owners or militia out at this time of night, they would arrest him on the spot.

All those slaves who had been at the ceremony would be returning to different places. They would be scattered and some of them would die, but this was only the first sally in their war. They needed to unite and form a more cohesive force if they wanted to carry the country. *He* would need to unite them.

There was time for that, and he had an advantage now, for he knew the story of what had happened at Bois Caiman, of how he had been possessed, would spread quickly, and many would soon know his name. He could use that story to bring the slaves together, to convince them that if they joined under his command he would give them their freedom.

First, though, he had to reach the plantation before the other slaves did. He had told them to kill only those who resisted, and who was to say that Bayou de Libertas would not resist? Toussaint's master was a good man, but he was proud, too, and he had a wife and daughters. He had books and possessions which he loved, and which he would no doubt die to protect, as stupid as Toussaint thought that sentiment.

As he turned a corner rounding a low hill, men who had been sitting on the grass leaped to their feet, shouting. He couldn't tell in the dark if they were black or white, so he clung to the horse, keeping his profile low. There was a bang and he saw dirt near the horse's hooves forced upward from a bullet. Swearing, he pressed the horse even harder, wondering if he would make it at all.

When he passed the cornfields belonging to the Comte Vendoux, he saw a black man there, a shadow in the darkness, putting a torch to the corn. Toussaint stopped, swung himself from his horse, and flung his cloak over the flames – small at this point, but greedy and devouring. When the thick fabric settled over them, they went out, and acrid smoke billowed up.

The slave shoved him. Toussaint noted that he had a flattened nose, twisted in places. Broken at some point in a fight with another slave, or more likely by his master.

— Why did you do that? the man asked. My blood fed this corn. Our blood. I have to burn it to be free.

— Only blood will feed you if you do this.

The slave looked at him blankly.

— When the country is ours, said Toussaint, what will you eat then? When you have burned your corn, what will sustain you?

A glimmer of understanding crossed the man's face and he sullenly lowered the torch.

— There will be soldiers, said Toussaint. From the commission, perhaps even from France. You would do better to burn them than to burn our inheritance.

Without looking back, he swung himself up onto the horse and spurred it toward the plantation. The revolution had spread quicker than he expected – he was surprised, in point of fact. He had ridden hard from Bois Caiman and yet it seemed that the flames of rebellion had spread even faster, and it would take a larger coat than Toussaint could tailor to put them out. He knew the rebellion was an idea that had taken root, sending tendrils through the ground more unstoppable than any weed. The idea had been sown in fertile ground, and once a seed is planted it cannot always be controlled, especially when that seed is fire. Toussaint had seen forest fires in the mountains;

63

they started small, but had the potential to consume everything. The irony was that this idea, like their slavery, came from Europe – it had been conceived by those revolutionaries in France who had declared themselves free and called for the dissolution of the monarchy.

When he finally drew near the plantation, dawn was beginning to break. Birds called from the trees around him. He saw the red stain of the rising sun on the eastern hills, and part of him saw it as blood, and part of him saw it as a new start.

He crossed the entrance to the plantation, relieved to see that no one was hanging from its posts. The other slaves were milling around in the courtyard, as if awaiting direction. They stared at him in a mixture of anxiety and anticipation. They already looked up to him, he knew. He had treated most of them when they were sick or wounded; he had told them stories. On a couple of the younger faces, though, he saw something, a kind of excitement, that troubled him. He recognized it as bloodlust. He scanned the crowd for his son, but the boy didn't appear to be amongst them. *Good*, he thought. He hoped that Isaac had remained inside the cottage, as he had instructed. Toussaint's son was a sensitive lad, although nearly a man, and not the type who should be involved in violence.

— Bayou is in there, said one of them.

Toussaint didn't know the man, thought perhaps he had come from one of the neighboring smallholdings. He was pointing to the door of the house.

— We'll pull them out, said another. Make them pay.

Toussaint raised a hand.

— Bayou has treated us justly, he said. Let's give him free passage to Cape Town.

— Why? said a woman. Tonight the whites die.

— No. Tonight the blacks rise, said Toussaint. And the whites flee, if they have any sense. If we kill those who surrender, we're as bad as they are.

He sensed their hesitation and seized it.

— Wait for me, he said. Arm yourselves. Look out for commissioners, for white vigilantes, but do not take up weapons to kill an old man.

Silent, shrugging, they let him past into the house.

Bayou de Libertas was abed still. Toussaint opened the door without knocking and knelt by the bed, taking pains to conceal his machete. Nevertheless, when he touched the master's shoulder and de Libertas awoke, he looked at Toussaint with anxiety.

— What is it? Is it the mulats?

The attempted rebellion by the mulats, and its brutal suppression, had occurred only a month before. That had been confined to the towns, though, where the rich mulats lived, spending their fathers' money on whores descended from their mothers' bloodline, and on wine grown by their French forefathers. The mulats' rebellion had never reached the countryside.

— No, he said. No, Bayou. It's the blacks.

De Libertas shrank from him then, and Toussaint felt his heart harden.

He suspects me, Toussaint thought. *After everything, he looks at me and he sees an animal.*

With an effort, Toussaint regained his composure. Madame de Libertas was awake now, too, and staring about her in alarm.

— I don't mean you any harm, said Toussaint. You've been good to me. But you must leave. Now. Tell anyone you meet that you surrendered, that your land belongs to the slaves who farm it.

Bayou de Libertas nodded – he was ever a man of quick understanding. He got out of bed in his nightcap and gown, and went over to the sideboard. He began to take items from its drawers.

— It's better if you take nothing, said Toussaint. No money or weapons. There will be less cause to kill you then.

Madame de Libertas began to cry and her husband shushed her.

— Gather the children, the master said, although he was master of nothing now. Toussaint will prepare a carriage.

Madame de Libertas hurried from the room, but not before turning and directing at Toussaint a look of fear and suspicion, an insult that needed no words to deliver its blow.

— Take horses, said Toussaint. A carriage will be too slow.

De Libertas continued to arrange items at the sideboard, taking a quill from a wooden stationery box, dipping it in the built-in inkwell – how many times Toussaint had replaced that ink! – and leaning down to scrawl something on a leaf of paper.

— Don't worry, I'm not taking anything, he said, noticing Toussaint's look of impatience.

He handed the paper to Toussaint, before hurrying from the room. Toussaint began to fold it, to put it in his pocket for Boukman to read later. But to his surprise the black scrawls jumped off the paper into his mind and formed words there. He stared at them in disbelief. *But I can't read!* he thought. Yet the paper offered itself to him and opened up its meaning.

He put his hand to his heart, felt it beating fiercely. The whole room seemed to swim, to breathe. *Is this magic? What happened to me in that clearing?* He felt at once himself and not himself. Wasn't it a fact – an undeniable fact – that he couldn't read? And yet here he was, looking at this piece of paper, apprehending the words written on it. He felt that he might faint, and steadied himself by seizing the corner of the sideboard. He stared, open-mouthed, at the paper.

I, Bayou de Libertas, being of sound mind and good health, do hereby declare that my Master of Horse, who goes by the name of Toussaint, is henceforth, from this night of 8th of August 1791, free. Please accord him all the rights and liberties of a French subject.

Stunned, Toussaint turned to the door, the paper rustling in his trembling hand.

— You cannot declare it, he said.

De Libertas had already gone into the dark chambers of the

67

house, so Toussaint spoke to the wood of the door instead, and the iron nails.

— You cannot declare it because I am already free. I am no one's subject, French or otherwise.

He stood still for a moment. So catastrophically did his old master seem to have misunderstood the enormity of what was happening that Toussaint could almost feel sorry for him. When you have been free, and then have been stolen and carried away to another country, you understand that things can change places. When you have always been master, this insight is closed to you.

Just then, there came a great banging from downstairs. Toussaint went to the window and looked out to see more slaves massed there, weapons in their hands, the moonlight glancing off blades.

Hurrying to the door, he paused and turned back to the side-board. He folded down the writing slope, brushed his fingers underneath to find the hidden catch, and released the drawer containing the pistol. He was certain that de Libertas did not realize he knew of this hiding place – but a good slave knows his master. He checked that the pistol was loaded with shot and powder, then resumed his course out into the hallway.

De Libertas was rushing to the stairs, breathless, a child under his arm. His mouth dropped open when he saw the gun and machete in his hands.

— Toussaint, no . . . You said yourself that I've been good to you.

— Be quiet, said Toussaint. Follow behind me. Appear

meek. Hobble, if your pride can bear it. This country will be mine but, as you say, you've treated me well. I'll get you out of it alive before it runs with blood.

De Libertas paled as there came a splintering sound from below, and a yell of triumph from the mob. Fear twisted in Toussaint's belly like a snake. He hoped Isaac was safe; hoped, too, that his son hadn't joined the angry mob. He would not see his son killed, but he would not see him kill, either.

As soon as I can, he thought, *I'll send Isaac away from here.*

— They're your brothers, de Libertas said, gesturing to the door. They'll kill you for resisting them.

Toussaint smiled.

— No, he said. That's not my destiny.

NOW

I wake and open my eyes. And for a moment I panic.

I'm blind.

Then I remember the darkness. It's strange, but it's blacker with my eyes open. When they're closed, I see the pulses and swirls of my blood, fireworks against my eyelids, and I remember this one time, when I was lying under the sun with my eyes closed, with Tintin nearby, floating on a rich man's pool, drunk on stolen liquor.

Only here, in the hospital, there is no sun.

Here, when my eyes are open, I see nothing.

The wound in my arm is itching. I'm thirsty again; my mouth is consuming me. Thinking of my mouth gives me a strange feeling and I remember that I had anpil dreams when I was sleeping, curious dreams in which I was Toussaint l'Ouverture and I was riding horses and clutching machetes and other weird shit. I think of Dread Wilmè cos it was Dread who first told me about Toussaint, the hero who freed the slaves and made Haiti independent. He was Biggie's hero, too.

Biggie loved Toussaint even more than Dread – he wouldn't stop talking about him.

Biggie, he was the general of Route 9, and before that he was the right-hand man of Dread Wilmè and a big dog in the Site. He did all the shit the government should have done in the slums. He funded the schools, provided security. He punished thieves and rapists.

He sold drugs and killed people.

He made me what I am today.

I have not forgiven him for that, not yet.

But Biggie, he knew about Toussaint, too, and would spout shit about him all the time. It's cos of that, I think. It's cos Biggie told me Toussaint's story, that's why I'm dreaming about him. But I'm not convinced. I know dreams and that didn't feel like one, and anyway, there was more detail in that dream than Biggie ever told me. I think of the burned smell of that corn, which I put out with my coat, and the sound of people hacking at a door with axes, and the feel of an ivory-handled pistol in my hand.

No, I think. I'm just going mad, that's all. It's the darkness and the smell of death. Mouri pourri, I think. Then I giggle.

I thought the worst thing would be to survive. Now I realize the worst thing would be to survive but to no longer be myself. If they dig out a madman from this hospital, then I haven't really survived: I've died and come back as a zombi.

Don't go mad, I think to myself.

That makes me giggle again. I pinch my arm, where the bullet went in, and that makes me scream.

— Don't go mad, I say.

Good.

I can still speak.

I saw two men killed before I was eleven years old, and my papa was the first. This was a long time ago – 2003, the tenth of February. I was eight. It was, like, a year after me and Marguerite found the baby.

Papa was a fisherman, you could say – he shared a boat with another man from the Site. It brought him piti-piti money, but enough to send us to a small school.

Manman told me afterward that Dread Wilmè wanted to pay for our education, but Papa wouldn't agree – he thought that someone like Dread Wilmè would want something for his money one day. He was right. I know these things now.

At this point, I mean in 2003, Dread Wilmè was in charge of the Site. Dread Wilmè was a big strong man with dreads down to his shoulders. If Dread Wilmè caught a man stealing, he'd cut off his hand. If he caught a man raping, he'd . . .

You understand.

Dread Wilmè was an old chimère, a drug dealer who had become so powerful he was like a mayor – in one part of the Site anyway. But he got his guns and some of his money from Aristide, to protect the Lavalas supporters, so really it was Aristide who was in charge of the Site; Dread Wilmè was just someone who

72

did Aristide's work for him, who kept his people safe. Only no one had jobs still, and no one had any money. So it seemed like not very much had changed, and people were starting to complain about it. There were rebels who tried to fight the government and assassinate people. Most of these rebels lived in the Site. So Aristide gave guns and money to Dread Wilmè to make his own private army and keep control of the slum.

In the end, though, he was only able to take control of half of it – the other half was controlled by the rebels who lived in a part of the Site called Boston. These two gangs, Dread Wilmè's and the rebels, they were always fighting, always shooting one another. At the same time, the attachés were coming into the Site and killing people.

Dread Wilmè began as a chimère and he ended as one. But he built schools, too. He paid for people to go to the doctor. Nothing is as simple as it seems, you'll come to see that. What's for sure, though, is that Manman and Papa did not agree about Aristide. Papa didn't like him – he thought he was as much of a robber as the French and Americans he hated so much. I would hear them arguing about it, and I always tried to block it out, cos I didn't really understand anything apart from that they were angry.

The week before Papa was killed, there was a big disagreement between him and Manman. It was cos of me and Marguerite. I mean, it wasn't our fault, but it was cos of something Manman had done with us that Papa found out about. Actually, it was something she had been doing for a while. It was just that Papa didn't know about it.

73

Till that day.

Till the week before he died.

I don't know if Manman has ever forgiven herself for that.

Thing was, Dread Wilmè was doing a lot of good in the Site the way Manman saw it. He paid for people to go to hospital, he had houses repaired, he supported the schools. For this, he got some money from Lavalas, but Manman felt it wasn't enough. I didn't understand anything much of this at the time, you realize. I filled it in later.

Anyway, Manman had come up with a way to raise money for Lavalas, for Dread Wilmè. And that was where me and Marguerite came in. That day, we were in a peristyle deep in Solèy 19, far from where we lived. This was where Dread Wilmè's power was the strongest. A mambo, a female vodou priest, was leading the ceremony. She did the call to Papa Legba to open the gates, the usual. This wasn't the first time Marguerite and I had taken part in such a ceremony, so we didn't really listen. The place was a basement and it was concrete and gray, filled with gray smoke. It was like a world with all the color taken out. All around the walls were people, gangsters really, it was obvious to me, but Manman didn't care. Dread Wilmè himself sat on a big chair, his dreads a deeper dark in the darkness. They all chanted along with the mambo – Dread Wilmè, too.

Me and Marguerite, we sat in the middle. We were special. We were like mascots for the Lavalas, you know. We were delivered by Aristide, the hero of the party. We were Marassa. We were capable of maji, of performing spells.

The basement was small. There were lots of people packed

in there: young, old, gangsters, and not gangsters. The room, it seemed to contract, to expand, and was filled with noise like thunder. After a while, we felt the atmosphere shift. We had felt it before; we knew what it was. It was like a prickling on our skin. Then everyone was looking at us through the smoke, and we knew that the Marassa were coming. We looked at the mambo, and we saw that she was drawing the Marassa veve on the ground, drawing it in chalk. I say we looked, but I don't mean I assume Marguerite looked as well. I say it cos I know. Everything we did in those days, we did together. I looked at the veve. That means Marguerite looked, too.

We were twins. We were one soul, halved.

Back in the day, Manman said, they would have taken two chickens and cut their throats, a gift to the Marassa, the pwen to make them pleased. But people didn't do that kind of thing anymore, even Dread Wilmè, who loved old vodou. Instead, a skinny kid came up to us with a lale, a basket kind of thing, and on it were all these sweets and chocolates and shit like that and we would have loved to eat them, but we knew that wasn't how it worked. We were smart, me and Marguerite, we didn't need to learn the same lesson twice.

No. We didn't try to take the sweets. We just nodded to the kid, and he went round the peristyle, scattering them on the floor. There were a couple of toys, too, cos the Marassa love toys – plastic things, figures, like tiny dead people. Even so, I would have liked them. I never had any toys; I never saw a toy till the first time Manman took us to the peristyle. But I

knew they weren't for me; they weren't for us. We were
Marassa, but we weren't *the* Marassa. Even at that age we
understood we were only a door. A pipe. A window.

The chanting started.

— Marassa Simbi,
Mwen engage dans pays-a,
Marassa Guinin, Marassa la Côte,
Mwen engage dans pays-a!

It was a song to the Marassa of Africa. It called to the
Marassa; it told them the people loved Haiti, and they knew
the Marassa loved Haiti, too. You know I don't believe in this
stuff – I've told you that already – but when you're in a dark
place and the mambo is singing, it's kind of powerful, even I
will admit that.

The chanting got louder and louder.

Me and Marguerite, we knew what we had to do. We did it
together, like we did everything. You looked at us, you saw a
person in a mirror – someone reflected to make two people.
We were in sync, like drums, man. We started to shake, and
then we went all stiff and weird; to anyone looking at us it
seemed we were possessed. It was a trick we knew how to do.

Then we chanted back:

— Mwen rele Marassa,
Mwen engage dans pays-a.

76

My name is Marassa. I love this country, too.

Around us, everyone went crazy. They were shouting and singing and throwing the sweets in the air, and I thought, throw one of those sweets over here. And now I could say it cos now I was Marassa, and Marassa could do what Marassa wanted to do. I glanced at Manman. I knew she would be pissed, but I didn't care.

— Give us sweets, we said, cos to be sure Marguerite was thinking the same thing.

— Give us toys.

People started to scrabble on the floor, picking up all this stuff that the kid had only just thrown there. They brought it to us. And when they put it in our laps, they put money, too, and sometimes they asked questions. It was hard to hear and it was hard to see, with all the people and the smoke. But we did our best.

— Will I ever have a baby?

— Yes. Yes, you will. Marassa bless you.

— Will I see my Nerese again?

— When the time is right, yes. Marassa bless you.

— Will my karamel come back to me? Will she leave her husband and come back to me?

— No.

— Will Aristide stay in power?

— Yes.

Always yes to that one. Always, with no hesitation.

You had to do the touch, too, of course. A blessing is not a blessing if it's just words, everyone knows that. Got to be

77

touch with it. So each person who drops money, you hold out your hand and you touch them on the hand, or on the head if they're kneeling, and they get this dumb expression on their face like they just saw the clouds open and angels fall out, or some shit.

Some of them, they only wanted the touch. No questions; they just came limping, crawling, even, and they waited there for the touch. I felt kind of bad about those people. You knew them: you knew them cos they had arms missing, or legs, and they stared around with blank eyes, or they had bits of them swollen up like watermelons, or they were just gray and thin – and those were the worst ones. We didn't like to touch them. But we did it. We did it cos we were told to, but also cos it was all we could do. We always gave them our blessing.

Well. Almost always.

And at the end, there we were, with toys and money and sweets in our laps. It was like a damn party, but we couldn't enjoy it right then cos we had to seem like we were wise and magical and from old Africa. Course, sometimes we had to be rude, or not make any sense, cos that's what people expect from Marassa – as lwa, the twins are powerful, but they're kids. They don't do everything all goody-two-shoes and clean and predictable.

— Is my husband cheating on me?

— Of course he is. You're ugly.

Sometimes, and this was the nasty thing, you had to turn away from the sick people, too. Marassa are childlike: the

78

twins take against some people, no fault of theirs, no fault of the lwa, either. Me and Marguerite, we hated doing this. We chose before the ceremony – like, every third man, we'll ignore him, OK?

Sometimes these people cried. It was fucking terrible.

So, anyway, all of this was like it always was. Manman, she went over to Dread Wilmè and was talking to him, and people started to file out.

We began to put the money together. What happened was that we gave this money to Dread Wilmè. The sweets, we could keep. Not the toys. Papa might see the toys and then he might know what we were doing, and even though we didn't really understand it, we knew that would be bad.

Daylight always came down from upstairs when the trapdoor was opened, but suddenly there was a solid shaft of light in the basement, like someone had thrown the trapdoor wide open. And in that shaft of light were the rickety stairs from the upstairs world.

Papa came down the steps. It hadn't seemed like a strange day till then, but at that moment it did. We were two liars, sitting with sweets in our laps that we didn't deserve.

Me and Marguerite, we looked down, ashamed.

— Come, said Papa. Now.

His voice was cold, like nothing I had ever heard before. Dread Wilmè stepped up to him and started to say something, but Papa turned away, didn't even reply. He picked us up from the ground, effortless, like we were light things. The sweets fell. He swung us; he carried us to the stairs.

— It's for a good – began Manman.

Papa held a hand up.

— They're not performing monkeys, he said.

After that, there was a lot of coldness between Manman and Papa. There was no shouting; Papa didn't shout. When he was angry he was quiet and cold, like the deep sea, and that was worse.

Me and Marguerite, we played outside on the street whenever they discussed something, which is what they called it when they argued. At first we thought we were in trouble, but it didn't seem like we were.

It seemed like it was Manman who was in trouble.

There weren't any other children on our street to play with us – no one lived on our street, not anymore. We were the last family on the street. On one side of our street was Boston, which belonged to the rebels, and on the other side was Solèy 19, which belonged to Dread Wilmè. Later, Solèy 19 became Route 9, cos that's the name of a big road MINUSTAH are building on our side of the Site, to join us to the rest of Haiti. They've been building it for years now, and it still isn't done yet.

Anyway, Route 9 came later. For now, all you need to know is that me and my family, we were living on a strip in the middle, between Dread Wilmè's territory and that of the rebels.

You understand? No man's land. Manman told Papa we should leave, but he didn't want to.

— It's not our war, he said. We're anyen to them. If we move to either camp, then we've taken a side. And they'll kill us for it.

Me, I think Manman would have liked to go to the Lavalas side, to Dread Wilmè's territory. I could see she was happy when we were there, playing at being Marassa. But she must have loved my papa, cos she never pushed it.

So, on the day I'm talking about, Marguerite and me were playing all by our ownselves, while Manman and Papa argued inside. Occasionally we heard a bit.

— They're just children!

— You're exploiting the sick!

I didn't understand what those words meant then, not really. But I do now. And you know what? I think Papa was wrong.

One: we weren't just children. There's no such thing as children in Site Solèy, only smaller starving people, only smaller dead people. On the road next to ours there was a morgue – *Morgue Privée*, said the sign. It was one of the first things I learned to read. On the sign also, which was really just paint on a wall, there was a little girl, and above her an angel, flying her up into heaven. You think this was meant to manipulate people; you think it's kind of sick. But it wasn't. It was a reality. You didn't take your husband to a morgue – you couldn't afford it, could you? But when your child died, then you found the money, if you could. Your family helped you, maybe. Unless it was a baby you didn't want. Then you just threw it on the trash.

That sign, it wasn't about manipulating your emotions. It was like a car-shop sign with a tire on it to say, we change tires. Only instead it said, we look after dead kids. And the Site was full of dead kids.

Two: exploiting the sick? I don't think so. Me and Marguerite, for sure we didn't like to touch them. But if you saw the expression on their faces when they thought they'd been blessed, your heart would fucking break. If some of those people didn't think themselves healed after they believed the lwa of twins touched them, I will turn myself into a parrot.

But back then we didn't really know what Papa was saying, and we didn't care, either. We were just glad we weren't in trouble.

We had a game: you had to flick bottle caps and make them jump into a tin can. It was a good game. We had five bottle caps each and if I won, then Marguerite had to be my slave for the day and do everything I told her. I could have been really mean, but I never was. If she won, which wasn't often, then I had to be her horse, and she'd sit on my back as I rode her around the street. I told her it wasn't as good as having a slave, but she loved horses. She'd never seen one, but she loved them all the same.

Biggie never saw a Cadillac Escalade or a bottle of Cristal, but it didn't stop him rapping about them.

Anyway, on this occasion I had lost, so I was on my hands and knees, Marguerite whooping on my back, pretending to whip me with her hand and laughing.

Suddenly there was a scream. It sounded like Manman.

I bucked Marguerite off and she landed in the mud.

— What's happening? she said.

— I don't know. Stay here.

I ran over to the shack and ducked inside. I saw anpil young men in there, with baseball caps on their heads. They were carrying baseball bats and machetes, and had scarves around their faces like bandis.

Manman was backed against the wall of the shack, screaming and screaming. One of the men grabbed me and held me tight, my arms against my sides. He held me a long time. I struggled and he hit me and the world went black, and I don't know how much more time passed after that.

More men came in from the street.

— The girl? said one of them.

— Done.

— No, not my – began my papa, but one of the chimères kicked his legs out from under him and he fell hard on his back.

— Shut up, another man said.

Papa got to his knees and swore. It was the first time I had ever heard him swear.

— Let my family go, he said.

The chimère who seemed to be the leader sighed. He made a little gesture and one of his friends slashed down with his machete, then Papa's arm was gone below the elbow. That's how easy it was. After that the others started hacking and stabbing, too, and I was struggling in the arms of the one who was holding me, and he was laughing, and everything was

83

flying blood and twisted faces and terrible, wet noises.

Eventually, I closed my eyes. I think I maybe fainted. I remember hearing someone say:

— What about the woman?

And another man said:

— He said she should live.

Another said:

— Well, yes, but . . .

And all his friends laughed.

Then blackness.

See? I've been in darkness before, with bodies. I know this place. I wonder now if the hospital is only the shack again, and maybe I wasn't shot in the arm but in the heart or the head, and all of this is hell, or the land under the sea where the dead go to be lwa of the Gede family. Maybe I'm back in the room after Papa's murder, and that's where I'll always be now.

I take a deep breath. Everything I remember is too vivid. My fallen-down hospital room is a cinema with the lights turned down – it's total blackness, and my life is too bright against it.

So, the shack.

At some point the darkness ended and I was looking up at one of the men with guns. He winked at me.

— This is what happens when you fuck with the Boston crew, he said.

Another chimère laughed.

— For sure, he said.

I didn't understand. Papa hadn't fucked with anyone. All he did was take us away from the peristyle, where we were pretending to bless people. Even then, though, I think I knew that this had nothing to do with that, cos I understood that the chimère was Boston, not Route 9. I clung to that.

I told myself, one day all of these Boston pigs are going to die.

Then there was a loud bang that I recognized as a gun firing. I looked up and Manman was standing with a semi-automatic in her hand. She was crying. One of the chimères, the one who had spoken to me, was screaming. Blood was pouring from his shoulder. I noticed that there were skulls and cross-bones on the bandanna over his face.

— Bastard, he said.

— Get out, said Manman. Get out now.

The chimères backed away. Manman stood for a long time holding that gun, and we waited in the silence. But they didn't come back.

I was still on the ground. Papa's blood was on my hands and my face; it was sticky and smelled of everything bad. Manman stepped over me and went out into the street, holding the gun in front of her. A minute or a day later, she came back inside. There was a flat, cold look in her eye. She was shaking, and I was worried that the gun might go off by accident. But then she seemed to seize control of herself and she was Manman again.

She picked me up and gently prised open my fingers.

— What do you have there? she said.

It was a bottle cap. I hadn't realized I had been holding it.

Manman carried me out through the back of the shack. She walked and walked, and I didn't know where she was going. Then I smelled the sea and I knew she was heading for the boat, the one Papa used for fishing, and she said we would sleep in there till we could find somewhere else.

— What about Papa? I said.

— We can't help him now.

— And the gun? Where did you get the gun?

— It doesn't matter.

— But what about Marguerite? What happened to Marguerite?

In my mind's eye, I saw my sister sitting on my back, smiling. I hoped she had run away.

Manman stopped and looked at me. That flatness had come into her eyes again.

— They took her, she said eventually. Those chimères.

— Why?

Manman hesitated.

— She's a girl, she said. And she's pretty. One day she might be valuable.

I thought that was stupid. I thought Marguerite was valuable now. Manman looked like she was going to cry, and I didn't blame her. But there was one thing I was grateful for: Marguerite was alive.

— I'll get her back, I said.

Manman, she kind of nodded her head.

— It's hard, she said. But we should count our blessings. We're alive and we're together, you and me. We have each other.

— Yeah, I said.

Manman, she liked to count her blessings. It didn't usually take long.

We walked across the sand to where the fishermen moored their boats. I could see the one Papa and his friend used. I wondered then if Papa really was a fisherman. Manman wouldn't tell me where the gun had come from, but what if it was his? What if he was a chimère, too?

Maybe I didn't wonder that, actually. It's hard for me to remember. But I do wonder it now.

— I'll do whatever it takes, I told Manman. I'll bring Marguerite home.

— OK, she said. OK.

I don't think she believed me – but she should have. If she had, I might not be in this mess. When you keep hurting someone, you do one of three things. Either you fill them up with hate, and they destroy everything around them. Or you fill them up with sadness, and they destroy themselves. Or you fill them up with justice, and they try to destroy everything that's bad and cruel in this world.

Me, I was the first kind of person.

THEN

In his dream, Toussaint rode back to Bois Caiman. He knew the blind houngan lived there. People said he could speak to the alligators and had become their king. They said there were dead people in the marshes, zombis who he had put there and that he could make rise up and kill anyone who threatened him. Toussaint thought those were good stories to put about if you wanted to be left alone, and anyway, he knew perfectly well how zombis were made – it was a process more of pharmacology than death.

He followed a dim light through the trees, careful of the swamp on both sides of the track. A small voice inside him said that this was not really happening, but he was still scared.

There was a rich, vegetable smell of decay. It was dark, the moon that had been so full and fat the previous night obscured by dense clouds. He could see very little other than the looming shapes of the trees, the spidery shadows of the vines. Last night he had been amongst friends – fellow slaves. Tonight he was a warm living thing in the midst of an indifference of chilly mud. He could easily imagine that the smell came from rotting bodies, that there *were* dead people, zombis, in the mud to either side . . .

He shivered, tightening his grip on the horse's bridle. He focused on the light, followed it until he came to a small hut. He dismounted, tethered the horse, and knocked before entering.

The blind houngan sat on a chair in a simple, clean room. Except for some jars of powder, two chairs, some veves drawn on the floor, the room was empty.

— You came back, said the houngan.

— Yes. Is this real? Am I here? Or is it a dream?

— Can't it be both? said the houngan. Tell me. This spirit that is inside you, do you want me to take it out?

— I want you to . . . I don't know. What is it? I told the others it was Ogou, but I don't think that's true.

— I don't know for certain what it is, said the houngan. It's not Ogou Badagry, I agree. I would've been aware of his coming. We all would – Ogou is the lwa of war, and when he possesses a person, there is usually violence.

Toussaint shook his head vehemently.

— I don't know if I want this, he said. I felt good to begin with. Righteous. But we'll have to kill so many if we want our freedom. Last night it was all I could do to stop the slaves killing my master. And he was never cruel to them.

The houngan nodded.

— Life must be paid for with death, he said.

He indicated the chair beside him, gestured for Toussaint to sit.

89

Toussaint did so, and he was aware that he had just lied, although he hadn't intended to. He might not want to lead the rebellion, not precisely, but he knew that he would. It was his destiny. And who was to say that it wasn't the very thing to possess him that would give him the strength to lead his people?

In his previous dream, he had been in a city like none he had ever seen before, with houses made from metal and people dressed in the clothes of lunatics. Yet he had known it was the future, and in that land blacks walked free everywhere and there were no whites that he could see. There, he was a boy, or he was in the dreams of the boy; he was not sure which. At the same time, he was himself. It was a strange sensation, one that had lingered long after he had woken, and even though he had forgotten much of his dream, he remembered one essential truth.

He knew that they were going to win, because the boy he had been in that strange future knew it was not right for one person to own another, not anymore. That was why Toussaint had no doubt that he would lead. No one else had the same conviction. No one else could pursue the cause knowing that it was not only just, but that it was possible.

The problem was that he didn't necessarily want to. He had never killed anyone in his life, and he didn't want to start now. He wanted to understand all sides of a conflict before he ever had to pick up a weapon.

— How do you feel, otherwise? the houngan said. What do you know of the thing that entered you? Because something did. I sensed it. We all sensed it.

— I like it, said Toussaint. That's what scares me. And I can read! I could never read before.

The houngan nodded slowly.

— The lwa bring strange gifts, he said.

— I'm not sure if it is a lwa, said Toussaint. Is there a way to tell? Can you . . . examine me?

The houngan put out his hands.

— Give me your head, he said. Lean forward.

Toussaint inclined his forehead and felt the old man's calloused hands gently cradle his head. Some time passed whilst the houngan made little noises of consideration. Finally he took a deep, deliberate breath, released it unevenly, and he let go.

— It doesn't make sense, he said.

— What doesn't?

— There is only one soul in you. There is only one you. It's as if . . . as if there isn't anything else. The houngan was talking to himself as much as to Toussaint. But I was there! I sensed you buckle, and be taken!

Toussaint stood up shakily.

— When I was a boy, a houngan said that I had half a soul. My twin sister died when we were young. The houngan told me about Marassa, said we had had power when we were together, but when my sister died the power was lost. My mother thought . . .

Toussaint had been about to speak of his twin sister, and how she had died, how it had made him feel, but he stopped. He did not want to speak of his life to the houngan. He kicked at his chair instead and sent it sprawling across the dirt floor.

91

— What should I do? he asked.

— I can't tell you, said the houngan. Boukman says you'll lead the people to freedom, but what do I know? I'm a blind man. The whites did that to me. So many of them will have to die. You said it yourself. So perhaps you should run to the mountains, live there with your son whilst the war wages. They may even win without you. Boukman says you're indispensable . . . unique, but you seem an ordinary man to me. One soul, one nose, two eyes.

Toussaint trembled. He was thinking of the future, where he had walked through streets of black people living all together in their own homes. He was thinking of how in the future he had glimpsed he had been a boy, and the boy had known the name of Toussaint. He stepped over to the chair he had kicked and he righted it. He was startled to see the houngan standing right in front of him all of a sudden, with some kind of pipe in his mouth. He took it out, made a circle of his lips, and blew.

Smoke drifted toward Toussaint, curled around his face until he was standing in a gray fog.

He woke.

He was lying in bed in his cottage. Slaves had already begun to gather in the courtyard of the big house, in the fields, awaiting his word. Yet, to his surprise, de Libertas had been able to escape and his grand house still stood, not yet burned.

Toussaint stared at the ceiling and the grayness around him, and he thought hard. He did not want to kill the whites – it was true what he had told the houngan. He was filled with an overwhelming desire not for vengeance, but for justice. He saw a world that crushed people beneath its wheels, and he determined to take its reins and steer it onto sweeter ground.

It seemed to him, lying there, that there were three kinds of slaves, three kinds of people. There were those who were so filled with hate by their experience, by their oppression, that they snapped and destroyed property or people. There were those who were so filled with sadness by their experience that they snapped and destroyed themselves; someone would find them hanging in the barn, or lying in the field with slit wrists; Toussaint had been that someone several times, had found them like that. It made him cry, always. The third kind of person, though, was filled by their experience with a fierce longing for justice, a fierce desire to make things right in the world, to redress the balance.

In the darkness, Toussaint fancied that he was the third kind of person, and to fire his soul, to fill himself with a sense of the need for justice, he called up the faces that embodied for him slavery's evil.

He lay there, and he remembered.

He remembered a baby.

This baby was not Toussaint's; it belonged to a Chérie, a woman slave from the neighboring plantation. Or, rather, it didn't belong to her – it belonged to her master, and this was the root of the problem. Toussaint had been fourteen when

Chérie arrived one moonless night at the small cottage where he lived with his father. She knocked at the door in the dead of night, startling them both badly and making them think something terrible had occurred. It hadn't, but it was about to.

Chérie had only just given birth and the baby was swaddled in rags she had torn from her own clothes. She had run, she told Toussaint's father, because she knew that otherwise the baby would be taken from her and sold. Black babies were worth many hundreds of francs, because eventually they would become black slaves.

— How can it be my master's? she said. He didn't make her.

Toussaint's father sighed.

— He owns you both, he said. It's the way of things. If he had made her it might have been better. Then she would have been a mulat.

Toussaint frowned. This was perhaps the first true intimation he had received that slavery might be wrong. He had never thought about it too much before, but now he wondered how it could be right for a man to sell a woman's baby.

— Please, said Chérie. Please, let us stay, just for tonight. The baby has a fever. I thought perhaps . . .

Toussaint's father was skilled in the mixing of simples. It was well known throughout the province that he could help when a child was sickly or a man was dying. Now he threw up his hands and made a tutting noise, but he moved aside and let the woman in.

No more than an hour later, there was another knocking at the door. Toussaint peered through the window to see men with torches, some on horseback. The torches threw his own shadow long and spindly along the floorboards. When his father opened the door, the men shoved past him, knocking his head against the wall. On searching the cottage, they easily found Chérie and her baby and they dragged both outside. Bayou de Libertas was also there – Toussaint saw him – but he said nothing; he just sat there on his bay stallion, his lips pursed.

Chérie was crying. She begged for forgiveness, hugging the baby to her.

One of the men – the master of a neighboring plantation, a man named Coste – dismounted from his horse and tore the baby from her hands.

— You stole my property, he said.

Coste tossed the baby to a younger man, a black. One of his slaves.

— I intended to sell it, he said, but it seems that this woman requires a lesson in the principle of ownership.

He made a brusque gesture.

— Kill it.

The slave betrayed no hint of emotion as he grasped the baby by her ankles, upended her, and snapped her neck. The bones broke, percussively.

Chérie sank to her knees, wailing. She did not stop wailing. Toussaint had never heard such a sound; it was inhuman. It was a horrible scream that knew no reason. It was the sound of a person's mind breaking, never to be whole again.

Coste turned to Toussaint and his father.

— Arrest that man, he said. For aiding and abetting a fugitive.

At this, Bayou spoke for the first time.

— No, he said. I've already permitted you to commit murder on my land, but I won't permit you to take one of my slaves from me. I vouch for the man – he has a kind soul and cannot abide to see a woman in distress. I ask you to forgive him.

Coste grumbled at that, but he got up on his horse again and had one of his men tie a rope around Chérie's ankles.

— Au revoir, Bayou, he said. Thank you for your assistance. I'll return this bitch to her kennel now and hope that the discomfort of her journey teaches her the value of obedience.

Then he rode off, the rope attached to his bridle, dragging Chérie behind, screaming. Toussaint looked away from the bumping, twisting body.

Toussaint's father tried to make eye contact with Bayou.

— Could you not have stopped them? he said.

Bayou would not meet his gaze.

— She belongs to him, he said. What could I do? Be glad I didn't give you to him.

He remembered a man.

Toussaint was younger at this time. Perhaps eight. His father had been called to a plantation five or six miles away, further up in the foothills. There was a slave who had been wounded, and his master – hearing of Toussaint's father's abilities – had requested his help.

They rode down an avenue of poplar trees that had been implanted from France, both on the same horse, for although Toussaint's father was well treated by Bayou de Libertas he was only allowed the use of one old nag. When they arrived at the property, all Roman columns and greenhouses, they were shown to an outhouse that had evidently, until recently, contained animals of some kind. Pigs, Toussaint guessed, from the smell.

The master stood imperiously in the center of the room. He was flanked by another white man, possibly his son, who was holding a machete in one hand and a rifle in the other. Both wore suspicious expressions on their faces – Toussaint thought they had that look all white men get when they find themselves in a confined space with blacks they've never met before.

By them was a canvas stretcher on which a large black man lay, face down. His back was a horror. A few thin, ribbon-like tatters of skin still adhered to the flesh, but mostly it was a mess of bloody muscle, in one or two places bone showing through, the whole thing like the map of some evil country. The stench was awful. Toussaint could tell at once that the flesh was rotting, for he had seen decaying meat often – had been fed it sometimes – and he knew what it looked and smelled like. There was a white fluid oozing from the wound – if it is possible to call a man's whole back a single wound.

Toussaint's father kneeled by the slave and examined his back.

— He was whipped? he inquired, his voice neutral.

— Yes, said the master. He stole from me.

— What did he steal? asked Toussaint.

His father shot him a look, but the master laughed.

— A curious one, your boy, he said. The man stole bread. Apparently he thinks that I don't feed him well enough. He's wrong. We always feed our slaves well, otherwise what use would they be in the fields?

He laughed again, and the younger man laughed with him. Both had double chins that wobbled as they laughed, and mustaches that quivered. Toussaint noted that their eyes were blue and pale, a color that he forever afterward associated with cruelty, to the extent that he could not bear an early summer's day, when there were few clouds in the sky.

— The whipping was perhaps . . . a little zealous, said Toussaint's father.

Even at his young age, Toussaint could tell he was measuring his words carefully, as if they were very expensive and had to be rationed out.

The master shrugged.

— It's a lesson to the others, not just to this one, he said.

Toussaint's father sniffed at the putrefying flesh, and opened one of the man's eyes. He sighed.

— The infection has spread, he said. See these red filaments running through his flesh? That is poison in his blood. I can make him some willow-bark tea for the fever, and there are plants that can be mixed to treat the blood poisoning. With careful attention he may live. He'll need plenty of food – I suggest porridge, thin enough to be spooned down his throat. And water, naturally. If he survives, it'll take weeks, possibly months, for him to recover. He won't be able to work for a long time. And there's no guarantee that –

— Enough, said the master.

He held out a hand and the man who might have been his son handed him the rifle.

The master shook his head.

The younger man handed over the machete.

The first blow didn't take the injured slave's head off. Nor did the second. The man woke up, of course – he whimpered and jerked, his eyes rolling. It took four great hacking slashes before the head finally dangled from a half-broken length of spine.

Toussaint began to cry.

His father was trembling, close to tears himself.

— The man was yours to deal with as you chose, he said hesitantly, but might not a bullet have been more humane?

— Bullets cost money, said the master.

He turned and left the outhouse.

That was when Toussaint fell to his knees and was sick. His father stroked his head and murmured, but that didn't make it better.

He remembered a woman.

This woman, like the baby, belonged to Coste. Toussaint had steered clear of this master and his slaves since the incident of the baby, but it proved impossible to avoid him forever.

Toussaint was older in this memory, perhaps twenty, and his father was growing more feeble by the day. So it was Toussaint who was sent to a woman in a nearby village, to give her succor during childbirth. He took with him several herbs and concoctions, and was relieved to find that, when the time came, he was able to remain calm and to ease the woman's pain, even as he delivered the baby. With scissors heated white-hot in the fire, he cut the umbilical cord, and by the early hours of the morning he was ready to leave mother and baby, and ride for home.

All of these medical skills would help him enormously when he became a general. He would be the first to start tending to the wounded after a battle, and the last to stop. His compassion, too, would serve him well when it came to leading men.

But it did not on that night.

Coming along the track to the Libertas farm, he passed a number of shadow-shapes moving in the sugar cane and the darkness, and heard a woman scream. He hitched his horse, then made his way through the tall stems of the plants. He came upon Pierre Coste, who was the old master's nephew, and several of his friends raping a black girl who could not have been much older than seventeen. It was she who had been screaming.

When Toussaint stepped into the clearing they had made in the cane, she did not even register him – her eyes were a white emptiness. She had been beaten, Toussaint could see. He had seen a lot of people beaten; he didn't need his medical skills or his compassion to recognize the signs.

No – he had seen a lot of *slaves* beaten. He had seen men whipped for not working hard enough; he had seen men whipped for working too hard and wearing themselves out.

— Stop, he said.

The men looked up at him.

Pierre Coste gave a snarl that was more animal than human.

— Be off with you, negro, he said.

Toussaint drew a breath.

— You're hurting her.

The young man sneered.

— You'd rather we hurt you? he asked.

It was a rhetorical question.

They hurt Toussaint – badly. When he finally crawled back to his father's cottage, he had one eye forced shut by swelling, three broken ribs, a crushed hand, a broken leg, and a cracked skull. He was bleeding from his mouth and his nose and his eyes.

Bayou de Libertas was horrified and saddened when he heard what had happened.

— Men like that give us all a bad name, he said.

Toussaint nodded, although he didn't agree, feeling as he did so the ache in his neck from the men's boots. He thought most men would become like that if they were presented with people and told that they were not so much people as belongings, as chattel. Toussaint had, at this point, already become acquainted with Boukman and his revolutionary ideas, but it was when he saw his own blood behind him in the dust of the road that something crystallized in his mind – something he had almost apprehended, but not entirely grasped, when he had seen the baby killed years before. *The blood of all creatures is the same, and mocks their uniqueness.* His, the baby's, the mother's, all the same, all indistinguishable from the blood of any animal, no different from that of a horse, nor of a pig. As he dragged himself back to the plantation, Toussaint saw the magic trick of slavery, and he knew Boukman was right.

This was the magic: it was merely an idea that made men into animals.

Yes, there were slave owners who were relatively kind and gentle – Bayou was one of them – but animals were disposable for good men and bad alike. Even Bayou, for all his natural goodness, for all his squeamishness, had stood by as butchery was committed on his soil. Although Toussaint could see that Bayou was truly pained to see his favorite slave's wounds, he would never seek real reparation for them. A man might love his horses, might not whip them as others do, but if his horse were to kick a wealthy neighbor, he would stand aside whilst his neighbor punished it.

This. This was the truth that Toussaint suddenly saw: that an evil idea makes bad men of everyone who believes in it.

And that, to Toussaint's regret, included Bayou de Libertas.

After the attack on Toussaint, Bayou didn't require him to work for some weeks, in order that he could recover. That was what passed for mercy amongst the whites.

So it was that sometime later, Toussaint was sitting outside under the eaves of the cottage, watching the sunset, when the young men from the Coste plantation came riding up the path to the Libertas house. They didn't even glance in his direction – perhaps they didn't recognize the slave who had tried to ruin their fun.

Less than half an hour later, the young men left again.

That night, Toussaint saw Bayou as he visited the cottage to check on his father. Bayou was ten years older than Toussaint, in the prime of his life, and he was vigorous in his habit of patrolling the perimeters of his property and checking all his belongings, including his slaves, before retiring to bed.

— Pierre and his friends . . . said Toussaint, as he let the man through the door. Did they come to apologize?

Bayou de Libertas gave a wan smile.

— They came to give me this, he said, drawing a money pouch from his pocket. My compensation for the time that you've been unable to work. Men like that, they don't apologize. To them you're just property. But Pierre's uncle was angry with him for damaging *my* property, so he told them to bring this money.

Toussaint stared at the pouch. *Compensation?* He had thought the beating painful, but this cut through him like a knife. He mumbled something – afterward he couldn't remember what. He could see that Bayou was angry with the boys, could see, even, that Bayou was ashamed by their behavior, but still, a thought echoed around his mind.

You didn't have to take the money, was the thought. *You didn't have to accept the compensation.*

His resolve to help Boukman stemmed from this moment. If there was to be an uprising, he would be part of it. He

103

could not live in a world where a man could break the bones of another, and then pay compensation if they felt like it, if their esteem for the man's owner was great enough to warrant it.

He remembered it all.

He remembered it all, and he wept.

His son woke. Isaac came to the bed and asked what ailed his father. Toussaint told him he had dreamed a bad dream, but it was better now. It was all going to be better now.

He thought, as he lay there in bed, of how he had never learned to read, as Boukman had. What point was there in reading when you were nothing but an owned thing, to be whipped or sold on a whim? When the only things to read were written in the language of the whites and did not speak to you?

Now he could read, despite never having sought the ability. It had been accorded to him, granted, a gift. This gift – and his visions of the future – were how Toussaint knew that he had been chosen. It is not given to the common ranks of man to suddenly know, in a single night, how to read and write and compute figures.

His decision had been made. He would lead the slaves; he would destroy the idea of *masters* for good, and there would be no more slaves. One could call a master a good master because he did not whip his slaves, but ultimately he was still an owner of men, and men were not made to be owned.

One could call a tiger a good tiger because it kills only to eat, not out of pleasure as a cat sometimes does, but it still kills. And Toussaint's father had always said, in the Creole that was his only language, ptit tig se tig.

The son of a tiger is still a tiger.

Like father, like son.

My father was a great man, thought Toussaint. *Perhaps I will be a great man, too.*

His determination coursing through his veins, he closed his eyes.

Then he was in Bois Caiman again, staring up at the night sky as something entered him, as something possessed his soul. If anyone had been watching Toussaint, they would have seen him tense, his eyes rolling back, before he unmoored himself from the world and floated into a dream.

He crossed worlds and time, and he was a boy, and loud music was playing – except he thought perhaps it was all in his head – and a man was saying something in English that Toussaint could not understand, and the notes and beats of the music were like a scream of furious anger, like a murder made sound.

NOW

I'm trying to remember all the words to *Ready to Die* by the Notorious B.I.G. – Biggie Smalls, they also call him. He's got two names, like I do. I don't know what his real name is. Was. He's dead now, just like Biggie, who took his name.

I have my own real name, but I stopped being called that when I started rolling with Biggie and Route 9. Then I became just Shorty, cos that's what Biggie called me. It means kid, and it means small, too. That's about right, I guess. I was the youngest in the crew.

Taking a name is dangerous shit, cos you can bring down a person's fate on you – Biggie learned that his ownself when he got gunned down just like Biggie Smalls.

But Biggie was proud to be called Biggie. He was always mouthing off about the East Coast Crew, about Tupac, all this stupid bullshit from a country he had never been to. He said someone got to carry on that legacy, someone got to represent. When he wasn't listening to his own songs, he was always listening to Biggie Smalls, especially *Ready to Die*.

Over and over. It makes me mad that I can't remember all the words, cos I must've heard those songs, like, a thousand times. The Notorious B.I.G. was a gangster before he was a rapper, and I think Biggie learned how to be a gangster from these songs, at least in some ways.

I got the first verse down, so now I try and remember the second one. This song, it's like it's in my blood, in my brain cells. It's from songs like this that I learned English. This is the verse where Biggie Smalls talks about getting a Lexus, getting a Rolex, getting paid. I always knew a Lexus was a car, cos I saw a couple of them on the road to the airport, but when I was younger I thought a Rolex was a car, too. Tintin laughed when I told him that, called me a cretin. But you think Tintin ever saw a Rolex in his whole goddamn life? You do, you're a fool.

I'm trying to remember the words so I don't lose my mind, all that shit about having a Glock, about making all the motherfuckers duck, but the third verse I can't remember.

Last time I slept I dreamed I was in a marsh, riding a horse. I've never ridden a horse in my life, but I was riding it easy. And I saw this old man, I think he was a houngan cos his place was like the truck that Biggie's houngan lived in. He called me Toussaint and spoke about Ogou Badagry, who Biggie wanted on his side when we went to war.

It was crazy, but it was like I knew everything that Toussaint was, everything he knew. How he'd learned medicine from his father. How his wife's eyes had been the precise color of polished amber at dusk. How Toussaint knew what that looked like – amber, I mean – cos his master used a piece of it as a paperweight in his study.

I forgot most of it when I woke up, but I remember those things. And it freaks me out, cos I don't even know what a paperweight is. And I'd never seen shit that was made out of amber, but still I can picture that paperweight in my mind, see the bubbles in the yellowy stone.

You feel me? So now I think, maybe I'm losing my shit, cos I can't be Toussaint l'Ouverture – that would be crazy. I keep telling myself I'm just dreaming, that I'm remembering this stuff cos Biggie was always talking about Toussaint, how he was just an illiterate slave who learned to read and write, and how he destroyed the French navy, how he was the hero who made us free. Sometimes he said that Dread Wilmè was Toussaint l'Ouverture born again, but as I lay there in the darkness after waking up I thought, no, that's not Dread – or maybe it was Dread once, but not anymore – that's *me*, I'm Toussaint. But then I made myself stop thinking that, cos it's completely mad, completely crazy.

Me, I never saw the big deal with Toussaint, anyway. I never thought we were so free as all that in the Site. We couldn't get out, except if we had a pass. We had soldiers guarding us, and the people were starving. I thought that made us kind of like slaves, but if anything Biggie had more of a hard-on for Toussaint than for Biggie Smalls, so I kept my mouth shut.

Yeah, I say to myself. You're remembering this stuff from Biggie.

But then I think, no. Biggie never said nothing about a

108

paperweight made of amber, and besides, I don't even know what amber is.

So then I've gone round in a circle, and I'm back to the start. I'm going mad with the darkness and the loneliness. The hand has stopped crawling toward me, making that rustling sound, and I think it was only doing that in my imagination to begin with. There's nobody else here. Just me. No wonder my mind is spinning out, making up this story for when I'm sleeping, and I try not to let myself think the worst thing – there's a part of me that's looking forward to going to sleep again, so I can see what happens next.

I get bored of saying the words to songs, so I sit and crack my knuckles instead. It makes a sound like guns going off a long way away. I wish I could see something. Anything. I wish I could see my hands. If I could see, I wouldn't feel so crazy.

I need to think about something, anything, so I think about Biggie. Yeah, Biggie. The mofo named himself after a dead gangster, like that was a good idea, like that was good luck.

Biggie, the first time I saw him, he was standing by Dread Wilmè's right-hand side, and that's not just an expression, man – that shit means something. It meant he was the second-biggest gangster in Solèy 19, the general who carried out all of Dread's black ops. And Dread got his orders from Aristide, so that made Biggie part of the government in the Site, almost.

We were in some shack somewhere, cos Dread was always moving around to avoid the militia who wanted to bring down Aristide's government. One of his guys found me and Manman in Papa's boat, brought us to see him. This was, I don't know, a few months after Papa got killed and Marguerite went missing. Dread, he was sitting on the bed, a gun tucked into the waistband of his jeans, his dreads hanging over his face – you didn't see Dread's face till he wanted you to see it. There was a smell of unwashed clothes in the air. Manman and me, we were trying not to look at the young men standing around us with guns.

Dread was younger than you would think – thirty, maybe. He had this music on when we came in, not rap like Biggie liked, but some real old Haitian stuff, maybe vodou songs. Dread wasn't looking at us, just reading some book. Biggie was standing next to him, only I didn't know he was Biggie then, if that makes sense. I just knew he looked cool, with his baseball cap and his low jeans, his underwear showing. I guess he was only fourteen, maybe fifteen.

Dread still didn't look up, but he tossed the book at me and my hands flashed out and I caught it.

— Read the third page, he said.

I fumbled with the book, got it open.

— Toussaint was a slave, yes, but he was a man of noble countenance and –

— Good, said Dread.

He looked up for the first time and I saw that his eyes were huge and black, like windows into something bad, like his soul was older than I could imagine, only not in a good way like Marguerite's. In a scary way.

— I heard you could read and I didn't hear wrong, he continued. Your papa raised you right.

Manman did this, like, half-choke, half-sob thing, and I looked down at the ground.

— I'm sorry, said Dread. I've heard about what happened to your husband. To your papa. Dread took a cell phone from his pocket and waved it at us. I've spoken to Aristide. He agrees with me. We're going to give you a house here in Solèy 19. We'll look after you, keep you away from those anti-government fuckers. And we'll send you to school.

— Oh, thank you, thank you, said Manman. There were tears on her cheeks. Merci, Dread.

— Don't thank me, he said. Thank the prime minister.

I turned to Manman.

— What about Marguerite? I asked.

Manman swallowed, then nodded at me. She took a step forward and put her hands together, like she was praying.

— Dread, you know I've been Lavalas all my life. Aristide, he delivered my children.

— We know, said Dread. That's why we want to do right by you, keep you protected.

— So, said Manman, the men who killed my husband, they . . . took my daughter. She's the same age as my son – they're twins. We . . . I . . . we need her back. Will you look for her?

Dread, he looked at her slow for a moment before he stood up and took her hands. I saw how big he was then. He reached the ceiling and it was like the room was too small to contain him, like anything would be too small to contain him. There were scars on his face and his neck, like someone had tried to remove his head.

111

— We'll try, he said. He turned to the guy next to him. Biggie, he said. And that was how I heard Biggie's name for the first time. Take them to their house, he told him. And make sure the boy receives an education.

At that moment, I didn't see the guns, I only saw the book I was holding, which I handed back to Dread.

— No, said Dread. Keep it. Read it. That book will open your mind, tell you how the Haitians rose up to throw off the yoke of oppression, man. These people who want to remove Aristide, they want to make us slaves again. Truth. Read that book, maybe you can help fight them better.

— Thank you, I said.

You know what? I never did read that book. I think I lost it, maybe, when we moved. I was thinking so hard about my papa, and about Marguerite and whether we would see her again, that I forgot all about it.

Right now, I wish to fuck I had read it.

My mind drifts off, and I start to think about vodou. Toussaint, he went to see a houngan, talked about some thing that was inside him. I saw a houngan once, too – right before Biggie shot him – and he said I was half a person. I thought vodou was bullshit back then, a lie for people who wanted to feel safe. I thought it when Dread was burned, and I thought it afterward, too.

Biggie was different. Biggie thought that cos of the bone dust the houngan had sprinkled on him bullets couldn't kill

112

him. Like I said, I thought that was about the stupidest thing ever.

But now I'm not so sure. I've seen Biggie talk to me, bullet holes all through him, like a bowl for draining vegetables. And I've seen . . . I don't know what I've seen. I've seen myself flying through the night air and rushing down and going into the mouth of a man, and then I was dreaming of Toussaint. I think, maybe there's something to this vodou stuff after all.

I reach into my pocket and I take out my pwen. I hadn't really thought about it till that moment. Dread Wilmè gave it to me. It's a stone with a god in it, from the old country. A gede lwa, one of our ancestors. It's meant to protect me, so I think, well, now is the time. I hold it in my hand. It's smooth, round. It's like it came from the sea it's so polished. I thought it didn't work when I got shot in the arm and ended up in here. But now I think, what if it stopped me getting shot in the heart? Or in the head?

I lift the pwen to my ear.

— Tell me, lwa, I say. Tell me if there's a way out.

Nothing.

I hold the stone tight. I ask it for strength. I ask it to stop me going mad. I ask it to find me food. My stomach is a tiny curled-up thing, like a cat, and it's got claws that dig into me. My mouth is a desert that stretches miles in every direction. My stomach is a creature hurting me from the inside.

The pwen is silent, but I'm feeling its smoothness with my fingers and I have another thought. I put the stone in my mouth and I suck it, and there's, like, a firework burst in front

113

of my eyes, even though there's no light. Saliva runs down my throat, and I swear it's like I'm drinking a glass of cold water, even though there is no water.

I think, maybe the pwen will save my life after all. I take the stone out of my mouth and I say:

— Thank you, lwa.

Then I suck it again.

I'm glad I didn't give the pwen to Tintin. Right now, it feels like it's saving my life. I know it's just a stone and all I'm drinking is my own spit, but there's a little part of me that believes something different – there's a little part of me that thinks the stone is giving me water, keeping me alive.

I told you I saw two men killed before my eyes by the time I was eleven years old.

This is how it happened the second time.

I was, like, one month from my eleventh birthday. Manman and me, we'd been living on our own for 877 days, and I'd been going to school on Dread Wilmè's dime, while Manman had been doing I don't know what for Lavalas. Only, that got harder, cos in between Papa dying and this time I'm talking about now, Aristide got kicked out of the country for, like, the third time, and you can imagine how happy Lavalas were about that.

I was playing again, but alone this time. I was in the middle of our street, trying to build a bike. I'd seen one on a TV which someone had set up in one of the squares in the Site, so that people could sit on the ground and watch it. I'd found

114

a couple of wheels from old prams, and some chains and other parts that were on the trash heap. I spent hours on that bike and never had much to show for it.

Like the night I was born, it was very dark. It seems like it's always dark when the big things go down in my life – when we were born, when my papa was killed, when Dread Wilmè died.

This was after Aristide had gone, like I said. The Americans made him leave, except Biggie said it was them who put him in the palace in the first place. I never understood that. I asked Manman about it and she said it was complicated. She said that about everything. Then when I asked too many questions she would say, chita chouter yon jour wap fait goal. *Careful, or you'll get what you're looking for.*

I think she meant that some answers are dangerous.

So, Aristide was gone. Some moun said he was in Africa, some moun said he was in South America. Others, they said he would come back one day, when he was ready. Maybe he's come back now. Maybe he was so pleased to see Haiti again he jumped off the plane and *pouf*, the hospital fell down. The way Manman talked about him, you'd think he was some giant, some magical big guy from a story, more powerful than any ordinary person, so that when he jumped up and down, you could imagine the buildings shaking.

But Dread Wilmè still lived in the Site. Before, he would send his chimères to fight the rebels. After Aristide left, it got worse. The new government gave more guns to the Boston guys, the rebels, and told them to go after Dread Wilmè, cos he had been Aristide's man. Also, the police would come into the slum and hunt for Lavalas supporters. With them were the attachés – they were like police, but they wore black masks and no moun could see who they were. Usually they made people they didn't like disappear, but sometimes they had the chance to kill people, and the best time for them to do that was during the demonstrations. There were lots of demos and Manman took me on some. You have to understand: the Site was the biggest base for Aristide. He said he'd make the poor rich, so the poor loved him. It makes sense, right?

When the military kicked him out, and the UN came, the Site fucking exploded. It stands to reason.

I remember one demo. It was Haitian Flag Day, and thousands of us went out on the streets of the Site, singing songs in support of Aristide, calling for him to come back, singing songs against Latortue, who was the prime minster of the government that replaced him.

— Trop de sang a coulé, Latortue doit s'en aller.

Too much blood has flowed, Latortue has to go.

We sang in French, so the reporters could understand, which was a joke, cos there were no reporters there anyway, even though we must have been, like, 10,000, minimum. We were all carrying Haitian flags and it was like a big party, all these people, all this color.

The attachés came when we were close to the sea, on the main avenue. There were UN soldiers behind them in armored trucks, but they didn't do anything. The attachés were in jeeps, and they got out with their black masks on and their rifles in their hands. Manman and me, we were near the

116

front of the crowd, so we saw them, and we started to back away. People were shouting out in fear, and then the shooting began. One guy in front of me, he went down on his knees, and he was crawling toward me like a zombi, man. I was screaming and screaming. I wanted to get away from him more than I wanted to get away from the bullets.

You, maybe you live in a world where people don't get shot. I know what you're picturing. I've seen anpil movies. You think bullet holes in a person look like little circular holes, like red coins. They don't. What a bullet does, it goes into a person and it tears, it rips them open, makes them into a monster. They're not human anymore.

This guy in front of me, he'd been hit in the face, and his whole cheek, the whole side of his face had been, like, blown out about half a meter from his body, like a horn, like a trunk, like some kind of awful animal thing. You have never seen shit like this in your life, mwen jire. He was like a zombi, I'm telling you, like something out of a horror movie. And he was still crawling toward me, this massive bloody growth out of his head, making this animal sound, too.

I don't remember much of what happened after that. It was all running and screaming. Eventually we found ourselves in an alley with lots of other people and we couldn't hear gunfire anymore.

The UN soldiers came and locked everyone into the slum so they couldn't escape. That's what they did to people in the Site during the break-bones time.

We called the UN soldiers casques-bleus, cos they wore

blue helmets. They put cargo containers on the entrances and exits to the Site, and they built checkpoints and put soldiers on them. They're still there – sometimes, me and Tintin, we drove as close as we dared and showed them our asses.

It was a dog fight and the Site was the pit. Manman said 3,000 people died in twelve months.

But in those twelve months, there was one person who didn't die. One person who moved around constantly, sleeping in a different place every night, evading the men sent to kill him.

Dread Wilmè.

We had moved to Solèy 19, thanks to Dread, and for a long time, our part of the Site had been safe, cos Aristide paid Dread Wilmè to protect the people. Manman knew Dread Wilmè from her time with the Lavalas party. She respected him. He sold drugs, but he didn't tolerate crime. He didn't let anyone steal, or commit murder for no reason.

It was bad under Dread, but it was good at the same time.

Now Aristide was gone, though, Solèy 19 was no longer safe. Some of the men who worked for Dread Wilmè had taken their guns and become chimères, working for no moun but their ownselves. Also, there were many men who wanted to kill Dread cos they didn't like Aristide, and that included the government, who were handing out guns like they were lottery tickets. Plus, the UN wanted to kill all of them, so there would be no more guns in the Site. Manman was always frightened during the break-bones time, which was basically the whole time after Aristide was banished for good, cos the people from the Site, they just wouldn't give up on him, on the dream he'd sold them.

OK, so now you know the lowdown on everything that was going on at that time, when I saw my second man get killed.

That night, Manman was outside, too, cos it was so hot. She had an old radio and she was listening to it, sitting on a chair outside the shack. She was keeping an eye on me, as I worked on my bike.

With no warning, the radio went off and all the lights.

I heard someone scream. That wasn't unusual in the slum, but then I heard another loud noise. A sort of rumbling. It was a little bit like the noise I heard when everything fell down.

Rrrrrum, rrrrrumm, rrrrruuuum, rrrrruuuuum.

I'm trying to show you the noise. I'm making it here in the dark and I'm not doing it so good, but still, if you could hear me, you'd understand.

But you don't hear me, do you? I hear your voices less and less often now – the voices asking if there's anyone alive down here – but you don't hear mine. You don't hear me when I shout back.

So, I have to describe the noise. It's hard to do. You'll have to use your imagination.

OK, you're in the dark. There's piti-piti light coming from the rich houses on the hill, but in the slum it's preske pitch-black. You can hardly see a thing except for candles, matches, the glow of cigarettes. You can just smell the salt of the sea and the fish. You can smell oil from the bike chain in your hand. But mostly you can smell sewage. From somewhere in the darkness this rumbling sound is coming, and then from somewhere above you another sound is coming, like, *thwup, thwup, thwup, thwup*, incredibly loud, a million bees overhead.

That was what it was like – and also not. I can't put it into words.

I dropped the chain. I thought I'd better run from whatever was making that noise, so I started to move.

But suddenly there was bright light everywhere, and I froze. A spotlight on an armored truck came on, blinding white. Fire was spitting from guns.

A bullet went, *fwwwwiiiiiip*, and pinged into the corrugated iron behind me.

I was terrified. I felt like I couldn't get enough air in my chest to move, like I was just eyes, watching, and ears, hearing the boom of the gunfire, and all of the rest of my body had disappeared.

I thought, very clearly, I'm going to die.

And I knew – really knew – for the first time that I didn't want to.

I saw UN helmets and under them machine guns, rattling fire. That sound above turned out to be a helicopter and it was shooting down into the shacks on the other side of the street.

There was more gunfire coming from the shacks. A man was running away down the street. I didn't know if he was a chimère or not, but it didn't matter cos one of the soldiers shot him in the back. I saw a little girl standing very still and screaming, screaming, on the other side of the street from our shack, till something hit her and the top of her face was taken off, and she swayed on her legs for a moment, then fell in the mud.

There was a door open and through it I saw Jeanne. She was this woman who lived opposite us with her little baby Willie. I never knew where the papa of this baby was; maybe he was dead, or maybe he'd just left her cos he couldn't afford to look after Willie. Anyway, she was lying on the ground in anpil blood, Willie on top of her. I wanted to see if he was alive, cos I liked Willie – he would smile when he saw me – but I couldn't cos there were still bullets flying all around.

I went down on my knees. I couldn't run; I could only stay there. I saw Manman standing outside our shack, shouting and shouting at me to run, but I couldn't – I was seeing these bullets flying everywhere and I was convinced that if I moved, one of them would hit me. I thought if I crouched, very still, then maybe they would stop shooting, and I would be OK. I turned around and there was this enormous tank coming toward me, still a little way off, but it wasn't steering away from me.

And the guns just kept firing. Dread's soldiers, they were trading fire with the casques-bleus, but I didn't see many MINUSTAH go down – they were all wearing armor and their guns were better. A couple of the gangsters dropped their guns and put up their hands, then the UN guys grabbed them and dragged them into an armored vehicle, a Humvee. I didn't know it then, but one of the people they arrested was Biggie.

He spent, like, a couple of years in prison after that night. They said he killed a soldier. Maybe he did, I don't know.

Finally I saw Dread Wilmè come out of a shack. I had no idea he was sleeping so near to us, but the chimères were always moving around, especially after Aristide was deposed. They never stayed in one shack for two nights running, in case someone found them.

Well, I guess someone found Dread Wilmè that night. His dreads were swinging crazily and he had a gun in each hand. I didn't know what his guns were then, but I do now. They were Uzis.

Dread Wilmè hit one soldier in the leg. But they were shooting him from the helicopter, they were shooting him from the tank, they were shooting him from the ground. Something hot exploded in my leg and I looked down to see a blossom of red on my jeans. I knew it was blood. The thing that shocked me was how much it hurt. I was already on my knees and now I fell down altogether.

Time slowed.

My leg pulsed with pain.

Lying there, I saw the ground stretching out before me, an endless muddy plane, and I saw my manman leave the shack and start moving toward me.

— No, I tried to say. Stay –

But then I must have fainted, cos I don't remember anything else. The rest is what my manman told me.

Manman was moving toward me and then something seized her tight. She was being held by a soldier – he'd come out of

122

the blackness and grabbed her arms, and she was struggling to get away, to run to me, but he wasn't letting her go. Me, I was lying in the mud, unconscious, and Dread Wilmè was between me and Manman. Coming toward me from the other side, still not stopping, was an armored vehicle, and Manman could see that it was heading straight for me, was going to crush me without hesitation to get Dread.

There were so many holes in Dread Wilmè, Manman said, you could see the light from the trucks and the torches on the soldiers' guns shining through him. I never believed that, but she swore it was true. Now, I kind of believe her. Now, I've seen shit that makes me think she was telling the truth. All these bullets in him, through him, my manman said, and he was still standing there, filtering the light, like that was his destiny.

Then – and this is the crazy bit – Dread Wilmè turned to me, and Manman said it was like he saw something holy, something that could save him. He started to move toward me. Bullets were still slamming into him, but he staggered toward me, the light flickering through the holes in him, like his body was the night sky and the bullet holes were the stars. And all the time that tank was continuing toward me – toward Dread Wilmè especially, but it was going to have to run me over to get to him.

Dread Wilmè did not want that to happen, it seemed. He staggered toward me without stopping for anyen, even as they shot him.

Dread Wilmè was still dying, still moving toward me, the

tank approaching. Manman couldn't believe how long it was taking, and she was screaming the whole time for the tank to stop. Manman said it took Dread minutes to reach me, not seconds, and he kept shouting:

— Ayiti viv, Ayiti viv.

Long live Haiti.

I don't believe that, though. If he was shot that many times he wouldn't have been shouting anyen. Me, I got shot in the leg and I fainted. In reality, all of this must have happened in, like, the time it takes to click your fingers.

Manman stood in the mud, constrained by the soldier who was pinning her arms behind her back. The street was running with blood like a river. That tank was just going and going, rumbling toward me, and she could see that some of the bullets were flying toward me, too. She knew that if the soldiers didn't stop shooting and the tank didn't stop driving I would be dead very soon. She was calling to the soldiers for help, but she was calling in the wrong languages. She found out afterward that the soldiers were from Jordan, which is a desert country far away – Manman told me they have camels there. What they were doing in Haiti, I don't know.

Finally, Dread Wilmè reached me, and he picked me up, Manman swore it, just as the Humvee was about to hit me. It was looming over us, like a moving wall. She was scared for a moment that it would hit him, and turn me and him into bloody mud, like the rest of the street. But Dread was just in time. He bent down, picked me up, and carried me to the side of the street. He pushed me against the wall of a shack and he lay over me, covering me. They continued to shoot him, again and again, till he didn't move anymore.

Then the soldiers got back in their trucks and their tank and the helicopter went, *thwup, thwup, thwup, thwup,* and flew away.

Manman crawled toward the body of Dread Wilmè. He was more holes than flesh and he was leaking all over the world, but she swears – mwen jire, mwen jire – that he opened his eye and rolled off me when he saw her. He was lying in a pool of blood, like the one that had grown between her legs when me and Marguerite were born, and she had a sense deep inside her of déjà vu. He had a socket where one of his eyes should have been and he was bleeding from a thousand wounds.

Dread fumbled in his pocket and took out this stone, a smooth pebble, like something worn by the sea. He pushed it into Manman's hand. She knew that it was a pwen, and there was a god in it that had traveled all the way from the old country in west Africa to be in her hand on that bloody street.

— For the boy, he said. He only has half a soul. He must be protected. One day soon, another soul will possess him and it could be good or it could be bad, but this shorty could be the one to . . .

He coughed, and blood flew from his mouth. There was a terrible, long pause.

— Ayiti, he whispered.

Haiti.

Manman tried to ask him more, to understand what he meant, why he had done what he did to save me. She had the feeling that she had heard a prophecy, but she didn't know what it was. She knew that Dread Wilmè was deep in vodou, was almost a houngan himself, and that he said and did nothing without meaning it. She couldn't stop thinking of him lying with me in that flaque of blood, and of the houngan who had told her that the baby inside her would be born and die in blood and darkness, but would live forever, too.

But Dread was gone. His blank eye, the one that was left, reflected only the blackness of the sky, as if the night had poured into it. Apparently, at the very moment he died, I took a deep breath and opened my eyes and squealed with terror and pain.

Manman held me in her arms, and she looked up and saw a black sky covered in stars, the same sky she'd seen through the hole in the church roof on the night we were born. Later, when she returned to our shack, she saw that the roof was full of bullet holes – from the helicopter, she guessed. She knew that if me and her had been in there we would have died, and she knew that this was a sign.

She just didn't know what it meant. Or, to be more precise, she was afraid she did. She was afraid Dread Wilmè's soul had left his body and entered mine, to take possession of Marguerite's half of my soul.

She was wrong, I know that now. It was not Dread Wilmè who became the other half of my soul.

THEN

Toussaint rode at the head of the small army. The soldiers, if they could be called that, were mostly on foot, dressed in mismatched raiment of multicolored cloth, ragged, their headdresses and weapons ludicrous and supplied by necessity alone. Some were even in women's dresses, their feet bare beneath, sporting with mockery the fine silks of their erstwhile masters.

He had gathered the slaves who had been at Bois Caiman, and they had quickly overcome the masters in this small corner of the country, meeting little resistance. As they went, they increased in strength, recruiting more blacks to the cause with each plantation that they liberated, growing larger all the time, as a baker rolls his dough about the board to incorporate the small pieces that have broken off.

However, the whites would be gathering their troops in the south, and it wouldn't be long before war began. Toussaint was determined to reach high ground before then. He had taken some maps from his ex-master's office, and had made a study of them. He reckoned that the mountains of the interior would make a fine redoubt, offering the advantage of height and secrecy, whilst providing land that they could cultivate. Many of the other slaves were thinking only of revenge, and several times he had intervened to prevent atrocities when they came to challenge the white self-styled owners of the land they freed. Toussaint was thinking further, though. He was thinking about what they would do when they had all quit their posts, and were free. They would need to eat. They would need to hold out against their foes, for surely the French would send reinforcements to destroy them?

Ahead, he was going to rendezvous with Boukman, who had ridden west already, with twenty men, to free the blacks and clear the land in front of them. Then, together, they would lead their people into the mountains and hopefully join up with the other leaders of the rebellion. Rumors had reached their ears that slaves in every part of the country had risen up, casting off their yoke of oppression and proclaiming themselves free. Toussaint had instructed all the men of his still-small army to spread the word that they were going to the high places to consolidate their power. He was confident that some blacks from other provinces would join him: the women and children, certainly; the cowards, no doubt; but also those with a longer-term view of the situation.

Toussaint could hear the men behind him singing of their victory. Already they had made up songs about the freedom they had won, and were chanting them more enthusiastically than they had ever chanted work songs, although the rhythms were the same, he noticed. He knew it would be a longer struggle than they suspected, but he didn't comment. He didn't think it would be good for morale.

At his side, Jean-Christophe was silent, riding with a thoughtful expression on his face. That was one of the things Toussaint liked about the boy and he was pleased to have him by his side. Jean-Christophe thought a lot, even if he was sometimes naive in his conclusions. Well, he considered, a little innocence would probably do Toussaint himself good in his new role – give him perspective.

The younger man had been trained by Bayou de Libertas to add up numbers and keep his accounts. Toussaint thought that could be useful, too. He'd had to prevent the men singing behind him from destroying everything in those old plantation houses. He had ordered them to be very carefully looted, and the gains brought with them, since they would need money as well as food. Inevitably, he hadn't been able to prevent deaths entirely, and he was sorry about that. The worst excesses, yes – he had saved some daughters from rape, some of the crueler masters from torture – but war was war, and he had been unable to help some. He thought he saw the dead whites behind him, too, traipsing at the rear of the rag-tag army, insubstantial, pale ghosts in fine clothes.

He was turning back in his saddle, regarding the motley soldiers, thinking about ghosts, and so he heard Jean-Christophe gasp before he saw anything. When he whirled around, his gorge rose, and he made a horrified noise. Ahead of him was a black man nailed to a tree by his feet, his head swinging upside down, his entrails hanging out and buzzing with flies.

Toussaint dismounted and stepped into the complicated shadow of the tree, lightness and darkness making curlicued patterns at his feet, as if trying to convey something by means of runes that no man could read, not even he.

When he drew nearer, he saw that the man was Boukman, and he felt something in his chest that might have been his heart breaking.

The younger man's throat had been slit – his head hung low because of it, the savage cut having severed the spine – and it was for this reason that Toussaint only recognized the features when he was close by. The stomach had been opened, too, and there was a bullet wound in the forehead.

— My god, said Jean-Christophe. It's as if they killed him several times.

— Yes, said Toussaint.

He was thinking of Boukman's pwen, and how the other man had always said that it would protect him and guard his life. *Perhaps it had*, thought Toussaint. *Perhaps Boukman had been difficult to kill, and so they had to mutilate him like this.*

Holding his breath – the smell was awful – he patted Boukman's clothes until he found what he was looking for. Boukman had sewn the stone into the lining of his jacket. Toussaint frowned at that and he wondered if Boukman had known, somehow, that he was in danger.

— What's that? said Jean-Christophe.

Toussaint turned the stone over in his hands.

130

— It's a god, he said. It gives protection.

— It doesn't seem to work, then, said Jean-Christophe.

— It depends when he died, doesn't it? Toussaint said. If a man has to be shot, knifed, and gutted before he dies, I'd say he was well protected.

Jean-Christophe blanched.

— I suppose so, he said.

Toussaint didn't know what the stone might do, or had done, but he knew it had been important to Boukman, as he knew that the rebellion was important to Boukman. He polished the pwen with his sleeve, then he slipped it into his pocket. This god had come all the way from Africa to live in Boukman's stone and Toussaint wouldn't let its journey end with Boukman's lifeless body. He crossed himself.

He took one last lingering look at Boukman's face. As he did so, an image proffered itself to his inward eyes: Boukman, at the card table in Toussaint's home, banging his hand on the table as he likened the whites to the house of a casino, and told Toussaint and the other influential slaves gathered there that they should no longer suffer their cards to be dealt to them, that they should take their cards for themselves. This was soon after Boukman had been brought to the plantation next to Bayou's to oversee the field labor. Boukman was smart, and the whites were smart enough to use him. They just didn't know how smart he was, or what *he* might use his intelligence for.

The card game had stopped – things tended to stop when Boukman spoke. With his hands, as he talked of the freedom they deserved, he rapidly constructed a castle of cards.

— This is the white nation of Haiti, he said. Nothing but a house of cards. We outnumber them. They hold their dominion over us through a kind of mental trick, making what is delicate and weak seem solid.

He blew on the cards, made them scatter.

— We are the wind, he said. We are the air and earth and mountains of this country, and we will take it from them.

Toussaint closed his eyes, remembering that voice, remembering the rapt expressions on the faces of the other men there. He only hoped he could inspire as Boukman had inspired.

He swung himself back up into the saddle. As they rode onward, they saw more and more bodies, all nailed to trees, but none as profoundly murdered as Boukman had been. *It was the stone*, Toussaint thought – no, he *knew*. He worried it in his pocket whilst he rode. The stone had protected Boukman, had made him hard to kill. He hoped its power would transfer to him, not because he didn't want to die, but because he wanted to fulfill Boukman's dream.

In point of fact, he was not afraid to die, not anymore. He now understood with a faith that he had never before possessed that he would see those he had lost when he died, that everything would be made whole, that he would talk to Boukman, and his mother and father and sister, again. It was true that there was no need on earth that could not be slaked and satisfied. When you are thirsty there is water. When you are hungry there is food. It is impossible to need a thing without that thing being available for the having. A man may want a green horse that flies, but he cannot *need* one, for there is no such thing.

At this precise moment, Toussaint felt that he needed Boukman, that he could not bear it if he never saw him again, and he knew, because this need existed, that it would be met.

After a while, they came to a large plantation; Toussaint didn't know its name, and it didn't matter. He stopped his horse abruptly when a shot rang out and a puff of dust rose from the track in front of him. The whites had fallen back, it seemed, and were going to defend the house. The sensible tactic would have been to go around the plantation to find a longer way to the mountains that would cause no bloodshed on either side. But Toussaint didn't see the trees and the dry track and the fenced fields full of sugar, waving in the breeze. He didn't see the white pillars of the house, shimmering in the heat at the end of the drive. He saw Boukman, swinging from that tree, a pool of his own blood beneath him, being feasted on by flies.

He turned to Jean-Christophe, who was the most agile man he knew, and a clever one.

— You'll go through the sugar cane, he said. Skirt around the house, and avoid the windows. Head for the woodshed if you can – it'll be at the rear of the building; the whites can't stand having things like that on display. They'll be watching the track, I'm sure of it. They won't see you coming.

— Then what? said Jean-Christophe.

— Set it alight, said Toussaint. We'll be waiting for them to come out.

A large man, who had distinguished himself as a fighter but showed a streak of terrible cruelty, stepped forward. Toussaint thought his name might be Matthieu.

— And then? he said. You want us to let them go again?

Toussaint ran his hand through his hair.

— No, he said. These ones you can kill.

NOW

I wish I could hear somebody talking. I wish I could hear Manman one more time. I remember when it was her shouting that made me come out of the darkness into the real world.

After I got shot, Manman waited till the soldiers had gone and then she carried me to the nearest checkpoint. She left Dread Wilmè there in the street, dead, where the MINUSTAH troops had abandoned him. They weren't mad, those guys. They were willing to kill the man – they had the balls for that – and guaranteed they were going to take some bullets for it, but they knew that take Dread out of the Site and they would have a fucking revolution on their hands. It wasn't worth it. Not only that but Dread was reputed to eat babies, man, and they'd seen him walk down the street with a thousand bullet holes in him. The white soldiers, the blancs, they didn't want that vodou with them.

Manman, though, she was pissed that they had left me behind. I was a child, bleeding; she thought that even in a war people should not leave children wounded in the street. She was afraid that I was going to die, and then she would be left with nobody.

I woke up again when I heard the shouting. I opened my eyes and I was in her arms. I wasn't light then, I was, like, 50 kilos or something. She had carried me all the way to where the street was blocked off by an orange shipping container and there was a barrier across the road. Sweat was beading on her face and her eyes were huge, they were so close to me. Everything was kind of bleached and washed out, and I was aware of the smell of my own blood. Casques-bleus were pointing guns at us and they were doing some of the shouting.

Manman was shouting, too, but not at the soldiers. She was ignoring them, and instead walking toward these people with cameras, with no uniforms, who were on the other side of the barrier. The soldiers were holding these people back, but they were squeezing past and taking pictures of us. I could see the flashes going off and they made my head spin even more. This was, like, dawn. There was a little light in the sky, like blood seeping from a wound, but not much.

The people with the cameras, I figured they were journalists. They were shouting and shouting – in English, I think. Manman didn't speak English, but she shouted in Kreyòl and she shouted in the broken French that she knew. She shouted:

— My son was shot by MINUSTAH soldiers in the slum.

She shouted:

— He was shot during a military operation to kill Dread Wilmè. Dread Wilmè is dead and my son is injured. Help me.

136

One of the reporters broke away from the group and turned to the soldiers. He thrust a video camera forward.

— Can you confirm that Dread Wilmè has been killed? he asked.

The soldier backed away, looking nervous.

Manman didn't stop shouting. She walked closer and closer to the barrier, and the soldiers were backing away from her now, unsure how to proceed.

— Please, she said. Please, let me through. Let my son have treatment. Please. You shot him, now just take him to the hospital.

All of this, the reporters were filming and taking photos of it. The flashes, they were a bit like guns going off, and they made me think I was going to be sick, or faint again. I didn't, but I kind of wished I would.

— We heard gunshots from inside Site Solèy after seeing vehicles enter there from the United Nations Stabilization Mission in Haiti, said one of the reporters in French. We also saw a helicopter. Did you shoot this boy?

She asked this young soldier near her, but really she was asking all the soldiers, and she was talking for the camera, too.

I saw one of them, who seemed a bit older than the rest, turn away and talk quietly and quickly into a walkie-talkie. The others had their fingers on their triggers, and not all the guns were pointing at us; some of them were pointing at the reporters. Manman, she was smart. She wasn't even looking at the soldiers; she was talking to the reporters the whole time, showing them the wound in my leg, telling them what happened.

— I saw Dread Wilmè die with my own eyes, she said. They filled him with so many bullets you could pick him up with a magnet.

The reporters were pressing forward then, trying to get into the Site, and the barrier was straining against them. One tried to duck under and a soldier brandished his gun, shouting. I think someone could have got shot right then, but at that moment the soldier on his walkie-talkie stepped forward and put a hand on the barrel of the gun.

— Let the woman and the boy through, he said to the men who were manning the barrier. Escort them to Canapé-Vert for treatment.

The reporters went quiet, then they were all shouting at once:

— Does this mean you confirm the death of Dread Wilmè at the hands of MINUSTAH troops?

— Can you . . . ?

— Do you . . . ?

— What is the status of Dread Wilmè?

— Did you shoot this boy?

The soldiers raised the barrier, and Manman moved through. Now she was ignoring the reporters completely, and it was like they didn't exist anymore.

— No comment, said the soldier with the walkie-talkie. No comment.

THEN

Toussaint looked down on the bay of Cape Town through the spyglass. He saw three fat-bellied ships, wallowing in the deep water. He and Jean-Christophe were up on a hill above the town, whilst the majority of the body of freed slaves still camped in the mountains near Dondon. Not all the rebel forces were Toussaint's yet, but he had faith that they soon would be.

He found that he was compelled to work deep into the nights in order to avoid sleep. For when he slept the dreams would come, and he would turn into a young man in a strange version of Haiti, where the blacks were free, but seemed to be imprisoned still in a city of shaky houses, encircled by soldiers. In this nightmare world there was loud music, with the insistent, repetitive beats of a vodou ceremony, and there were strange signs and lights that burned bright as the noonday sun, even at night. There were so many odd sights and sounds that he always woke feeling dizzy and disoriented, despite this world seeming familiar to him, as if part of him belonged there.

Other nights, he was not in this city, but in a small black space, like a cave, and it seemed that the world was pressing itself down on him. He was convinced that no one would rescue him and that he was going to die. He screamed, but there was no one to hear.

What if it was something terrible that entered me at Bois Caiman? he wondered. *What if it's hell I'm seeing in my visions?*

These thoughts troubled Toussaint, but his people needed him. He should have been back there in the mountains, training the troops, ensuring that the land was being cultivated as he had planned, drawing maps to show how the country could be managed once it was fully in their hands. And he had done these things tirelessly for the past several months. He also wanted to be where Isaac was. His son was sixteen now, practically a man. But he was no soldier, and that wasn't merely because Toussaint did not want to see him die. Isaac was a sensitive boy, intelligent, a smooth speaker and a reader of books. He was better off – safer – in the mountains.

However, he had heard of these ships that had sailed all the way from France and wanted to see them for himself. So, leaving his son in the safety of the hills, he had brought a small detachment, the finest amongst his troops, to camp just above Cape Town and observe what the French were plotting. The other two generals, Jean-François and Biassou, thought him a madman to travel all the way to Cape Town.

— The commissioners have given us our freedom, they said. We've achieved our goal.

Certainly, this was true. The commissioners had surrendered

to the black troops, and the island was theirs inasmuch as it was now a free republic of whites and blacks, no longer subject to France. This had been an ecstatic moment, the culmination of all they had fought for. Toussaint himself had taken delivery of the document in which, in formal language and precise copperplate script, the commissioner had confirmed the freedom and victory of the slaves. It had been as light and as fragile as any other sheaf of paper, although every letter was written in blood and behind every word were dead men.

But it was in vain that Toussaint tried to explain that what the commissioners did and said was of less import than the beatings of a fly against a windowpane. The commissioners might be white, but they were not French, not truly, for in the most part they had not been born on French soil. When they arrived, the authentic French would take the freedom of the blacks that the commissioners had declared and they would wipe their white arses with it.

Biassou and Jean-François hoped they could simply throw off the yoke of slavery and be happy for evermore. It didn't occur to them that the French were already plotting how they could take the freedom of the blacks back, and bury it with the bodies of those who resisted. Now, particularly because Boukman was dead, it was Toussaint who had to think about crops, and governance, and what happened when the slavers wanted their land back. It was Toussaint who had to think about justice and order. It was Toussaint who had to think about the various negotiations still to be concluded with the commissioners. Amongst those, and chief in his mind, was the release of the many black prisoners they held – some taken before the uprising for a litany of feeble pretexts, some captured in the course of the fighting. As long as those prisoners remained in jail, and the commissioners remained in power, Toussaint did not consider the slaves entirely free, no matter what the commissioners said.

He sighed, feeling sweat trickle from his forehead into his eyes. The hill they were on had never been cultivated, so it offered the cover of thick vegetation. Broad leaves concealed them from below, and granted them a little protection from the fierce sun. Toussaint knew that all on Haiti were slaves to the sun – it burned the backs of owners and workers alike.

He lowered the spyglass and took in the entirety of the view – he still had good eyesight despite his age. These three French ships must have set sail from France as soon as news of the slave rebellion arrived on her shores. To the naked eye, they didn't look so large. They were dwarfed by Cape Town, a shambolic port that hugged the bay with sprawling spiky arms. Many of the houses were grand, in the French style, but there was also an embarrassment of wooden structures, little shacks and houses that clustered on the flanks of the hills like barnacles on a whale's side. He clicked his tongue against his palate, thinking of the French envoy, seemingly stuck on that ship of his.

— You're sure he didn't land? he asked.

Jean-Christophe nodded.

— The French envoy left his ship once, on a rowing boat. He reached the shore and the commissioners met him, but

142

they must have sent him back. There were several armed men with them and the envoy didn't look happy about it.

Toussaint considered this for a moment, glad he had sent Jean-Christophe ahead of him.

— The spirit of revolution has reached these commissioners, too, he said. They think to themselves, perhaps *we* should own Haiti. They think to themselves, perhaps we should no longer bow to a government half the world away. The whites want to be free, too.

— They deny the power of France, said Jean-Christophe. It's madness on their part.

Toussaint shook his head.

— No. They deny the power of the Revolutionary government in France. Who's to say the monarchy won't be resurrected in France, and these commissioners won't be ennobled for resisting the Republican usurpers?

The three ships below did not fly the king's colors – they flew the tricolor flag that stood for the Republic. In France, only recently, the king had been deposed, his head cut off, and an assembly had taken his place. It was one of the events that had convinced Boukman, and others like him, that it was time to assert their independence from the slavers.

Toussaint could almost admire the risk the Haitian commissioners were taking. They were refusing permission for the French government's ships to disembark – if the new Republic did not fall, it would go badly for them. Galbaud, the envoy on board the largest of those ships, had been sent by France to take control of Haiti and to enslave the blacks once more. He would not take kindly to being imprisoned on his own vessel.

Well, Toussaint thought. *Let the French and the commissioners fight amongst themselves. It will make my task easier.*

He continued to study the ships. They sat low in the water – too low. Sluggish water, made lazy by the hot sun, tapped against their hulls. A single figure bustled on one of the forecastles.

Birds banked and dived in the blue sky above.

Toussaint put his nose close to the ground and breathed in. He smelled mud; he smelled the richness of fertile vegetation. He smelled the spirit of Haiti. He smelled opportunity.

— How many are on the ships? he said. I mean, how many have you seen?

— Not many, just a few who mill around on the decks. Sometimes the envoy, in his silly hat.

Toussaint frowned. Not many. Yet the ships were large. He might have thought them laden with cargo – millions of francs' worth of sugar cane, indigo, potatoes, and the like – except that cargo left Haiti; it never arrived. The only things that had ever arrived on ships like that were slaves. Slaves such as Toussaint's father, who even on his deathbed had spoken of the endless days of sickness, of bodies being thrown overboard, of weeping in the darkness, of manacled legs and hands, of flesh rotting from contact with the human effluvium that was omnipresent belowdecks.

Why are they sitting so low in the water? he wondered. *What's on those ships?*

He clapped Jean-Christophe on the back.

— I want to see what's on those ships, he said.

— But they're out in the bay – the commissioners still won't let them into port.

— I know, said Toussaint. I hope you can swim.

Toussaint stood on the beach, looking out at the gray water. A path of moonlight on the sea led out to the horizon. He had the sense that if he followed it he would end up with the dead in their resting place, and for a moment he was tempted not to swim to the ship, but to just swim, until he ran out of strength, until the sea took him, until he could see Boukman again, and his father, until he could clasp their hands and say:

— It has been too long.

Gazing at the moonlight, he remembered something Boukman had told him: that the sea and the moon were linked, the moon guiding in some mysterious way the motions of the tide. Toussaint felt that the sea was indeed more of the moon than of the earth. It seemed an alien place, full of strange creatures, whispering to him, but cold. He took a deep breath, ignored the impulse, and concentrated on feeling the wind on his bare skin.

Jean-Christophe stood beside him, shivering. Toussaint stepped forward so that his feet were in the water, and suddenly he was afraid to go on. He perceived the surface of the sea not as a simple plane, but as a membrane, a horizontal border into somewhere foreign and not of this world. He took a step back.

Jean-Christophe touched his shoulder.

— Look, he said.

He pointed to a shape in the gloom beside them, half-buried in the sand. Toussaint peered down and saw the face and bust of a beautiful woman, her eyes of peeling paint, her form of wood. He identified it as the figurehead from the prow of a ship, a mascot and no doubt source of comfort to the men who had sailed with her. Presumably that ship had long since foundered, but the sight of her carved hair and heaved bosom gave a strange access of courage to Toussaint. He stooped to touch her, noting how closely she resembled icons he had seen of la Sirene, the lwa of the sea and of the dead.

The wood was warm to the touch, and he smiled. He had seen the ocean before, with his father, and seen the things that swept up on the beach: pieces of polished wood, glass, sometimes even human bones, or barrels of still unperished food and drink. The sea, he realized, was not foreign at all; it behaved like humans. It took things – the driftwood, the drowned – and loved them, but always, like a person who dies and leaves behind their possessions, it ultimately abandoned them, casting them up onto shore, and moving on. Nothing belonged to the sea forever; it would always end up on some beach somewhere, forgotten.

The sea expels these things, he thought, *these mementos of the lost. It does not want to remember.*

He understood that. He did not want to remember, either, did not want to think about his ancestors who had come, suffering, to this land over this shining sea. But what he wanted and what he did were two different countries at war with each other. He wanted to be with Isaac, yet here he was. He wanted to ignore the past, yet he fed on it for his anger, for his impetus in his fight against the slavers.

He touched the warm face of the wooden lady once more, then walked out into the ocean and let it embrace him. Behind him, he heard Jean-Christophe gasp as he entered it.

The water was slippery, almost greasy, against Toussaint's skin. He swam breaststroke, his hands meeting before him like prayers.

He thought of the fish swimming beneath him, their silvery grace drinking in the light from the moon above, reflecting it with their flashing scales. The taste of salt was in his mouth. He was not a particularly strong swimmer – having only swum in river pools before – but he was stronger than Jean-Christophe. He could hear the younger man struggling behind him, his breathing heavy and labored.

Ahead, he could see the glow of the ship's lights on the water. From the hill he had observed a ladder with his spyglass, and he made toward it. He knew himself to be invisible – he was black, and so was the water. Cape Town had a port patrol, but it was over to the east, close to the shore. They were guarding the quays against the men in the ships – it had not occurred to them that someone might go from shore *to* the ships.

There was the rope ladder hanging from the side of the first ship. For a moment he simply hung from the bottom of the ladder to catch his breath. The black water tapped against the hull with a soft, rhythmic clapotis. He glanced back, saw Jean-Christophe nearing the ship, and gestured to him to follow. Then he began to climb and soon reached the height of the portholes. Swinging himself from side to side, he gathered some momentum. This was the dangerous part. He caught hold of a round opening and hauled himself up, until he was looking inside the ship.

His eyes widened.

In the hold, men sat in row upon row, or slept in hammocks and on the small spaces of planking afforded them by gaps between barrels of powder. All wore some semblance of uniform, although many had taken off their heavy surcoats and draped them over spars and beams. Weapons were arranged in metal pyramids on the floor.

Soldiers.

One of the men who was opposite Toussaint, facing toward the porthole he was looking through, paused and frowned. He cocked his head to peer at the space where Toussaint was. Toussaint held his breath. He closed his eyes, hiding their whiteness in the darkness.

He counted to twenty.

Opening his eyes a crack, he saw that the soldier had turned his attention to one of his neighbors, and was sharing some tobacco with him. Toussaint breathed out very slowly. Then he quietly rejoined the ladder and climbed down. The sea when he reached it was shocking cold and as bracing as a baptism.

He swam to the next ship and climbed its barnacled hull. Inside, arrayed in rows or lying in sleep like discarded toys, not in use at present, were hundreds upon hundreds of soldiers.

The third ship was the same.

It was what he had expected, but it was still terrible to see. The number of them! A host such as Haiti had never seen, the country having relied upon fear and intimidation more than military force to subdue its black population. He and the other generals had overcome the commissioners, but how could they hope to overcome such as these?

By pure chance, he was clinging to the side of that third ship when an officer entered the hold where the soldiers were sleeping, or playing cards, or drinking from small bottles of rum concealed about their persons. He rapped his sword against a beam, and the soldiers scrambled to attention.

— The commissioners defy us, he said. Therefore, tomorrow, before dawn, we invade by force.

— Vive la – began one of the soldiers, amidst the hubbub of voices.

— Hush, said the officer. Do you wish them to hear us?

Yes, thought Toussaint. *Yes, I do.*

Galvanized, he entered the water once again and struck out for shore. He swam with a sure, swift stroke. The moonlight still made a path on the water that looked as if it must lead somewhere for anyone brave enough to follow it. Toussaint had been to enough vodou funerals to know that the adherents of that hybrid faith often floated their dead down that road to sink them into the ocean.

For a moment he considered that luminous road, but then he thought of something. Even with the help of the commissioners, he wondered how they could vanquish the army that France had sent. *But not all of my men are free yet.*

— Are you well? asked Jean-Christophe, drawing level with him.

He smiled.

— Very well, thank you, he said.

He swam back to the land, the scented and beautiful land, nourished with the blood of his people, rising like the curves of a woman above the night-black water.

NOW

The week after Dread Wilmè died they had his funeral in the
Site. They drove his body through the streets on the back of
a pickup truck, and everyone went and sang songs against the
government:

— Grenadye alaso, sa ki mouri zafè a yo!
Grenadye alaso, sa ki mouri zafè a yo!
Nen mwen papa, nen mwen mama, sa ki mouri zafè a yo!

They sang that they were going to war and they were
prepared to die. Well, a lot of them died, but they never went
to war – except against each other. A lot of those chimères who
worked for Dread, they ended up joining Boston, or other
gangs, and they shot each other and cut each other to pieces.

But right then, they were together. It was the last time the
whole Site was together, I guess, like a big party.

Me, I had to beg Manman to let me go, cos my leg was band-
aged from being shot, and I had crutches. She wanted me to

stay in our shack, said it would be safer for me there. She said I was lucky the UN had paid for my treatment; me, I thought maybe they shouldn't have shot me in the first place.

I wanted to see Dread, who had saved my life.

I begged and I begged, souplè, Manman. Eventually she said, OK. We went out and it wasn't hard to find where the funeral was, cos anpil people from all around were heading in the same direction. We came to the wide street that led to the sea, the one where Marguerite and me found the baby, and we saw the pickup truck carrying Dread's body, and the people following behind it, singing.

We heard that there was no power for lights or music – the UN had cut off the electricity to the Site, so there could be no funeral.

But someone went to see a guy called 50 Cent; he had a diesel generator that he let out, only this time he gave it for free, cos it was for Dread. Then there was power, and light, and a beat to walk to.

A man was beside us. He had a machine gun in his hand, but it was pointing at the ground. There were no MINUSTAH anywhere. People said they were too scared to come near the Site on this day.

— I heard he isn't dead, said the man. I heard he's a zombi, so he only seems to be dead. I heard his houngan has arranged it all. Some moun, they say that he cannot die, cos of the babies that he eats.

I stared at the man. He had a scar that ran down one side of his face, like someone had tried to cut his mouth out. I knew

152

about zombis. I knew they were rare. Like, if someone wanted to be a houngan, then they would have to become a zombi first, or sometimes if someone had to be punished they would be made into a zombi. What would happen is that a houngan would give you some drugs, make you seem like you were dead. Then they'd bury you, two days, or three, before digging you up again. Moun said that they saw Baron Samedi in that time, that they were able to communicate with the lwa, that they were never the same again when they were reborn. Manman, she said it was why houngans had these eyes that looked very far away, cos they'd been dead and had come alive again.

— Dread's not a zombi, said Manman. He's dead. I saw him die.

— You saw it? said the man. He touched Manman, like it could give him luck.

— Yes. It was in the street outside our shack. There was this army truck, it was going to run over my son here. Dread pulled him out of the way, saved him. But he was all bullet holes in the end. No way he's coming back to life.

— But his houngan –

— No. He's dead.

The man was smiling. I noticed then he wasn't as old as I thought at first.

— He saved the boy, though. That's strong maji.

Manman frowned. She pulled me away and we fell into a different group, all girls chanting and crying. Eventually, we came to the sea. There was no beach, just a row of shacks and some fishing boats, a stink of fish in the air. There were gulls doing circles overhead, screeching. Behind us, the other Port-au-Prince rose on its hill up toward heaven, all clean and bright, but we were down in the trash heap, down in the Site, and Dread Wilmè was dead.

Everyone stopped chanting.

This old man, he stepped up beside the pickup truck where it had stopped, gestured for the men around him to take down the coffin. Someone lifted me up then, so I could see better. It hurt my leg, but I didn't mind cos I was above the heads of most of the people. The coffin was open. Dread Wilmè was lying inside in a suit, looking totally indemne, like you wouldn't believe that he had a thousand holes in him.

The old man, he was obviously a houngan. Dread Wilmè's houngan, I guess. He had a bone rattle and a gourd, an ason and a clochette; he was shaking them. He called out:

— I need Baron Samedi!

He called out:

— I need la Sirene!

A couple of volunteers stepped forward to be ridden by the lwa. I recognized them: they were soldiers for Dread Wilmè. The houngan nodded and made a motion with his hands for the people around the pickup truck to back away. Then he and the two men lifted the coffin and put it onto a little boat. The houngan took a canister and poured what was in it all over the boat, all over the coffin.

A stillness came on the crowd then, a hush. They knew that

154

was petrol the houngan was pouring; they knew what was going to come.

Then the houngan picked up his cane and he began to draw in the sand. I couldn't see everything, but I guessed he was drawing veves to bring the lwa down. People stepped forward and put offerings on the ground – cakes and sweet things for la Sirene, rum and cigars for Baron Samedi, who loves anything that reeks of death. There was a bucket of water, too, for la Sirene, cos she can't be out of the water for too long, else she dies.

The houngan arranged the offerings, then he raised a hand. Everything went quiet. He began to sing, first the song to Papa Legba, to open up the gates.

Vodou, yeah: it's complicated. Some of the lwa we brought from Africa, some we found on this island, took them from the Indians. And some of them – we call them the Gede family – are the spirits of our dead ancestors.

You die on Haiti, you become a god. Me, I try to tell myself that, as I lie here in the darkness. I tell myself, if Manman is still alive and I die, I can still talk to her – all she got to do is visit her houngan.

These lwa can come down and possess a living person, ride them like a horse. For an hour, or whatever, that person *is* the god, speaks the god's words. But it's not easy. First, you got to open up the gate between our world and the world of the lwa, and for that you need Papa Legba, the lwa of the crossroad. He's, like, the phone line between humans and the lwa.

So, first thing you do when you have a ceremony is you invoke

155

Papa Legba. Then you can call on other lwa: Baron Samedi, maybe – he's the one who takes you to the land under the sea when you die; or la Sirene – she's the one who looks after you there; or Ogou Badagry – he's the lwa of war, but you don't want him unless you're crazy; no moun wants to be ridden by him. See, a person is like a horse and a lwa is like a rider. Ogou Badagry, he's a rider who uses a whip. A heavy whip.

So, yeah, the houngan, he called on Papa Legba, and I guess the gates got opened, cos suddenly it was raining, in the middle of summer, and then the houngan was stomping in the wet sand and singing again, this time to Baron Samedi. The guy who was holding me on his shoulders, he tightened his hands on my legs, and I knew he was tense about this part. Baron Samedi, he may not be Ogou, he may not be that badass, but he's still some dark vodou. You got to be afraid of the lwa of war, but if you're not a cretin, you're afraid of the lwa of death, too.

— Papa Gede, nou moun nou cè
Nou moun nou cè, c'est rond ago yè!
Papa Gede, nou moun nou cè
Nou moun nou cè, c'est rond ago yè!

The houngan sang, and he was shaking the snake tail bones in his ason, and dancing, dancing.

Suddenly one of the men who volunteered – he was kind of skinny and short – went stiff, then he laughed, big and loud, like a boom box. He didn't seem so skinny and short anymore.

He turned to the houngan, and he sang back at him. His voice was deep and dark and sounded like something echoing in a grave.

— Sonnin cloche là, Papa, moin Gede!
M'apè vini tout en noir joind houngan!
Ti wa we Gede vini tout en noir joind houngan!
Ti wa we!

Ring the bell there, Papa, I am Gede, he sang, cos Baron Samedi is also father of the Gede lwa, the lwa of the dead, so he is Baron Samedi, but he is Papa Gede, too.

I am coming all in black to meet the houngan, he sang in his deep voice. *Little ones, you will see Gede coming all in black to meet the houngan. Little ones, you shall see.*

— We see! said one of the children there.

— We see! said another.

— We see you, Papa Gede, Baron Samedi!

Papa Gede, Baron Samedi, whatever you want to call him, picked up a cigar from the ground, and he put it in his mouth. He lit it with a flame that just appeared in his hand – that's what it looked like from where I was watching. Then he took the kleren, which is like a moonshine kind of whiskey, and he bit off the top and tipped the bottle upside down and drained it. He turned, and saw a pretty girl in the crowd. He walked up to her, picked her up in his arms, like she was a doll, and kissed her, long and deep. Baron Samedi loves girls, man.

Then he let her drop.

— Nen zam pou mwa? he asked.

A guy, one of Dread's soldiers, handed him a gun. Baron Samedi, he pressed the release and the clip fell out. He caught it smooth with his other hand. He popped out a bullet, put it in his mouth, and swallowed it.

— Ah! he said.

Gunpowder is one of the symbols of Baron Samedi, one of his objects – you want his protection, you carry it with you always. Don't say I don't tell you anything useful.

The houngan walked up to him.

— Will you take him? he said. Will you take Dread Wilmè into death?

Baron Samedi looked at Dread, lying still, those massive dreadlocks fallen around his chest like a great black octopus. Then he threw the empty kleren bottle into the coffin.

— Dread Wilmè is a hero of this country, a soldier. I never took him before, the times he got shot. Now the whites have killed him so bad I have no choice. I will take him.

The crowd fucking erupted; they were cheering and jumping. I nearly fell off the shoulders of the guy who was holding me, he was so happy.

Then the houngan was singing again, and dancing. He sang:

— La Sirene, la Balene, chapo m tombe nan la mer,
La Sirene, la Balene, chapo m tombe nan la mer,
Map fou kares pou la Balene (chapo m tombe nan la mer),
Map fou kares pou la Balene (chapo m tombe nan la mer).

That's a song to la Sirene. It calls to her and tells her our hat has fallen in the sea – I don't know why. It calls to her and says that we caress her, that we caress the mermaid, that we caress the whale. She's a mermaid and a whale, too, this lwa; she's the embodiment of the sea.

The other volunteer, he was in the circle with the houngan and Baron Samedi, and he went stiff; it was like there was a wire running down through his head and his spine, and someone had taken hold of it at both ends and pulled it taut. He gasped, finding it hard to breathe, and he stumbled. The houngan caught him under his arms, held him up. La Sirene, she has the tail of a fish and she lives underwater, so when she rides someone, it isn't easy for them to stand. This guy, he was big, strong, with a beard and a big chain around his neck, but suddenly he looked smaller, weaker. He turned to Baron Samedi.

— Ah, handsome Baron, he said – and his voice was high and like music.

— La Sirene, said Baron, la Balene, you are beautiful as always.

The men stepped forward, the houngan supporting la Sirene, and embraced with a passionate kiss. The weird thing was that no moun thought of it as weird, cos it was Baron Samedi and la Sirene, not two of Dread's soldiers, kissing like movie stars. I turned to look at Manman – she was staring at this scene with, like, rapt attention, as if it was beautiful. Me, I thought it was a charade, the whole thing. I didn't doubt that the men had been paid to do this, or had agreed to do this, cos it was a good send-off for Dread.

159

There was no such thing as a lwa, that was what I thought then.

Now I know better.

Anyway, then la Sirene broke away and turned to the houngan who was holding him or her, and said:

— Water.

The voice had gone all dry and croaky.

The houngan gestured to one of the men standing outside the circle, who picked up the bucket of sea water and tipped it over la Sirene. She made this *ah* sound that was a bit like when Baron Samedi ate the bullet, only more grateful, more relieved.

— La Sirene, said the houngan, will you take Dread Wilmè into your land under the sea and look after him there?

She made a movement with her hands, graceful, like a dolphin.

— Dread Wilmè is loved by all the lwa, she said.

Her voice was still a woman's, and you could almost imagine you heard the water in it, the echo of the deep, the whale song.

Almost.

— Of course I will take him, she said. He is a hero. He is Haiti.

Again, the crowd completely lost their shit. I was kind of worried Manman might get pressed to death, but she was dancing with the others, clapping her hands and laughing.

After that, it was quick. The houngan spoke some words, and the two men who had been ridden fell to the ground, just

160

lay there and didn't get up. He turned to Dread's other soldiers and gestured to the boat. It must have been planned, cos it happened without many words. The men picked up the boat and carried it to the sea, then they set it on the water and gave it a push so that it drifted out. The houngan lit a stick covered in rags. He didn't say anything, only tossed it onto the boat, and *whoooosh*. The little boat went up in this ball of flame, bright like a setting sun on the water, hissing in the rain that was still falling lightly.

The boat was drifting out to sea even as it burned, crackling, hot even from the distance I was at, like, twenty meters, at least. It blazed, and it drew further from the beach, till it started to break apart and fall into the water. Soon there was nothing but a slick on the sea, and a smell everywhere of burned petrol.

Later, some of Dread Wilmè's men swam out and dived for the pieces of his body that had not burned, and they brought them out of the sea for luck. One of the pieces ended up with Biggie's houngan – that's how come Biggie got Dread's bone dust sprinkled on him, to make him indemne against bullets. But that was after, when everyone else had gone. I didn't see it, so I don't know if it was really Dread that Biggie had on him, or if Dread just stayed on the bottom of the sea, became the sand and dirt of the beach.

The man who had been holding me up grasped me under my shoulders and put me back on the ground beside Manman. She looked out, past the people, to the stain that was on the sea.

— Well, I guess he isn't coming back now, she said.

And you know what I think now? I think she was wrong. I think everything comes back – that's what's so fucked up about the universe. Everything comes back, whether you want it to or not, all covered in dead earth and stumbling like a zombi, and you can't say no to it, cos there's always time, flowing in and out, and eventually time brings the wreckage of the past up on the beach for other people to find.

Toussaint came back and he was Dread Wilmè, and then he was me.

My sister came back and everything changed.

Everything comes back.

Everything.

THEN

There had been no time to call upon the forces encamped at the mountain stronghold in Dondon, so Toussaint had only the hand-picked men who had accompanied him here to Cape Town. This included Jean-Christophe, whom Toussaint had sent ahead to gather the cavalry.

The commissioners had more men, true, but the truce that existed between them and the blacks was built, like much of Haiti, on shaky ground. Toussaint knew that he must needs use his knowledge and his cunning to bring the two forces together in order to repel the French and push them back into the sea from whence they came.

Hours before dawn, he rode into the town with Jean-Christophe back at his side, his other soldiers commanded to wait just outside the gates. The guards balked when they saw him, but he raised a calming hand.

— We are only two, he said. We need to speak with the commissioners. They will be grateful for the news we bring.

— You're slaves, said one of the guards with a sneer.

— No, said Toussaint. Your masters declared us free. Would you go against their word?

The guards grumbled, but they let Toussaint and Jean-Christophe in, reserving their most aggravated looks for Toussaint, Jean-Christophe being blessed with a countenance that not only inspired trust, but that could move more easily than most between the two worlds of black and white. Toussaint envied him that. He was a handsome one, Jean-Christophe, a fine young gentleman. Toussaint himself was a very ugly man, he knew. Already the men of his army, like his lost wife before them, had taken to calling him the Ogre, as if he were a monster out of a fairy tale. And who knew? Maybe to the whites he was.

He didn't envy Jean-Christophe his upbringing, though. His mother had been a mambo, a vodou priestess, his father a petit blanc who owned a small parcel of land in the north of the country. From his mother he had acquired a firm knowledge of vodou, and a passing acquaintance with most of the many African tongues spoken on the island. From his father he had inherited pale skin and light eyes, the only indications of his other heritage being a certain curl to his hair, a certain curve to his lip. In his eyes sparkled a lively and insubordinate intelligence – one of the characteristics Toussaint admired in him. The young man's father had tried to beat this apparent devilry out of him many times; Toussaint had seen the scars. Evidently, it had not worked – Jean-Christophe was as clever as any devil.

They followed narrow, winding streets, working their way

up the hill toward the residence of the Commissioner of Haiti. On one corner was a cage and as they passed it monkeys hurled themselves against the bars, screeching at them. Hearing that noise and seeing the sharp teeth in their wide-open mouths, the hate in their wide-open eyes, Toussaint felt his heart stutter in his chest.

Eventually they reached the residence, which sat squat behind low garden walls, bougainvillea and other perfumed flowers growing in great profusion; Toussaint was aware of them more by smell than by sight. The guards on duty stopped them as they drew near.

— What do you want? said one of them from behind a musket.

— I'm here to speak to Brandicourt, said Toussaint.

— To say what?

Toussaint smiled.

— I'll tell that to him, not to you.

The guard's whiskers trembled with fury. He took a step forward.

— Insolent nigger! he shouted. I'll have you killed.

Lights flared on the other side of the garden wall, and a general ruckus broke out. Toussaint saw candles flicker into life behind the windows of the residence, too. Another guard made as if to secure them.

— Leave them, said an imperious voice, the accent unmistakably French.

Brandicourt himself appeared out of the gloom, coming through the garden gate, a ghost in reverse, becoming detail and color and contrast out of the darkness.

— You are Toussaint, are you not? he asked.

Toussaint nodded.

— I have that honor, he said.

— I lost many men to your troops, said Brandicourt. He turned to someone behind him, a woman. The man has a certain low cunning – for a slave, he added.

Toussaint kept his face expressionless, felt Jean-Christophe tense beside him.

— Why have you come? asked the woman. You have your freedom. Do you demand our lives also?

With a faint shock, Toussaint noticed that she was holding a knife, that her husband, too, was armed, holding some kind of pistol. *Do they so fear us*, he thought, *that they would arm themselves against two of us, in their own town, in the middle of the night?*

— I've come to warn you, that's all, he said.

— Ah. We have a month to vacate the island, or we all die? Do I have the measure of it?

It was Brandicourt who spoke this time. He motioned to his guards afterward.

— Seize them, he said. But be careful. There may be some vodou witchery here.

Toussaint held up a hand.

— No. I'm here to tell you that the French will land soldiers before dawn. We advise you to prepare to repel them.

Brandicourt bristled.

— But they wouldn't –

— Dare? interrupted Toussaint. Yes, they would. I swam

out into the bay and saw for myself that each ship carries three hundred men, at least.

The wife drew in a sharp breath. Yet strangely, although she had been roused from her bed by a black man bearing ill tidings, she did not seem afraid.

— For the income that this island generates? she said. Of course they would take it back by force.

— Well, said Brandicourt. Then we'll welcome them.

His wife laughed, a soft, short sound.

— And what will you say? That we're sorry we gave away their most valuable possession? That we're sorry we freed the slaves and declared ourselves a republic? That we wouldn't allow their envoy on shore? Don't be so bloody naive. They'll mount our heads on pikes.

Perhaps Brandicourt had gone pale, but it was hard to tell in the darkness.

— We cannot fight them. Our troops are depleted and –

— I have troops, said Toussaint. They're camped just outside the town. And you hold two thousand black men in your jail.

Brandicourt snorted at this.

— You can't honestly believe that I would free criminals in the interest of a single –

— Be quiet, Robert, said the woman.

Toussaint was starting to admire the steel in her voice. She faced him, and he could see the strong line of her brow, the reflection of moonlight in her eyes. There was a scent about her, too – something feminine over and above the minor notes of the midnight flowers.

167

— Two thousand unarmed men, even freed criminals, won't last long against crack French troops, she said.

— No, said Toussaint. But I can arm them.

Of weapons, he was well supplied. Many of the properties the slaves had overrun had possessed small arsenals, the better to allow a minority of plantation owners to dominate a much larger population of laborers.

The wife of Robert Brandicourt, Commissioner of Haiti, stepped forward and put a hand on Toussaint's arm.

— I think you had better come inside, she said.

Deeper into the night, Toussaint ran a soothing hand down the neck of his horse. The white troops of the commission were now stationed further up the hill alongside his own men. He, however, had concealed his horse in a side alley in the warren of streets that led up from the port. Beside him, astride his own horse, was Brandicourt.

— You had better be right about this, said the commissioner.

— Oh, I am, said Toussaint. I have seen the future, and it does not include the French. Besides, if I were wrong, the men would return to the jail.

In the gloom behind them someone laughed at this, and Brandicourt blanched. All two thousand of the previously imprisoned slaves, murderers and rebels, rapists and thieves lay in hiding in the streets around them, armed with machetes and guns.

Toussaint trained his spyglass on the ships, dimly illuminated by the crescent moon. Several rowing boats had detached themselves from the mother vessels. He saw, too, the heads of the soldiers as they swam toward the shore, the whole thing silent as death.

— They come, he said.

It begins, he thought.

He turned to the men behind him, crouching in the muck of the alley. On the other side, under an awning, lay the bodies of three monkeys that had been taken from their cage and snapped at the neck before they could hiss and shriek. Toussaint had to acknowledge that their deaths, after they had frightened him earlier in the night, had afforded him a certain satisfaction.

— You are free, he said to the men in a low voice. He was certain that the message would be conveyed. Yet these French will make you slaves again if they're allowed to remain on Haitian soil. Make sure that soil runs with their blood.

One of the men sniffed and said:

— I'm not sure this is soil.

The others around him laughed quietly.

— Well, said Toussaint. Even more fitting then.

The men laughed again, and he knew they were with him.

It was his last lucid thought for some time, because soon afterward the first of the French soldiers started to haul themselves onto the dockside, dripping, like invaders from some watery realm. They moved lithe and fast up into the streets, padding soft on bare feet. There were no lights; there would have been no warning had Toussaint not overheard the stratagem.

One of them passed the alley and Toussaint pressed his knees into his horse's sides and moved forward. The French soldier stopped and stared at him, open-mouthed, the whites of his eyes very bright.

— Wh–what? he stammered.

Toussaint read terror on the man's face. He placed himself for a moment in the man's shoes, a trick he had learned many years before.

He imagined himself a Frenchman, come to the West Indies for the first time. He saw himself in a strange town, amidst the smell of tropical flowers and night soil, of sweat and rain, as birds cried overhead. He saw himself thinking that he was safe, that the people in this sprawling fetid town knew nothing of his coming.

Now he saw the looming mass of the land behind the port, all rock and forest. He saw a big ugly black man in front of him on a horse, grinning blacks with weapons behind him, and he remembered the tales of pagan magick told in the Paris streets.

Yes, Toussaint thought the man was entitled to be afraid. He pointed to the soldier and turned to his men.

— Get these intruders off our island, he said.

Then there was carnage.

The soldiers were taken by surprise and were pushed back to the docks by the mass of freed criminals. Bodies fell to the ground and into the still, black vastness of the water, but they were professionals, and the prisoners for the most part untrained, and the French forces quickly rallied. Toussaint and Brandicourt were protected by a contingent who had held back, otherwise they might have been overwhelmed.

— Now, said Toussaint.

Brandicourt maneuvered his horse around, toward the hill. Turning his horse, Toussaint followed Brandicourt back up the alley. He had seen slaughterhouses in his life and had no wish to see another, even if he had commanded it. The soldiers of Toussaint's own detachment parted to let them through, then he and the commissioner pressed their horses into a canter, making for the higher ground that would allow them to see the night's work.

As they settled into position at the top of the hill, Brandicourt raised his horn to his lips and blew.

On this signal, the standing army of the commission – what was left of it – and the small army of blacks Toussaint commanded flowed down the hill, horses in front, a cordon of infantry behind. Toussaint thought he could just make out the silhouette of Jean-Christophe, leading the cavalry.

It was from that moment on that the tide turned, and it swept down the hill in a black wave, pushing the French out to sea as piles of bodies.

For a long time after that, it was hard for Toussaint to see what was happening. There was an impression of movement in the shadowy streets, of men running in all directions. Church bells and ship bells alike were ringing out their alarum. Toussaint was sure that down there it must be hell, that the streets would be rivers of blood as the rout continued, but he could see none of it from up here.

Then the fires started.

At first there were just one or two blazes, then whole sections of the town were burning. Soon everywhere seemed to be a bonfire; flames took up half the world that Toussaint could see. He was surprised to find that there were tears in his eyes; they made the conflagration shimmer and blur.

I didn't want it to burn, he thought. *I didn't intend that.*

From out of the flames came men in their hundreds, walking with a grim triumph in their eyes and in their gait. They were white and black, but mostly black, and they walked together.

— The French are destroyed, said Jean-Christophe, walking up the hill.

— For now, said Toussaint, pleased beyond measure to see the young man alive.

He looked back toward the ships, and as he looked he saw one of them explode: a dull *crump* and then – as sudden as that – it was just a ball of flame bobbing on the water. He guessed that some of the slaves, or perhaps the whites, had decided to swim out to the ships, as he had done the night before, and set the gunpowder kegs off. Later, he heard that for days and weeks afterward, it was possible to walk from the port out to the ships over French corpses the entire way. He doubted it, but it made a good story. Regardless, the completeness of the victory almost shocked him.

Brandicourt turned to him.

— Thank you, he said. For warning us.

Toussaint inclined his head.

— No. Thank you. For trusting us.

— You must thank my wife for that, said Brandicourt.

I do, thought Toussaint. *Believe me, I do*.

— Speaking of which, I should rejoin her, said Brandicourt. We need to leave this town before it's nothing but ashes.

Jean-Christophe, who had been standing at a discreet distance but still in earshot, walked over. Toussaint dismounted from his horse and handed the younger man the reins. Behind them in the bay, another ship turned loudly to flames.

— You have the gratitude of the whites, Jean-Christophe said.

— No, Toussaint replied. They have mine. We have just won the island.

He was sure of it, as sure as he had been of anything. The war was by no means over, but they had just won Haiti's freedom – as a *slave* republic, even if Brandicourt didn't realize it yet. Soon, whether months or years from now – and he was prepared to wait either – there would be no commissioners, only a government of blacks.

War, he understood, was not simply a matter of taking up arms. It was a matter of thinking.

He had put into motion an idea that would spread over the country quicker than the fire that even now was consuming the wooden shacks of Cape Town, licking its way closer by the moment to where he stood, turning the three ships in the bay into three torches, pouring upward in the form of black smoke their hulls and sails, their wood and canvas and coil rope into the star-scattered sky above Haiti.

And the idea was this:

The whites had to free the blacks to save their own skins.

He turned, exhausted but satisfied, and he pointed his horse toward the jungle of the interior.

— Home, he said.

He melted into the darkness.

NOW

I've been singing songs in the darkness. I sing the rebel songs from the time of Aristide, which my manman taught me, the songs they sang at the funeral of Dread Wilmè.

— Grenadye alaso, sa ki mouri zafè ya yo.

Soldiers attack. Those of us who die, that is their business.

This has been a battle cry in Haiti since ancient times – since Toussaint, at least. After Dread Wilmè died, the supporters of Lavalas changed the words; they started singing:

— Sa ki mouri vanje ya yo.

Those of us who die, we will avenge them.

I wonder how that worked out for them. In my experience revenge doesn't help anyone, least of all the dead.

I wonder if the people out there can hear me singing. I wonder if there even are people out there. I'm still not 100 percent convinced that I'm not a ghost, that this is not the land under the sea, where the dead go.

But if I am a ghost, then who am I haunting? Everyone here is dead, too.

The smell from the bodies is very bad now. It's been a long time since I reached out and touched the hand that lies near me. I think if I did it would be bloated now and slimy. It smells slimy. I have a fear that keeps coming back that the hand will crawl toward me, like a fat spider, and cling to my face. When I close my eyes, that's what I see, when I'm not seeing ships and burning houses.

I'm getting weaker, I can tell. To begin with, I would crawl around, try to find a way out. Now I just lie here, mumbling to myself. I try to remember what they say about survival. I know that you die quicker from not drinking than from not eating, and I guess that I'm only alive cos of drinking the blood.

I'm not a ghost, I think. I'm a vampire.

I click my tongue against the roof of my mouth, which is something I did in my dream, when I was someone older in a different version of Haiti. Don't worry, I'm aware that I'm going mad. I'm in this hospital and, in my dreams, I'm commanding an army. Or the other way round, maybe. I know that's not normal. Soon, I think, that hand-spider will come for me, and if they do dig me out of here it won't be me they dig out. It will be some crazy person.

To stop the madness, I see if I can remember Biggie's lyrics again. Biggie always wanted to be a rap star, like Biggie Smalls. He would drive around the Site in his car – no moun had a car in the Site, apart from the chimère bosses – and his arm would be out of the window and he would spit along to his CD of beats.

There was this tune he recorded once. He put it on a CD

and he tried to sell it in the Site, but people had anyen to eat; they weren't going to buy a CD when they were starving. Biggie sent the CD to some record company in New York, too – he got the name from Stéphanie, I think. He said that guns wouldn't help us forever and if we wanted help for our country then the only way to get it was with music. He did the song in English. That was the thing about Biggie – the man was a gangster, but he wasn't stupid. He could speak French and Kreyòl and English and even a little German, cos before he was fucking Stéphanie he was fucking a German chick from Médecins Sans Frontières.

In the darkness, I recite the lyrics to his song:

— Mwen thug, mwen gangster, mwen bandi,
Think I care, think you can hurt me?
You start this war, but I'll be here when it's over,
Livin' in yo' house,
Drivin' yo' fuckin' Range Rover.
Casques-bleus, attachés,
Get your asses out my Site –
Don't come in here wit' yo' forces
Cos I got gangsters ridin' whips like horses,
I got mad guns like Toussaint and his slaves,
I fuck you up, no one gonna be saved,
Fifty rounds semi-auto in the head,
We keep shootin' till you all be dead.
We chimès, we ghosts,
We got fire to make you roast.

177

We take your hands off,
We take your heads off,
We leave you helpless, like a baby.
You kill us? We come back like a zombi.

Me, I never saw how lyrics like that would help Haiti, but I never said that cos that would have made Biggie mad. He was always writing songs about how the government had screwed him over, how MINUSTAH arrested him for being a gangster even though he had been forced to kill people, cos the government gave him no money, only weapons. For ages he was part of Aristide's private army, and he never seemed to get over the shock that this didn't make the UN love him.

The truth was he liked killing people – that's what I thought. You see why I never showed him or Tintin my silver half-heart that I got from Marguerite? They would have said it was lame. Biggie would've taken it from me and mocked me for being a pussy-boy.

But Biggie could be a good man, too.

After Papa was killed, when we ended up in Solèy 19, it was Dread who sorted everything, but it was Biggie who actually did the work, who looked after us. He found Manman a job putting petrol into tin cans to sell to people as fuel. Me, I would sit out in the mud and watch the world go by. Mostly what I liked was to watch Biggie in his car. He would drive slow, always stopping to talk to people, to find out what their problems were. He would hand out money: to kids, so they could go to school; to mothers, so they could feed their kids.

He was a good man, sometimes.

It wasn't Biggie that I liked so much, though; it was his car. He called his car a whip – that was something he got from his rap songs. I had a car that I had made from sheet aluminum and the wheels from a shopping cart, but it wasn't so fly as Biggie's whip.

I was always inventing things – that was what I liked doing. After Dread died, Biggie continued to pay for me to go to school and I learned lots of things, but what I loved was to make maps and diagrams. I would make a map on my note-book of where all the pretty girls were in Solèy 19. I would make a map of Boston, only I didn't know anything there so it was a very blank map, and in the middle I would put a cross and mark it, *Marguerite*. I had not forgotten about her, you see. I was going to get her back.

One day, I was sitting in the mud, and in front of me I had two bowls of ice. I had made something to help my manman, and I was feeling proud. Suddenly I heard the rumble of a car engine. Biggie stopped in the street right by me. I looked around to see who he wanted to talk to, but he beckoned to me. I turned and looked behind me. He laughed.

— Come, he said. Ride with me.

I stood up and went over to him. I saw that in the back of the car there was a blanc, a white girl. I had seen her with Biggie before, but I didn't know her name, and she didn't much look at me anyway.

— What is that you're doing? he asked.

I glanced at the bowls. I had baked them from mud, a bit

179

like the cakes that people eat, only with no butter. One of them had just ice. The other had a smaller bowl inside full of ice, and there was wet sand between the two bowls. Manman was always complaining that when we did get food, which was not often, it would soon perish in the sun. I'd thought about this and I'd seen the way that the dogs in the slum panted and their tongues steamed. I thought that maybe when water burned into the air, it took some heat with it. So I thought to myself, if there was a way to surround food with wet sand, maybe the water would dry from the sand and take the warmth from the food away with it. That was the story with the bowls – and it worked, cos the ice in the normal bowl was half-melted and the ice in my sand bowl was still frozen.

— Nothing, I said to Biggie. Just a game.

Biggie nodded, like he understood, but he didn't cos it wasn't a game – it was a fridge. I didn't tell him, though.

Biggie put his head out the car window. He had his hair in cornrows and his face had a scar that ran from the forehead across the nose and all the way to the jaw. They said he was hit with a machete during a fight. He was good-looking all the same, though. He had sharp eyes that sparkled. I liked his eyes right from the start. They were clever and they said he liked to laugh.

— I hear you're good at maps, he said.

I shrugged.

— I'm OK.

He leaned over and popped the passenger door, then he

gestured for me to get in. I couldn't believe it – Biggie was going to let me inside his whip.

I climbed in. The car smelled like weed and sweat, and it was the coolest place I'd ever been. Biggie was wearing jeans and a baseball cap with the cap pointing backward. He had no shirt on and I could see that he had grand muscle, ripped, like we say. He had a blunt in his mouth and he was breathing smoke out his nose. Between the seats there was a shotgun. Biggie pressed a button and a beat came out of the speakers, anpil loud. It was *MVP Kompa* by Wyclef Jean, which is the song where he talks about zombis. I'd heard it before. There's a bit where Wyclef goes, like, you disrespect us, you're gonna be put in the ground. Biggie, he shouted it out alongside Wyclef, and right then I thought it was the coolest thing I'd ever heard, so I started singing, too. Course, now it's me that's in the ground, I have a whole other perspective.

— Wyclef, he's representing the Site, Biggie said. He's a real gangster.

Me, I'd heard that Wyclef came from Croix-des-Bousquets, which is kind of a nice place, or so they say, outside Port-au-Prince, but I didn't say anything, cos it was so cool to ride in that car, shouting that we weren't scared.

We rolled out of there and onto a wider street. I was laughing and laughing. Biggie thought that was funny, too.

— You're the kid that Dread Wilmè saved when he was dying, he said.

It wasn't a question.

— Yes, I said. That's what my manman says, anyway.

181

He gave a long slow nod. He didn't seem to remember me from when Manman and me went to see Dread, after Papa died.

— Dread Wilmè was a hero, man, he said. A true Haitian. Rebel spirit, man. I was in his crew back when we were just Solèy 19, you know, before we became Route 9? Yeah, I ran with those Aristide soldiers when I was a shorty. Dread saved your life; that's some fucking powerful maji.

I shrugged. I didn't know then that Biggie had sprinkled Dread Wilmè's bones on his ownself to make himself proof against bullets. Maybe he thought cos Dread saved my life, nothing could kill me, either, so I'd make a good chimère. A chimère who couldn't die; it would be a special thing, like a gun that never runs out of bullets, like a wallet that's always full.

— I want you to make a map for me, he said. He gave me a pencil and a sheet of paper. The teacher says you're good at that kind of shit. I want to be able to see where everyone lives. Customers, aid workers, school kids. Those who owe me money, those who don't. Who has guns.

— Tu ne penses pas qu'il soit un peu jeune encore? said the girl in the back.

Biggie replied in French. I was kind of surprised. It sounded like he had been to school and had actually paid attention, which went against the image I had of him.

— Le gosse est anpil intelligent, c'est ce qu'on me dit. Et bientôt ça sera la guerre. On aura besoin de soldats comme lui.

The girl sighed.

Even though they were speaking in French, not Kreyòl, I understood some of it. I understood that Biggie had said I was intelligent, and it made me proud. I understood that Biggie had said there would be a war, but I didn't really think about that.

— Stéphanie is UN, he said. From Paris. She worries too much. She should mind her own zafè.

She flipped him a finger.

— When you give guns to kids, that's my zafè, she said in Kreyòl.

I was surprised again. I'd never heard a blanc talking in our language before. Also, I thought the UN were all soldiers.

— You're UN? I asked her. For real?

— Yeah, but from the office, she said. Not the troops. My job is to protect people, to help. You understand?

I shrugged. I didn't know what Stéphanie was doing in Biggie's car if she was UN, but I didn't say anything.

— Here, he said. For your map.

We drove around Solèy 19 for many hours, never going out of Route 9 territory. We drove past stalls with VCDs on them and banks that Manman said weren't banks, only money-lenders. There was no moun selling food.

It was slow, cos Biggie always had to stop and talk to people. There was a woman who told him that the chimères were fighting every night outside her house, and she could no longer rent out rooms cos people were too scared. Biggie said he would sort it. Also, he and Stéphanie were handing out tins of food and medical kits that were stacked in the trunk. Stéphanie had brought them from the UN, I guess.

— We can't get our trucks into the Site, Stéphanie said to me in Kreyòl. That's why we work with the chimères.

I didn't really care about any of that. I was thinking about the map. As we drove, I filled in streets and houses. I marked the things Biggie told me to mark – people's names, what they did. Pretty soon the map filled the whole page. Down one side of the map, there was a big dark line, and I wrote under it, *Boston*. Sometimes, I looked at the shotgun between me and Biggie.

I thought, Biggie is Route 9. If I can become Route 9, too, then maybe I can fight Boston and get my sister back. I was sure she was still there in Boston, cos it was the Boston crew who had taken her, who had killed Papa. Besides, I knew she wasn't in Route 9 cos I'd never seen her, and I was sure I would recognize her, even now, four years later. She was more than my best friend. I wondered if she would recognize me, though.

— How can I become a chimère? I said to Biggie.

I wanted a whip, too. I wanted everyone in the street to like me how they liked Biggie.

Biggie laughed.

— It's easy, he said. Just ride with me.

The next day, Biggie picked me up again. It was evening, in fact. Stéphanie was in the passenger seat this time, riding shotgun. In the Site, riding shotgun isn't just an expression – she was holding the gun. I was surprised by that, cos I'd seen aid workers before and they didn't usually have guns. I noticed that she was pretty, much prettier than I had realized the previous day. She had blue eyes and kind of light-brown hair, and her face was a little oval. She was young, also. Mid-twenties, no older.

— Salut, she said over the boom of the bass.

I said hello to her, too. My face was burning, cos looking at her made my skin tingle. Biggie turned and grinned at me, and I began to shake cos I was sure he knew what I was thinking.

— You still want to be a chimère? he said.

I nodded.

— Bon. Bon. Route 9 till you die, yeah?

— Yeah, I said.

— Those Boston motherfuckers, they killed your papa, n'est-ce pas?

I was surprised he remembered that, cos the day before it didn't seem like he knew me from when me and Manman went to Dread for shelter.

— You remember that? I said.

Biggie laughed.

— I remember everything, he said. I know you were pulled from your manman by Aristide, too. I know Dread Wilmè lifted a tank off you to save you, even though he was full of bullet holes.

I didn't tell Biggie that Dread didn't pull any tank off me, he only got me out of the way of a tank, but it didn't seem important, and anyway, I was pleased that Biggie knew who I was. It was like a famous person took the trouble to stop and talk to you when he noticed you. Like that. Back then, I thought Biggie was awesome. I thought he was a stone-cold gangster, g-star, cooler than the other side of the pillow. I was, like, Biggie's groupie; it was fucking embarrassing, looking back.

Stéphanie sighed. It was something she did a lot, I came to know.

— Fucking UN, she said. Dread Wilmè distributed more food and medicine than we ever could, and they fucking kill him.

I don't know what surprised me more. The way she could swear in Kreyòl, or the way she was criticizing the UN. I thought the UN and the blancs were the same thing. But I thought of the way that Stéphanie brought those tins of food and medical supplies into the Site and helped Biggie to give them out, and I thought she was pretty cool for a white person.

— If you want to be Route 9, you have to prove yourself, said Biggie. Do you know what I mean?

I didn't know, but I nodded.

— We just got one thing to do first, he said.

Biggie continued to drive. As we turned onto different streets, I saw my map in my head, so when we pulled up outside a shack, I knew it was the address of a Route 9 chimère called Tintin.

Biggie got out and told us to follow. We went inside. Tintin was sitting on a petrol drum. He wasn't much older than me. He was rocking back and forth, making a whimpering sound. I saw that there was blood on his chest, and he was

186

clutching it as if he wanted to stop it leaving his body, or to push it back in.

— Aiie, said Biggie. That's got to hurt.

— It's not a party, said Tintin.

Biggie laughed.

— And the Boston guys?

— I took them by surprise. Two of them are dead, for sure. The other, maybe not. I shot him in the hip, not the stomach.

Stéphanie made that sighing noise again.

— You were attacked, yes? she said. By militias loyal to the new government? They hate you cos Route 9 used to fight for Aristide. Yes?

Tintin looked at Biggie.

— Just say yes, said Biggie.

— Yes, said Tintin.

— Good, said Stéphanie. Right, you were wounded in political violence, so the blancs have to treat you.

She said that like she wasn't blanc her ownself. She rooted around in her pocket, came out with a plastic-sheeted card.

— Show this at the checkpoint, she said. Say I sent you. The soldiers are to escort you to Canapé-Vert Hospital, OK?

She took something from another pocket – it was a bundle of cash.

— Show this, too.

Tintin looked grateful. He took the card and the money and we left, but not before Biggie clapped Tintin on the back. It looked like that hurt, but Tintin didn't say anyen at all.

After that, we drove onto another street, and then another. As we slowed, and Biggie turned the engine off, I noticed that we had come to the shack of one of Biggie's customers; I knew it from the map I had drawn. What his customers bought, I didn't know.

No, that's a lie, and I don't want to lie to you. You're the voices in the darkness, and I have to tell you the truth, or maybe you'll never let me out of here. I knew even then that they bought drugs. I just didn't care.

Would you care? I was living in a place where it was common to eat mud. Don't you judge me, motherfuckers. People call us gangsters, but who's helping the people here apart from us? No moun wants to pay for education; no moun wants to pay for hospitalization. NGOs don't come into Site Solèy. You want free food, the only place you get it from is a chimère. Biggie and Tintin threw sacks of food that Stéphanie brought to them out of a truck every Friday, fed half the Site like that.

As we sat there outside the house, Biggie turned to me.

— Can I see it? he said.

— See what?

— The pwen. The one you got from Dread.

I stared at him. Everyone knew Dread saved me, but I didn't know they knew about the pwen. Biggie saw the expression on my face.

— My houngan, he said. Your manman goes to him, too.

I nodded. That made sense. I took the stone from my pocket and showed him.

— Can I touch it? he said.

— Uh, yeah, sure.

He rubbed the stone.

— Smooth, he said. Who's in it?

— I don't know. An ancestor spirit, my manman says.

Biggie handed it back.

— You got protection, Shorty, he said. That's good. You got his stone. Me, I got Dread's bones. Me and you, we bullet-proof. You go in there, ain't nothing can touch you when the shit goes down.

— What shit? I asked.

Biggie just looked at me, and he knew that I knew what was going down. We got out of the car, but Biggie didn't open the door right away. I understood then that he had turned his engine off before we stopped, and I told myself I was stupid for not noticing it at the time. He didn't want no moun to hear, I guessed.

Me and Stéphanie got out the car. Biggie handed me the shotgun.

— You know what to do with this, right?

I suddenly became aware of my heart in my chest. It was banging like it wanted to get out, like it didn't want any part of this.

— Yeah, I said.

— This guy inside, he robbed from me, said Biggie very quietly. He took my stuff and he sold it to Boston. Can you believe that?

I shook my head. I couldn't believe it, but he was right. Shit like that could get you killed.

— I should never have trusted him, Biggie said. Dude used

to roll with Boston. I've heard him stand tall about all the men he has chopped with machetes. I only let him live cos he always has money; he's always able to buy.

I thought of the men – the boys – who had killed my papa, of the machetes they had held. Was it possible that this man in the shack was one of them?

Yes, I thought. Yes, it was.

— Buy what? said Stéphanie, but I could tell she was joking.

— Food, of course, said Biggie. He put his hands together as if he was praying, like he was a saint or something, and that made me laugh a bit on the inside, and my heart calmed down a little.

— You want me to . . . ?

— Yes, said Biggie. Yes.

I was thinking about that night my papa died, the blood everywhere. I was looking at the door and picturing the man behind it, and I wondered if he really was one of the bandanna men. I decided he was.

I remembered how my papa had looked, the fear in his eyes, as the machetes came down. I began to hate the man behind that door.

Stéphanie stood in the street, her arms folded. I noticed that she stood at such an angle that no moun could shoot her from inside; it was like she'd done this before. She looked bored, I remember thinking.

Biggie reached into the back of his waistband, took out a pistol, and moved to the door. He made a gesture to me that I didn't really understand, then he kicked the door open.

I was in front of the door and I raised the shotgun as the shadow of a man loomed before me. I pulled the trigger. It was that quick. There was a *boom* so loud, like the world was falling down, and I saw a spray of black and red. I was thrown backward, and my shoulder was screaming where the stock of the gun had blown back into it.

I staggered forward to see what I'd done. There was a dead man lying on the floor, but I was only half-conscious that it was me who had killed him.

I turned around. Stéphanie was kissing Biggie, her tongue in his mouth, and that made me nearly as sick as the blood all over the place. She pulled away and she smiled at me, a strange smile.

— Bon, said Biggie. Welcome to Route 9.

I was twelve.

THEN

Toussaint spread out the map on which, in a few strokes of ink, he would plan the doom of the French. They had landed more troops: an inevitability. It had been many weeks since the immolation and slaughter of their first landing party. For now, they held only the ashes of Cape Town and some scrubland that lay around it. The French would needs move into the interior if they wished to regain the country.

Toussaint would be waiting for them. Not for the first time, he blessed the features that allowed Jean-Christophe to blend in with the French, or at least with the mulats. He looked down at the map before him. He had drawn it himself, marking the places where there were mountains, where there were woods, and where there were plantations that could sustain them. He had traveled to all these places himself, had covered the length and breadth of the land on horseback or on foot.

The French could look at their imperfect maps and think, *oh look, there is a valley that will lead us nicely into the foothills, with plenty of fresh water to drink, and far from any of the known negro strongholds.* But Toussaint looked at his own map, and he saw the hidden caves that he had marked along the side of the valley, the trees below that obscured them from view.

The other generals, Jean-François and Biassou, thought it was hubris that motivated Toussaint to confront the French on open ground, but Toussaint believed he had something the French didn't have, certainly not in so much detail. He had the streams and the potato fields; he had the ravines where an army could lie concealed. He had the land.

As he had maintained from the beginning, there was no point taking Haiti if they couldn't hold it afterward. So as he had traveled, he had encouraged and cajoled, too. He had convinced bloodthirsty soldiers to put down their swords and to take up plowshares, for a time at any rate, before they picked up their weapons again. He had devised a simple system of two bowls, one inside the other, with watered sand between, which allowed food to remain cool for longer, and therefore not spoil. As he traveled the country, he taught people the principle of the cooling bowl, and in this way the vittles and viands that were required by citizen and soldier alike were made to last a little longer.

He had ordered the cultivation of everything that could be cultivated, and that included his staff, whom he had instructed to seek out literate soldiers, and to learn to read and write from them. He had put aside stores of dried foods, of simples, of water. Others suggested these things, too – his army weren't ignorant beasts, much as the commissioners might like to think it – but it had been given to him to unite the efforts of all, to hold the plan, whether it was a sequence of steps in his mind or a map that lay before him.

He traced a finger along the road to Marmalade, north of Cape Town. He had stopped short of crossing Cape Town off his map, but the place was all but destroyed, burned in a vengeful fire. Sometimes, in his sleep, he saw people screaming in the flames, and he asked himself if he should have taken on this mantle, and not simply have run when the revolution began. Yet where would he have gone? He would have been caught up in the violence, whether he liked it or not. Besides, he had seen what was to come. He *knew* slavery was going to end, and so he had to bear the duty of being the one to end it.

He comforted himself, too, with the knowledge that things would be worse if he were not present. The troops he and his fellow generals commanded were a ragtag bunch, attired in many cases in the ill-fitting clothes of their masters, armed with bric-a-brac weapons. They were difficult to lead, much prone to mindless obedience or brusque refusal, with no response in between. Yet lead them he had – to several notable victories on the way to their conquest of the mountains.

His only injury, so far, was his left front tooth, which had been knocked out by a shell ejected from his rifle. He liked to smile at people now and show this hole; he had even styled himself Toussaint l'Ouverture for this opening in his teeth. The men in camp put it about that he was called l'Ouverture for the openings he was able to create in enemy lines, and he smiled even more at that. It had not been his intention in taking the name, but it was good nevertheless, for he understood that when a soldier takes pride in his leader, it is his own self-respect and bravery that benefits. He had been a slave – he understood the power of names. His French master had named him Toussaint, for he was born on the feast day of all saints. Now he named himself, and if his name spoke of his military prowess, not a foolish injury, then all the better.

Unfortunately, whilst he had created his own legend almost without meaning to, he had been unable to erase completely the fearsome reputation of his troops. They were still given to excessive cruelty when it came to the whites, and they had too much of an appetite for blood, destruction, and rapine. Biassou all but encouraged this behavior.

But eventually, there will be no Biassou and no Jean-François, just me, Toussaint thought. *Then the soldiers will do as I command, all of them, and bring no shame upon our enterprise.*

— Their plan is not stupid, he said to Jean-Christophe as he studied the terrain. Marmalade is the only place the French can repair to. I hold Dondon, and Biassou and Jean-François control la Grande Rivière. The French must flee from Cape Town or be destroyed, yet they cannot hope to face us here in open battle. If they gain a foothold in Marmalade, however, we'll have to fight them for the interior.

— They move next week, said Jean-Christophe.

— Very well. He indicated the map. They don't know about these caves, I'm sure of it. We'll be ready.

— Ready for what? said Biassou, who was sitting near the entrance to the tent.

He was a fat man, and he liked to be close to a breeze if possible. Even so, sweat was darkening his shirt and running in rivulets down the creases in the flesh of his face. Toussaint forced a smile onto his face. Jean-François was otherwise occupied, strengthening his defenses to the east, but he knew Biassou was a threat to his leadership.

— An ambush, he said. I'm hoping I can take their main force without a drop of blood being spilled.

Biassou laughed, a sound like a pig eating.

— And how will you do that? he said. By vodou? Will Ogou Badagry take them all down to the land under the sea?

— No, said Toussaint. He held up the map. With this. And with words.

Biassou shrugged.

— To hell with words, he said. Swords are better. He touched the sword at his side. I killed my own master with this one. I never felt anything sweeter. I say we face the French on the open field, like men.

— You're right, said Toussaint. It's good to avenge oneself on an enemy. But remember – if we inherit this earth, as the meek should, then we should share that inheritance. Slaughter all the whites and mulats, and we'll only create a blood feud that echoes throughout history.

Biassou sighed.

— You would have us be merciful? he said. After all that they've done?

Toussaint shook his head.

— No, I would have us be pragmatic. Listen. We'll try it my way. If it fails, we'll kill them all.

Biassou smiled.

— I like that plan, he said.

The following week, Toussaint sat on his horse, looking down a long and gently sloping valley. The French soldiers progressed upward like some great insectile horde. He had not been a general long enough to have the knack of counting men at a glance, but he reckoned that there must be thousands of them. They preserved a semblance of discipline, even in the heat, and despite the skirmishes Toussaint's men had visited upon them as they left Cape Town, although he noted through his spyglass that many in the rear ranks were borne on stretchers.

— Is everyone in position? he asked.

Biassou grinned.

— Ambuscades have been set up on all sides, he said.

He pointed to the treeline on either side of the valley and the caves beyond. From here, Toussaint couldn't see their men, but that was the point.

He and Biassou were concealed behind a mound of earth just near the top of the valley. They had ridden at night to take these positions. Now they watched as the serried ranks of men, the steam-breathing horses, the dragged cannons processed steadily uphill.

— Now, Toussaint said.

Jean-Christophe, who was reined up beside them, nodded and spurred his mount, cantering down toward the front line of the French army. A white flag fluttered on the pole that he carried at his side. Toussaint could not hear what he shouted to them, but he knew what it was because it was his words in the other man's mouth. Jean-Christophe was telling them that General Toussaint l'Ouverture requested the opportunity to treat personally with the leader of the French army, and invited him to ride ahead of his force that they might parley.

After much commotion amongst the troops, a man in a hat emerged from the fray, mounted on a magnificent stallion that began to trot up the hill beside the young mulat. Toussaint nodded to Biassou, and they rode to meet him.

They encountered one another some hundred yards before the advancing army. Toussaint dismounted and bowed to the French admiral, or lieutenant, or whatever he was. For his part, Biassou stayed on his horse; he wasn't the type to learn that bowing doesn't have to mean anything if you don't want it to. In fact, he darted a quick frown at Toussaint, as if *he* were betraying weakness. *Well, let Biassou wait and see what happens*, Toussaint thought.

The French leader remained at saddle also; a Frenchman would not meet a black on equal terms. Toussaint smiled inwardly. Here he was, abasing himself, the only one of the three to dismount and bow, and yet he would carry the day.

The Frenchman was tall and arrogant of feature, perhaps

fifty years old, but with a strong thick chest and a narrow waist, a shining sword at his side.

— Do you wish to negotiate the terms of your surrender? he asked.

His accent was pure Paris.

Toussaint laughed.

— I wish to negotiate the terms of yours.

The Frenchman made a show of looking around him, casting his eyes over his thousands of men.

— It would seem I am at a numerical advantage, he said.

— Then you place a lot of faith in appearances, said Toussaint.

He raised his hand and his soldiers moved forward from their positions, from behind rock and tree and earthen redoubt. He knew how many men *he* had – five thousand, some half of them armed with guns taken from the slave masters, or the white army. Indeed, many of his men were white – soldiers who had fought with the commission but who had afterward joined his cause, desiring the permanent expulsion of the colonizers and the unification and independence of Haiti.

The Frenchman blanched and reached for his saber, but Biassou was already pointing his rifle at him, and his hand soon stilled.

Toussaint gripped his reins and, with an ease that belied his age, swung himself up onto his saddle again. He made his mount uprear on its hind legs, and shouted for attention from the white soldiers:

— Lay down your weapons!

— Do you dare to address my men? the Frenchman asked. Toussaint ignored him.

— You are surrounded by the men of Toussaint l'Ouverture and Biassou of the free Haitian army! he shouted. We are men of honor. You have many wounded – recommend them to the care of our women and our healers. They'll be well treated, as will you. Any man who surrenders to us will be allowed to live.

Some of the soldiers began to lower their weapons. Toussaint smiled – the plan was working. He raised his rifle in the air, in a display of power.

— Yield, and you'll live, he shouted. I swear it. Fight, and every last one of you will die.

He did not know if it was his supplication or the realization on the part of the French that their situation was hopeless, but suddenly the weapons began to fall, with a cliquetis of metal on wood, of metal on hard stony ground. Soon the great army had unarmed itself.

Biassou uttered a cry of triumph. He turned to the closest of his soldiers, the ones hidden in the bushes to the north.

— Now! he shouted. They're defenseless. Kill –

He did not get any further. Smoothly, Toussaint brought his rifle to his shoulder and fired, tearing the top off Biassou's head, hot blood spraying into the air. *Damn him*, Toussaint thought. The man collapsed at the waist, his feet still caught in the stirrups, and his startled horse carried him uphill, flopping like a rag doll.

— DO NOT FIRE! Toussaint roared to the men.

A good half of them were Biassou's, and the air trembled with the metallic resonance of the possibility that they would mutiny, turning on Toussaint, then slaughtering the French.

He took a deep breath.

— Any man who kills a prisoner will answer to me with his life!

There was a terrible pregnant moment, as Toussaint observed the hesitation on the faces of the free blacks, the mulats, and the whites who had joined them.

A moment passed, eternally.

Another.

Sweat beaded on Toussaint's brow and nose, dripped down, and landed on the warm skin of his horse; he fancied that he could hear the tiny splash it made.

To Toussaint's relief, though, absolutely nothing happened. No one moved; no one fired. A bird called somewhere, and a frog sang.

— Collect their weapons, he said to Jean-Christophe. Take the wounded to our infirmary tent. Any soldier who wishes to join us is welcome; we accept no segregation in this army. Tell them there'll be freedom, and food to eat, and some English to kill soon, I warrant.

— English? said the French leader, who looked pale and shaken.

— Yes, said Toussaint. I gather His Majesty's Royal Navy has landed at Guildive.

— What? Why?

— I presume, said Toussaint, that they've observed France's loss of control over the country and think to take it for themselves. I imagine, further, that they would like to enslave us once again. We, and the sugar we grow, are very valuable, are we not?

The French leader nodded, slowly.

— So. We eat and drink. Then we ride to Guildive, and any of your men are free to join us, provided you pledge allegiance to myself and to Haiti. You French love killing the English, so I hear.

One of the soldiers nearby laughed, and didn't stop when the French leader shot him an angry look.

I have them, thought Toussaint. *I have them.*

Only at that moment did he realize his hands were shaking, and he turned to see if Biassou's corpse was riding around still, but the horse had disappeared. He felt sickness wrapping its clammy hands around his belly, and he saw the Frenchman looking at him as if he were some kind of monster.

Good god, he thought. *Now they'll start saying I took my name from the time I opened up Biassou's head.*

But he had sworn that the French soldiers would live if they laid down their arms, and Biassou would have massacred them. Toussaint was many things, but most of all he was a man of his word.

NOW

I think maybe the oxygen is running out in here. I can hear my heart – *boom, boom, boom* – it's like one of the beats that Biggie used to rap to. I can hear my breathing, too; it's loud and shallow. I don't want to die in the darkness, so I start to cry, but then I think I shouldn't cry cos it's a waste of water.

But I'm not going to die without a fight. That's what Biggie used to say. He used to say:

— Don't come after me. Don't come after me or my soldiers, cos I will come after you a thousand times harder. Come after me, mwen apè mange, you, I'll eat you up, man. I'll come at you in broad daylight.

Broad daylight. I think about that. I want to see the daylight. There's no moun coming after me, but maybe the walls of this place are my enemy; maybe I should fight. I crawl over to the closest pile of rubble and I start to pull at it. It's stupid cos I saw the building from above – I think I did, anyway – and I know I can't dig myself out.

But I try.

I'm a cold gangster, real G, motherfucker. Gangster for life. That's what I say to the plaster and the metal and the concrete, cursing that stuff as it cuts my hands. I can't see it, but I throw it behind me. I'm crying, I think, and I'm grabbing this stuff and just throwing it into the darkness. I don't even know if I'm going in the right direction.

I just dig, and once I start, I can't stop.

Soon after Biggie took me into the crew, I was hanging out at a corner near Boston territory. I was on the lookout; shorties always get the lookout when they're starting coming up. I didn't have a gun, then. My job was to ring Biggie if anything went down. I had a cell phone in my pocket. It felt cool, like I was a real chimère. There wasn't anyone I could call with it – it only had Biggie's number and he never put much prepay on it. But sometimes I took it out and held it to my ear and pretended to talk to someone – real high roller, that was me, shot caller.

Right then, though, I wasn't on the phone. I was sitting against the wall in the dust and I was throwing my pwen up and down, up and down, catching it in my hand, and it made this smooth *thunk* sound when I did.

Tintin walked round the corner and stared at me. He had this bandage on his chest; it made him walk kind of funny. He was wearing baggy pants and I could see his Calvin Klein boxers. He had this, like, little goatee under his bottom lip. It wasn't really growing right, but it was cool anyway. There was a gold chain round his neck and he had on a baseball cap. I thought he was looking dope, even though he wasn't much older than me. Me, I was just a shorty in a T-shirt and jeans, throwing my stone.

Tintin stood over me.

— What's that? he said. He looked pissed.

— What?

— That. In your hand. What is it?

I looked at the stone.

— It's just a stone, I said.

I don't know why I said that. I guess I could see in Tintin's eyes that he wanted it. I put it back in my pocket.

— Bullshit, said Tintin. It's a pwen. Biggie said you had one. How'd you get it? You steal it?

I guess my mouth fell open.

— No. Dread Wilmè gave it to me.

— Yeah, said Tintin, and I've got a watch from Toussaint l'Ouverture. You expect me to believe that? Where'd you get it, Shorty? What makes you so special, huh?

I started to lever myself up, but Tintin kicked my hand out from under me, and I went down on my ass.

— I think maybe you'd better give it to me, said Tintin. I got shot and I don't want to get shot again. A pwen would protect me.

I should have given it to him – I could see in his eyes that he was the kind of guy who would hurt me for refusing him – but for some reason I felt angry.

— No, I said.

205

Tintin took a deep breath. He didn't say anything, just seized me by my T-shirt and pulled me up. He punched me, but his fist hit my belt buckle, and he went:

— Fuck!

He clutched his hand with the other. He came at me hard, grabbed me with his good hand, and headbutted me, only he didn't aim it right, or maybe I ducked, and it was his nose that hit my forehead. I reeled back – my head was ringing – but he staggered into me, nearly fell over. He was holding his nose, and there was blood all over his hands, dripping over his mouth.

— Mother*fucker*, he said. His voice was thick and trembly. That stone *is* protecting you, right? You give it to me.

— No, I said.

— Man, you've got a death wish, said Tintin.

He kicked at me, but I took a step back and he went down hard on his back. The whole front of his shirt was covered in blood now. It looked like I'd kicked his ass bad, and I hadn't even hit him once.

Tintin got up, and there was murder in his eyes, I'm telling you. Then I saw something out the corner of my eye – a reflection maybe, a flash of light – and I turned my body the tiniest amount. All this was happening without me thinking at all, and I saw a car drifting slowly down the road. It was a Ford, I think, gentle, gentle, gentle, like a boat, making no sound at all, or at least I wasn't aware of any, and sticking out the car window was something long and dark.

I pushed Tintin hard in the chest and he went down again. This time I heard his head hit the ground and I could smell his blood, and it seemed like the moment went on forever.

— Motherf— said Tintin.

Then I couldn't hear him, cos it was all just the *boom, boom, boom, boom, boom, boom, boom* of guns, like a drum 'n' bass beat. I didn't have time to go down; I just stood there waiting to die, like the Notorious B.I.G. in the song. I was ready, man. I couldn't describe to you how it felt, or what I saw. It seemed like I didn't see anything apart from the sun on the chrome of that car, the fire from the barrels, and I don't even know if I saw that, or I just imagined it afterward.

A moment later, the car was gone. There was a buzzing noise in my ears; it sounded like, *bzzzzzzzzzzzzzzzzzzzzzzzzzz*. Tintin said something to me from down on the ground, but I could only see his lips moving, I couldn't hear anything. I couldn't smell blood anymore. Instead there was this smell like something burning and metal, all mixed together, and underneath it the smell of toilets. I looked down and I saw that I'd pissed myself. I could feel it, too, this spreading warmth in my crotch, on my thighs. I figured I should be embarrassed, but my head was just full of this voice going, you're alive, you're alive, you're alive. All I could hear was buzzing and all I could see was the sun in the sky. I didn't think I'd ever seen anything better.

Then I saw Tintin's hand wave at me, like he was saying to give him a hand.

I put out my hand and I caught his and pulled him up.

He said:

— . . .

I put my hands to my ears, then did this shrug and spread my hands out to show I couldn't hear.

He leaned in close.

— HOLY SHIT, he shouted. HOLY SHIT.

— Yeah, I said. It was all I could think of.

— That was cold, he said. *Cold*.

I stared at him.

— You saved my life, said Tintin.

He was looking at me with this strange expression. No, not at me – he was looking past me.

— What? I said.

I don't know if he heard, but he pointed behind me and I turned round.

That's when I saw it. The wall behind me was full of bullet holes, great big craters in the plaster. There was a window that was shot out, bits of broken glass everywhere. Above my head, to either side of me, all bullet holes. But none of the bullets had hit me.

I noticed something, though: my shadow behind me was pinned to the wall by these bullets; it had been killed and good. It was weird, looking at my own shadow all full of holes. I wondered, if your shadow gets shot, is that bad luck? Is it like dying in a dream? I took a little step to one side, and for a moment I feared that my shadow would stay stuck to the wall where it had died, and from then on I would walk everywhere with no shadow and old women would make the sign of the devil at me. But that didn't happen. My shadow slid with me along the wall, and now there were no holes in it, none at all.

— How did they miss you? said Tintin.

I touched the pocket with the pwen in it.

— I don't know, I said.

— Man, said Tintin. The stone. Biggie said you was the kid Dread saved. I didn't believe it. Now I do. No wonder you got a stone.

He held out his hand for a high five.

I was looking at the blood all over his face, shocked, and it took me a while before I realized he wasn't joking. When I slapped his hand, it made a noise like a gunshot very, very far away.

I looked at his face.

— You broke your nose, I said.

— Yeah? he said. You pissed yourself.

I started laughing, and then he started laughing, and then we were both bent over, holding our stomachs, laughing so hard we cried. We held each other's shoulders and we laughed and laughed. The sound of a car engine interrupted us. We looked at each other and ran deep into Route 9 territory. We kept going till our breath ran out, then we sat down and waited to breathe again, and when we did, we started laughing again.

After we finally stopped laughing, Tintin lifted his shirt and wiped the blood off his face with it.

— Guess the stone wants to stay with you, he said. Sorry I tried to take it.

After that, we were best friends.

It was that simple.

Tintin was my friend, but he was one crazy mofo, too. A few months after we got shot at, he picked me up in Biggie's car.

— I've been collecting, he said, but now I gotta go out of the Site, make a delivery. You want to come for a ride?

A delivery meant heroin, I knew that, but I didn't know that Tintin was a delivery driver.

— You're leaving the Site? I asked.

— That's what I said, isn't it?

I stared at him. I'd never left the Site – at least, not since the soldiers killed Dread Wilmè and put the whole place on lockdown.

— Well? said Tintin. Are you coming, or what?

— Shit, yes, I said.

I jumped in the car and Tintin gunned the engine and we shot off down the road. When we got to the UN checkpoint, Tintin rolled down his window. He handed a pass to the blanc soldier on duty.

— This pass says one, said the soldier in French.

— My brother's sick, said Tintin. I got to take him to Canapé-Vert.

The soldier leaned down and looked through the open window at me.

— Doesn't look sick to me, he said.

— It's malaria, said Tintin.

The soldier pulled his head back, like he thought I was a mosquito or something.

— You got papers for him? said the soldier.

Tintin leaned over me and opened the glove compartment.

— Yeah, they're in here somewhere, he said.

He started pulling out all this stuff – papers and trash and a torch and other things. He dropped some of the papers between the seats and started trying to fish them out.

— Forget it, said the soldier. He waved us through.

— You've got a pass? I said to Tintin as we pulled away from the checkpoint.

— Yeah, Stéphanie got it for me.

— Can she get more?

— Maybe, I don't know. But Biggie wants only one person to do the deliveries. Right now, that's me.

He put the pass back in his pocket and I looked at it longingly as he did so. That pass was freedom.

We turned onto a bigger road and started climbing the hill toward where the rich people's houses were. I wound down my window and pushed my head out, and I felt the breeze on my face. It was a feeling like freedom. I yelled, like:

— Whooooop!

Tintin laughed. He yelled, too, so we were like two wolves in that car. Then he saw this dog on the side of the road, limping. It was a mangy dog, a stray. Tintin swerved the car toward it, and he leaned over me and howled:

— Arooo! Arooo! Arooo!

My stomach did a dance as the car fishtailed, and I grabbed the steering wheel without thinking.

— Don't! I said.

Tintin laughed again. He wrenched the wheel back from me at the last moment and the car squealed on the tarmac, skidded back onto the road. The dog looked at us as we passed, like it wasn't even surprised. Tintin kind of punched the air and revved the car hard.

— This is freedom, man! he said. We can do whatever we like.

My heart was beating – *pit-PAT, pit-PAT, pit-PAT, pit-PAT* – in my chest and everything seemed brighter and more colorful, like everyday things were lit with neon. This car went past us going the other way, and as it drifted by its wipers went off, spraying soapy liquid onto the windscreen, into the air, light sparkling through it, and I thought it was like the car was a whale, something big and alive, blowing air and water through its blowhole, cruising.

I looked over at Tintin. He was grinning, trying to make out like it had been a joke with the dog, but I knew it wasn't – I could see the coldness in his eyes behind that grin. I knew him, and I knew he'd have killed that dog if I hadn't been there.

That was the thing about being with Tintin. Sometimes I'd look at him and it was like he'd forgotten to put the shutters over his eyes, and I'd see down inside right to his soul, and see how much he was hurting. He was unprotected, is the best way I can say it. His manman died when he was little, and there was anyen about him that could keep bad stuff out. I figure that's why he wanted my pwen, cos maybe it would have been like a shield for him.

He *is* unprotected, I mean. I forget that there's still a present, out there where there's light. When I think of Tintin leading Route 9, I think, shit, they'll have some fun, but a lot of people are going to get hurt. The thing about Tintin is, it's like . . . it's like he's got no skin, right? Like, everyone else, they walk around and they've got skin all over them to keep out the sun and the rain and the dirt. Tintin's got none of that. He's just cartilage and muscle and veins, something out of a horror movie, no barrier between him and the sharp edges of the world. He feels *everything*, and it hurts him. So he hurts other things first, so they can't get to him.

You see what I'm saying?

So, yeah, Tintin was whooping and going on about the dog, and did I feel how the car slid, and did I see the dog look at us, the expression on its face? Me, I thought the dog didn't really care, but I laughed, too, and said:

— Yeah, it's dope.

I was just glad he hadn't killed the thing.

— Look down, man, said Tintin.

He stopped the car. We could see the Site stretched out below us, all low and rickety and enormous. It spilled right out to the sea; from this angle, it was like the city outside the slum was pushing it, trying to shove it into the water, like trash. But from up here the Site seemed smaller, too – escapable, I guess.

It was like it had been the whole world, and now I was outside it. We were climbing up this road that switched back and forth on the hill, twisting and turning cos it was so steep, and the houses were getting bigger and bigger, and some of them even stood on their own in their own patches of green land.

The sea, it sparkled like jewels, like something precious, not a mess of sewage and petrol, which was what it really was. I could see gulls, pelicans diving. Around us, at our level, was a sea of green, punctuated by detached houses, gardens everywhere, full of trees and flowers and birds singing. It was beautiful. Right next to us, there was a grass lawn, smooth and green, like something you could eat, not just something to walk on.

— Gardens, man, said Tintin.

— Yeah, I said.

I wished I could get out the car and go lie down on that grass, it looked so cool and soft and green.

— This is it, said Tintin after a while.

We were parked outside this white house with pillars at the front and steps up to the porch. On the other side of the car was the hill, and at the bottom of the hill was the sea, and the garbage heap that we lived in.

— This is what? I said.

— Where the doctor lives, said Tintin. He buys most of our stuff, distributes it to the rich people.

Tintin opened the car door and led the way toward the house.

— Where's the stuff? I said.

I knew the gear usually left the Site in big sports bags, but Tintin didn't get anyen out of the car.

— I'll get it later, said Tintin. Chill.

He went up to the door and rang the doorbell. It made a chime, like, *ding* DONG, *ding* DONG, *ding* DONG, and I was worried it was so loud people on the street would turn and look at us and see our gangster clothes and wonder what we were doing.

We waited, and nothing happened. No one came to the door.

— Oh, said Tintin. I guess he must be busy, or something. Maybe we should check round the back.

He started to walk round on the grass.

— You think this is a good idea? I said to his back.

He shrugged, and I saw the gun butt sticking up from the waistband of his pants, and I started to get a really bad feeling. In my mind's eye, I could see that dog limping along and the car wheel racing toward it.

Tintin stopped at this high metal fence with barbed wire on top of it. He tapped a code into this little pad, and a gate opened. He beckoned for me to follow him. We walked past bushes covered in small yellow flowers. The whole place smelled like . . . I don't know, cos I'd never smelled such things before; it was all fresh and nice. If I'd been on my own, I would have stopped and smelled those flowers, but I knew Tintin would say that was some weak-ass shit, so I just followed him.

We came round the corner, and there was this big pool with water in it, blue like the sky. Next to it were white chairs, and there was a BBQ and this big bar thing. I stared at the pool; I'd never seen anything like it. Tintin grinned.

— This is the life, huh? he said.

He walked over to the bar and slid this rolling kind of lid open.

— What can I get you? he said. Whiskey and Coke?

I looked round. Behind us were these huge windows that went all the way up from the ground to the first floor, and behind those was a kitchen, but I couldn't see anyone inside.

— This isn't a delivery, is it? I asked. I was feeling nervous, but excited, too.

— I kind of lied about that, said Tintin. Sorry. The doctor is away. Holiday in Miami, or some shit. When we get back, you tell Biggie we had a problem collecting.

— Biggie doesn't know we're here?

— Hell, no. We'll say some asshole from one of the scrap stalls didn't want to pay. Say we had to fuck him up; he slowed us down.

— But wouldn't we have to do it? Find some guy and beat him up? I mean, Biggie would check.

— Already done, said Tintin. Already done, and you don't have to worry about it.

I opened my mouth, then closed it again. I was thinking, shit, Tintin. But I didn't say anything. I could see right into Tintin's eyes at that moment and I could see his soul shining inside, but not shining in a good way, like light on a knife blade. I just nodded.

— OK, I said. OK, whiskey and Coke.

Tintin clapped his hands.

— My man, he said.

He started pouring the drink.

I don't know how many whiskey and Cokes we had. A lot, I guess. We sat in those white chairs and drank, and it wasn't long before I forgot about the dog in the road, and the guy, whichever guy it was, that Tintin had fucked up so we could have this afternoon by the pool. Tintin was funny – he was making jokes, imitating Biggie, stuff like that. He was always good at imitating people, at making like he was a real person, not a thing that was rotten inside.

Pretty soon, we were drunk. Tintin took off his top and jumped into the pool – *splash!* – and I jumped in, too. I'd swum in the sea before, in the salt and the sewage, but this was unbelievable. It was warm, but cooler than the air, and the water was smooth and all around, embracing. I thought of Marguerite, how, when we were in the boat with Papa, she would look up at these houses and say that one day she would live in one. It felt weird to be floating under the sun in her dream of the future, swimming in her pool and drinking her drinks.

We swam over to these floating ring things and got into them, and then Tintin said:

— Hey, we should get our drinks.

After that, we just floated around the pool, drinking, drifting. It was the best day of my life.

I closed my eyes. The sun was overhead, just a little to the west, huge in the sky and beating down fierce. With my eyelids shut, it was like an explosion in front of my eyes – red fireworks, sparks flying. I knew the fireworks were my blood, and that was even more amazing.

I opened my eyes and turned to Tintin.

— Man, I said. This is . . . I don't know. It's amazing.

— Yeah, he said. I thought you'd like it.

I looked at him seriously.

— I'll give you the stone, I said. I'll give you the stone, if you give me the pass.

— You're kidding, right? Tintin said.

— That pass is freedom. That pass gets you out of the Site. It gets you here.

He laughed.

— Only cos the doctor is on vacation, he said. Keep the stone, Shorty.

It pissed me off that he called me Shorty – he wasn't much older than me – but I didn't say anything. I just floated.

— Seriously, man, you can have it, I said. Swapsies.

He shook his head.

— I saw those bullets, he said. The stone is yours. I don't even want to think about what shit could go down if you gave it to me. But listen, Shorty – you're fun, yeah? I'll bring you again.

— Cool, I said.

I closed my eyes again.

I must have fallen asleep, cos when I opened my eyes again I could hear shouting. I sat up quick, felt blood rush to my head. I stared through blurry eyes at the side of the pool. I felt dizzy, like I was going to puke.

Tintin was standing on the tiles, in his baggy jeans. There was still water dripping from his hair, and he was holding his gun out in front of him, flat side down, like a true gangster. He was shouting, but I couldn't tell what he was saying – I felt like someone had filled my head with engine grease.

— . . . Solèy 10 bitch, I heard.

That really got my attention, cos Solèy 10 is where the Boston crew have their territory.

I rubbed my eyes. Standing in front of Tintin was this girl in a maid's uniform, a young girl, like, 16 at the oldest. She was trembling, and there were sheets lying on the ground in front of her, like she'd been carrying them and had dropped them. I kicked off the floating ring and swam to the side of the pool, pulled myself out. I walked over to Tintin.

— What the fuck, man? I said.

He turned to me. His shutters were down again, and I could see that sick light.

— There wasn't supposed to be anyone here, he said.

He was scared, I could see it. I took a step away from him. He was scared, and it would be bad to stress him out more. That would make him act crazy.

— It's cool, I said. It's cool. She's just a maid. Listen, T—

— No names! screamed Tintin.

I blinked. I was seriously wishing I hadn't had those whiskey and Cokes.

— She's Solèy 10, said Tintin. She's Boston.

I looked at her.

— How do you know that?

He smiled this thin smile.

— I asked her, man. You Solèy 10? he asked the girl.

She nodded. Her eyes cut to me, and they were big and terrified. I was thinking, I wish this was a dream, and I could just open my eyes and be back in the Site.

— Just cos she's Solèy 10 don't mean she's Boston, I said.

She nodded again, harder this time.

— I'm just a maid, she said. I'm just a maid and I didn't see anything, I swear. Let me go. I'll keep my mouth shut.

Tintin was stepping from foot to foot, and the gun was swaying like crazy.

— No way, he said. The shit we'd be in . . . No way. She's got to die.

It was like he was talking to himself. The shit we'd be in . . . He took a deep breath, steadied the gun.

— Chill, I said.

But it was like he didn't hear me at all.

— She's hot, huh? he said to me.

— What? I said.

He turned to the maid.

— Take your clothes off, he said.

I was just staring at him. I could see this girl trembling, and she was pretty much the same age as me and my sister; she even looked like Marguerite a bit. Yeah, she was pretty, but she was scared to death. I even wondered if she was Marguerite for one moment, but the eyes were different – no one had eyes like Marguerite. I felt sick. The whiskey in my stomach was swirling round and round, like water going down a drain.

I didn't think, I just walked toward her, and I put myself between her and Tintin.

— Put it down, I said. She's just a girl.

Tintin hesitated.

I turned to her.

— You never saw us, right?

She nodded again.

— I never did. I was here, and I put out the laundry. That's it.

— Get out the way, said Tintin. Get out the way, Shorty.

Before he said, no names, but Shorty was cool. Shorty wasn't really a name, anyway.

— No, I said.

Tintin's finger was white on the trigger, and I thought, I'm going to die here. Then I remembered something. I put my hand in my pocket, took out the stone. I remembered Tintin trying to hit me, but just hurting himself instead.

— The stone says she's telling the truth, I said.

It was total bullshit, but I saw some of that light dimming in his eyes, like some kind of reason was taking hold again, like he was starting to be that real person he sometimes pretended to be.

— Yeah? he said.

I could tell he wanted to be convinced, he needed to be convinced. He didn't really want to hurt the girl. He was just afraid she'd hurt him, that she'd tell the doctor what he'd done and he'd pay for it, that Biggie would make him pay. Biggie was a ruthless motherfucker when it came to punishing his soldiers.

221

— Yeah, I said. I swear. That's why I'm standing over here. We do this, it'll go bad for us. Bad luck. Bad vodou.

I said *we* instead of *you*, cos I figured that might help him get some perspective.

Tintin's gun was wavering even more now. I turned to the girl again.

— Listen, you got to promise us, I said. Promise you won't say you saw us here.

— I don't even know your names, she said.

— Yeah, but you know we're Route 9. Listen – just promise, please. You say anything, we'd have to come back and find you.

I felt like an asshole saying that, but I had to make Tintin put down the gun. I was shaking inside at the thought of what he'd do if her clothes were off, and I kept seeing my sister. Marguerite was flashing in my eyes like those red fireworks, like the hot shadow of something you've been staring at in the sun, something that burns itself into your eyes.

— I promise, she said. Please, just go. I won't say anything. I promise.

Tintin lowered the gun.

— The lwa are on your side, girl, he said.

I knew he was thinking of the stone, and how it had protected me. He tucked the gun in his waistband.

— Come on, Shorty. Let's blow this joint, he said. We got to get back to the Site. They'll be wondering where we gone.

He picked up his T-shirt and walked back round the house, and I followed him.

We never spoke about that day afterward. It was the best day of my life, then it was the worst, and then it was this worry that was always at the back of our minds. But I guess that girl kept quiet, cos we never heard shit about it after. Biggie never even knew we'd left the Site.

I never left it again, till the day I got shot.

Listen. I was with Biggie two years after that.

This is what we would do in Biggie's crew:

We rode high on chrome bright as sky, rolling to heavy beats.

We had nothing but love for our crew, nothing but steel for the haters.

We sold drugs.

We killed people.

Mornings, we did our deliveries. We rode two or three in the car, one on shotgun – except it wasn't always a shotgun, sometimes it was an AK or a Glock. The gangs got all these guns from Aristide, back in the day. Now we had anpil guns, but bullets were much harder to find. So most of the time we tried not to use the guns if we didn't have to. Sometimes we used machetes.

As we passed, everyone said hello.

— Bonjou, they called. Bonjou.

Me, I smiled at them, but I'm not so good at talking as Biggie. I have a tattoo on my arm, though, an AK, to show that I'm a killer. So if I was shotgun I showed my arm out the window, so that people could see. Then they knew not to fuck with me. Me, I know how to cut heroin. I know how to cut people. I know where to shoot people so that they die.

Now, I think these are things I never should have learned.

This one time, we passed my manman. She saw me in the car and she made a noise, like, *tssssuuuu*, sucking air through her teeth.

Biggie stopped the car.

— Y'a pwoblem? he said.

— Gen pwoblem, said Manman. Not with you, anyway, Biggie. But that's my son in your car. My kid.

Biggie laughed.

— I don't see a kid, he said. I see a soldier. My frère chouchou. This kid's one of my bodyguards. I love him, man. I love all my soldiers.

Manman looked at the gun in my hand. She said:

— Chita chouter yon jour wap fait goal.

That's something Manman used to say to me a lot. It means, if you keep shooting, you'll make a goal. It means, if you keep doing like that, you'll get what you're aiming for. It means, basically, stop doing that, or you'll get what you deserve.

Usually I laughed when Manman said it; it's such an old woman thing to say. But then I had a gun in my hand and she was talking about shooting and it made me uncomfortable.

— Bullshit, I said in English. I put up two fingers in the peace sign. Peace, Manman, I said. See you around.

Her face went hard.

— What about school? she said. Aren't you going to finish school? You could have a job, you could make money . . .

— I have a job, I said. I make lots of money.

Manman's eyes went all narrow, like she was closing something to me.

— You will end in blood and darkness, she said, like the houngan told her when she was ansent with us.

Biggie gunned the gas.

— Wow, your manman is a hard-ass, he said as he pulled away.

— Word, I said.

That's what I always say when I don't know what to say.

Biggie was nearly always with us. When we rolled, he leaned out the window. He would be smoking a blunt – he was always smoking. He grinned at people, and he rapped to them about how the government threw him in jail and he was too young for it. I thought he still was pretty young, so he can't have been in jail long, but I didn't say that.

We handed out bags of drugs, and people gave us cash. We put the cash in the trunk of the whip. Some of that cash went to the kids in Solèy 19. It was for them to go to school.

Biggie said:

— No moun wants to help us in the Site, so we got to help ourselves. Give the kids an education.

Biggie has a daughter who's three. She's cute. Biggie said she'll go to America, go to college. I hope so. Sometimes when I looked at her I thought of Marguerite. She wasn't far away – she was in Solèy 10, where the Boston crew hang. She's my twin, so she was 14 then, too. I wondered what she looked like; I thought about it all the time. I wondered if she

225

was as tall as me, if she was good at mending things and making things work like I am. I pictured her in my head, but it was difficult – the image was all blurry, and it was hard for me to know how her child face would change as she got older. I hoped she was pretty, and had lots of friends, and didn't roll with any gangsters.

Afternoons, we handed out food from one of the trucks, or we just chilled. There was a game we played, too, and I was the best at it. It's called ghost-riding the whip. This is what we did: we took Biggie's whip and we found a nice long street. Then we took a brick and we jammed it down on the gas – only not too hard, cos then the whip rolled too fast. We made the car roll and we walked alongside, and the game was to rap a whole song before the car drifted and we had to reach in and grab the wheel.

I was good at it cos I'm the best with machines. Sometimes Biggie even let me drive the whip. And I always fixed it if it broke, which was often. Once Biggie got so stoned he fell asleep at the wheel and crashed the car into some people and a wall. One of them had a gun, so some shit kicked off right there, and Biggie had to kill that guy. Me, I had to repair the car. I didn't have to repair Biggie, cos Stéphanie got him some bandages and she did his stitches herself.

Biggie was pretty good at ghost-riding, too, but he wasn't so interested in the car; he was more interested in the rapping. He rapped all the time. It got a little annoying, actually. So mostly he just let the car crash while he rapped. He thought that was funny. It kind of was, I guess.

Sometimes they went on missions. Me, not so often. The guys called me the Mechanic. A gun jammed, they brought it to me. Biggie crashed the car, they brought it to me. Dust got in the carburetor – that happened a lot – they brought it to me.

As well, I did the accounts. I wrote down who owed what, how much we'd handed out. I wrote down who we were sending to school. I updated the maps. Biggie loved this. He said before I came we were losing anpil money, and now we were rich. Tintin called me a geek.

But sometimes I did go along. Sometimes we went on missions to Boston, and then I rode shotgun if I could. Usually the fights were for show – everyone hid behind houses and shouted a lot and shot without really looking. No one wants to die.

— I don't want to die, Biggie said. I got a kid, man. I don't want to die.

He said that, but he was still a gangster. So sometimes, yeah, people died. Sometimes people just got hurt, and then Biggie had to call Stéphanie and ask her to help. She helped a lot – more than she should have, I guess. But I could see from her eyes that she loved Biggie. Stupid, I think. Still, it's her life.

Listen. I'm telling you all this for a reason. So you understand the routine, so you understand the life, so you understand what happened next.

This is what happened next.

This was the end of 2009. I was 14, and it had been 2,501 days since Marguerite was taken.

227

We were down near the sea and we were standing in the back of a truck, Tintin and me, throwing bags of rice and flour to the people. Some of the other Route 9 soldiers were standing by the truck with their guns up. Sometimes people got too desperate, then they mobbed the truck. The guns were to stop that.

Stéphanie was on the truck, too. She was watching to see how much food was being distributed. It was NGO food that she'd got her hands on somehow, you see. She couldn't get her trucks in here, but she could get inside herself if she was prepared to take the risk. For her, it wasn't much risk, though. She was the girlfriend of a hardcore chimère leader.

Someone asked if we had bandages.

— I'm sorry, Stéphanie said. No medical equipment. Just food. We'll try to bring some next time.

The guy got pretty angry, but a chimère stepped forward with his gun. What was the guy going to do? He backed off.

Just then, a shot rang out. One of the people below us in the crowd – a woman with a baby slung on her front – went down on her face. Someone screamed, then more people screamed. In a flash, it wasn't a crowd anymore, but a riot.

Boom.

That was a shotgun. It took one of the chimères below us in the chest and he flew – *bang* – against the wall of the truck. I was on the metal floor, and I didn't know if I'd dived down or if someone had pushed me. There were people screaming and screaming, and I heard the whine of a bullet as it went over my head. Our guys were shooting back now. Tintin was swearing as he emptied his AK.

I stood up, and there was my pistol in my hand. I stared at it in surprise for a moment, then I looked out over the crowd. I saw a guy in a balaclava pointing a machine gun at us. I aimed and pulled the trigger, calmer than I felt, and I smelled the sulfur and cordite as my gun bucked in my hand. I didn't wait to see if he was down. I turned and looked for other chimères, and saw another balaclava running toward the truck. I shot his legs, and he went sprawling.

Then I saw someone else.

I saw a girl. She had bandannas on that covered her mouth and hair, but I could tell it was a girl just from the eyes, and she was pointing her gun at me. It was a Heckler. Expensive weapon. She was my age, and her eyes were big. She was no more than ten meters from me.

I'm dead, I thought.

I'm dead cos I can't shoot her.

She was wearing a Jay-Z T-shirt; she had little bud breasts. She must have been my age, maybe even younger.

And then I thought, oh, shit.

This girl, she was my age and she wasn't shooting, either. I could hear Tintin next to me, shouting something to me, but I wasn't listening. Everything was chaos, but in the center of the chaos there was this girl. She was all I saw. I was looking at her eyes and I *remembered* those eyes. They were small, like almonds. They had freckles either side of them, like I have freckles. They were the precise color of the sea at dusk.

They're my eyes. They're my sister's eyes.

Slowly, I lowered my gun. I stared into this girl's eyes, into Marguerite's eyes, all the time.

I counted:

Time since the bullets started: 1 minute.

Time since I last saw my sister: 2,501 days.

Time since I was a whole person: 2,501 days.

Time since I loved her: forever.

Behind me, Stéphanie said:

— Down! Down!

But I ignored her. I nodded to the girl and she hesitated, then she nodded back.

People always say, like, time stood still, when something big goes down. It's a thing that people say. But, mwen jire, that's what happened at this moment. Everything stopped, and nothing and no one was moving. There was this gull above me and it just froze in the air, hung there, and I could see the people holding the guns, the people cowering on the ground, and they weren't moving, either.

There was just Marguerite, and her eyes, and I could see that glow coming out of her, that glow I remembered, like her soul was just shining out of her, like she was a burning thing made to build, not to destroy. She had this little half-smile on her lips, and I could see her – she was filling my eyes – but in the corner of my vision I could see the street where we found the baby, too, and I could see the bit of beach where Dread was pushed, burning, into the sea.

Both those moments were happening at the same time as this one, and also the time when Marguerite found the baby

230

rats, and the time she handed over the baby, and all these other memories, too, like all the times we were on the boat with Papa, looking up at the Site.

I swear, man, mwen jire, this moment went on forever. I could see those freckles on her nose, like a constellation. I could see that everything was going to be all right now. My heart was something so, so slow in my chest; there was a rushing in my ears, like the sea, like holding a shell to the side of your head.

She's alive, I thought.

And then I thought, of course she's alive.

No one could ever hurt her, no moun in the Site ever said no to her, even – she was that special. She was, like, this angel in a human body; she was the picture on the wall of the morgue, floating in the air, too perfect to stand on the filthy ground. Anyone could see that.

She raised one hand, and I raised my hand, too, or maybe it's better to say that my hand raised itself, and gave a little wave. I didn't have shit to do with what my body did really, cos I was just looking at Marguerite. The whole world had shrunk down to those eyes and those freckles. It could have turned to night and I wouldn't have noticed, cos now Marguerite was the sun.

Flash.

A gun went off next to me, and suddenly time started again. I saw Marguerite duck as someone – some fucker – shot at her. There was a smell of cordite in the air, the gulls were wheeling in the sky above me again, and I could hear screaming.

Marguerite looked up as I dived against the wall of the truck for shelter. For a moment I thought, she'll come here, she'll run toward me. But then a guy in a balaclava – he was clutching his arm and there was blood coming from it – grabbed her and pushed her, made her run, stumbling, beside him. I snapped out of it, and saw that the truck guard, who was still alive, was coming round to where we were.

We've won, I realized. There were several bodies lying on the ground below the truck, most of them wearing balaclavas. But there were a couple of citizens, too. I thought, those Boston motherfuckers. We were just giving out food and they came and shot us up.

But that wasn't all I was thinking. I was also thinking about Marguerite.

She's alive.

She's with Boston.

She's everything – she's hope, she's life, she's the future – not this gangster bullshit of the cars and the cribs and the hos.

Together, we're Marassa. We have power. We can heal. We can see the future – we can change it, even. I didn't believe this before, but then I thought, what if it's true? Marassa can make broken things whole, make people walk whose legs are wasted. What if Marassa can heal the Site, too? What if Marassa can mend these streets, put Route 9 and Boston back together? We got nothing but love for our crew; we got nothing but steel for the haters. But what if we had love for everybody? With Marguerite, I could do anything. We think together. We are two halves of one person. We could use our power. Fix things.

But alone I am nothing. I have to have her with me if we're going to be able to do anything to heal this Site in which we live, to change its future.

I have to rescue her.

THEN

Toussaint l'Ouverture gazed at the town of Guildive on its little hill by the sparkling sea. Once again, he was lying on his front, breathing in the earthy smell of his country.

This was it. This was hope, this was the future, this was the freedom of the Haitian republic.

This was everything.

For months, he had ridden tirelessly. It was said of Toussaint that he and his horse were one compound being, for he was only ever seen riding on it. He had maintained control of his stronghold at Dondon, he had held Marmalade, he had held la Grande Rivière, expulsing all the French soldiers who had dared to land on Haiti. All of these places he had held by his tenacity, and his omnipresence. Early on, he had understood that to inspire the troops he must be everywhere. So he went everywhere, on his horse and sometimes on other horses, because a horse did not possess the same energy he did, the same drive. He slept three hours every night, and the rest of the time he rode.

If there were battles, he fought at the front of them. If there were wounded men, he was at their side. If there were crops to be planted, he was at the head of the row, singing the old songs, dictating the rhythm of the working.

The French had been defeated. The Republic of France had declared the slaves free, and this was no mere martial trick; this was a solemn declaration of the French government. Right now, though, he had one final problem to deal with, and then Haiti would be truly free.

Guildive.

The English had landed at several port towns, and had been repulsed from all of them eventually. But still they clung onto Guildive, which they had fortified with cannons taken from their ships. Haiti was a rich prize, one well worth the expenditure of the lives of English sailors. Toussaint had learned the value of the nation's slaves alone from Brandicourt, who had inspected the country's balance sheets himself, and swore it was the larger part of one billion francs.

Toussaint had been surprised to learn that Haiti's slaves were worth more than its exports, and Brandicourt had explained that an export is a fixed quantity, whereas a slave can keep on growing food or rearing animals or building all his life, and that their tenure can be lengthy if the master is not too cruel.

Slaves: nine hundred million francs.

Exports: two hundred million francs.

No wonder the whites had been so desperate to keep Haiti enslaved.

Now the English wanted that money for themselves, and it fell to Toussaint to stop them. He put away his spyglass and crawled back through the undergrowth to Jean-Christophe.

— I see new fortifications, he said. Ditches, and the like. But there are soldiers milling around outside the walls. They don't know we're here.

— Are you sure?

Toussaint smiled.

— I'm never sure. But it's worth the risk.

The two men walked back to a carriage that had been halted under the trees whilst they examined the fortifications at Guildive. Six of Toussaint's picked men stood around it. Toussaint approached the door and swung it open. Peering in, he saw a terrified woman, in the autumn of her life, her jowly cheeks wobbling. Beside her sat a rigid gentleman in a cravat, with gray whiskers.

— Please, sir, the man said, revealing himself to be French. You can take everything. Everything. Just, please, leave us our lives.

Toussaint tried not to be too offended by the man's assumption that he was a bandit.

— Where are you going? he asked.

— To Guildive, said the man.

— Why? Tell the truth, or my men will kill you.

The man seemed about to lie, then thought better of it.

— What's the point of staying? he said. We have no country here. I thought . . . I thought if the English won, we would be on the right side. And if they didn't, well, perhaps I could pay our passage on one of their ships.

236

— What do you mean, you have no country?

The man quailed.

— You . . . I mean, the blacks . . . they took our land.

Toussaint sighed.

— We took no such thing. We are not thieves, sir. We took our freedom. We require some measure of the land, of course. We must needs eat. But it has always been my intention to restore much of the land to the plantation owners.

— Really?

— Yes, but it doesn't matter now. Since you have declared for the enemy, the English, now you are prisoners of war.

— Oh no! Please don't kill us, cried the woman.

Toussaint smiled.

— I don't intend to. I merely intend to take your carriage and your riches.

He peered further into the carriage, seeing the rolled-up carpets, the chandeliers, the candlesticks, and the silver cutlery.

— You said you weren't thieves, said the man.

Toussaint was almost impressed. A moment ago the Frenchman had seemed entirely without backbone; now he was showing some spirit.

— We're not. In fact, we're going to give your goods away. The money, too.

The man frowned and seemed about to say something, but Toussaint was bored of the conversation. He waved to one of his lieutenants.

— Take these fine people and remove them to Dondon, he

237

said. This man wishes for land. Give him a plot on one of the south-facing hills, a good one – use your discretion. Our men will help him to build a house if he agrees to share the bounty of his land when others are hungry.

— Oh, dieu soit loué, said the white man.

Praise be to God.

Toussaint gave the man the benefit of his gap-toothed smile.

— Vous pouvez m'appeler simplement l'Ouverture, he said.

You may simply call me l'Ouverture.

Jean-Christophe burst out laughing.

Toussaint allowed himself a laugh, too. He wasn't aware that he had ever made a joke before, but he was in a good humor. If all went well, soon the entire country would belong to her people.

When the man and his wife had been escorted away, Toussaint turned to Jean-Christophe.

— You don't have to do this, he said.

— Of course I do, said Jean-Christophe. I'm the mulat. They wouldn't believe it if a black came looking for shelter in Guildive.

Toussaint stepped forward and embraced the man. He was surprisingly wiry for one whose actions had so influenced the course of the war. Toussaint felt emotion brimming within him. Jean-Christophe was young enough to be his son, and he knew he would be proud if his son grew up to be half so brave.

— They'll call out your name all over the land, he said. They'll make up songs about you.

— They already do, said Jean-Christophe. The women, anyway.

He kissed Toussaint on the cheek as Toussaint rolled his eyes, then stepped up into the carriage.

The next morning, Toussaint led his army to the base of the hill of Guildive – not within firing distance, but close enough that the English could see him there, arrayed in all his force. Jean-François rode beside him. After the death of Biassou, the man had been more than happy to defer to Toussaint as overall commander.

It was Toussaint's habit in war to attempt some kind of parley, ever since he had forced the French to surrender in that valley. He preferred to avoid fighting, if at all possible. But there were always exceptions. The English had never had any claim to this land; they were merely opportunists who had landed here in the hope of securing nearly one billion francs' worth of slaves. They were not like the French, who genuinely believed they had some right to the territory, who defended it from what they saw as the depredations of the blacks. These English had no business being here, and Toussaint did not intend for any of them to remain to foment rebellion and undermine his government once he had control of the country.

He intended that they should depart the isle or die.

Still, there were such things as appearances, even if some attached too much importance to them. He rode close to the town walls, a white flag fluttering above his horse.

An Englishman with a shock of white hair leaned out over the wooden parapet.

— Surely you can't hope to take us by force, he said in heavily accented French. We have cannon, muskets, and enough shot to last two months.

I'm counting on it, thought Toussaint.

He had prevented the English from landing at a dozen points, so the town of Guildive was crammed with soldiers and equally crammed with guns and gunpowder. Seven Royal Navy galleys lay at anchor just beyond the reach of Toussaint's guns.

One of the things that had surprised Toussaint, along with his sudden and miraculous ability to read, was the fact that his French had improved enormously. He had spoken French before, with his master, but not often, and he was more comfortable in the Creole of the slaves. When he spoke French he had always felt as if he were wearing one of the restrictive suits the whites wore, with those neckties that choked the throat. Now, though, with whatever spirit that had possessed him at Bois Caiman inside him, he wore French as if it were something he had always owned.

— I don't hope anything, he said. I know.

— Pardon? said the man on the parapet.

— You will lose this battle, Toussaint said. Better to go to your ships now and leave this country.

The man laughed.

— We're the British Navy, he said. You're untrained negroes. If you insist on fighting, you'll be crushed.

Toussaint shrugged.

— Have it your way, he said.

He turned and rode back to his troops. It didn't matter what he said; it didn't matter what the English said. They thought themselves incapable of losing, much less of losing to a black rabble – that was the only thing that mattered.

He lifted his hand and gave the signal for attack. A sorry, bedraggled row of soldiers staggered forward under the blazing sun. It was nearly midday, a terrible time to fight a battle. That was precisely why Toussaint had chosen it.

Jeers and catcalls went up from the English soldiers on the parapet as the pathetic troops advanced, unsteady on their feet, their weapons barely raised.

They think we're an army of péquenots, he thought. *Untrained peasants. And that's all to the good.*

He was surprised that the English had not yet noticed that to all appearances his army was not black.

But then, just as he began to despair of their intelligence, a cry of alarum went up from one of the town's defenders.

At almost the same time, the men in the front ranks of his army began to clamor, the fear of the guns bristling on the parapet outweighing the fear of the bayonets and machetes and guns behind them, which had been forcing them forward.

It doesn't matter, thought Toussaint. *The more chaos the better.*

— We're English! the ragged front line shouted.

— Don't fire!

— Don't shoot – we're English!

The English prisoners, captured by Toussaint's men at other port towns and reserved expressly for this purpose, began to wail, and their line broke. An over-exuberant black, one of Toussaint's army who was herding the English prisoners forward, stabbed one of them in the back and he went down. Then there was confusion and a mêlée. There were black soldiers in amongst the English captives, too – Toussaint had made sure of that – and whilst the men in the town would not fire for fear of killing their compatriots, these black soldiers, hidden within the mass of captives, were shooting upward. Toussaint saw a body fall from the ramparts, two, three . . .

This is awful, he thought. *But if we win, it will be worth it.*

He glanced up. The sun was halfway through its progression over the sky.

Any moment now. Succeed in this and the bloodshed can stop.

His army continued to press forward the English sailors they had captured in Cape Town and Port-au-Prince. Ragged, walking as slowly as they could, the English prisoners were pressed against the walls of the town. They never stopped calling for mercy from the troops above, and indecision continued to reign amongst those troops. They began to fire tentatively, even as Toussaint's cannon regiment came close enough to hail down balls on their position. Simultaneously, the advance guard pushed through and began to climb the mounting bodies of the English prisoners, nearing in this way the top of the town walls.

Just then, there was a sound so loud it seemed to rip the

day apart, and the ground shook. Toussaint felt an unaccountable terror, and a sense of overwhelming déjà vu. For one terrible instant, he was in bed in a strange place of white walls and machinery, from which came regular, high-pitched noises, as of baby rats squeaking. There was a tube of some kind stuck into the back of his hand, as if he were part machine himself. The ground shook violently, and then there was only blackness. He blinked. Then he was watching a metal vehicle on rubber wheels explode, tearing apart the people standing too close to it.

Where was that? he thought, as he opened his eyes. *Was that hell?*

No. Hell is what I'm looking at now.

A second sun had appeared, and it was burning in the center of Guildive, a fierce fireball beneath the sky. A great cloud of smoke was rising from this blazing fire, and shrapnel and cannonballs flew screaming through the air in all directions, as if the town had been a great repository of trapped spirits and vengeful ghosts, which now careered out in flaming arcs.

The ammunition store had exploded.

Toussaint breathed a sigh of relief. He could only imagine what Jean-Christophe had been through to achieve this; how he would have had to convince the guards on the gates that he was a poor downtrodden mulat, reviled by the French for his part in the original uprising, condemned by the blacks as a turncoat and an agitator for both sides. How he must have handed over the riches stolen earlier from the carriage as a bribe for his safety. How, on gaining entry, he must have waited for the darkest moment of the night to sneak to the ammunition store, and found his way in.

It was remarkable how so many events had conspired to put Jean-Christophe there. And lucky, too, that the cache of ammunition was as great as Toussaint had hoped. He had known of the hoard even before the English took the town – and had projected to capture Guildive himself in order to avail his forces of all those weapons. Then, fortuitously, the English had added to them, bringing their cannon and their powder and their shot from all those ships.

It had been the largest store of gunpowder on the island, and it was spitting fire all over the English forces.

I hope Jean-Christophe got out, Toussaint thought. *I hope he used a long fuse as I suggested.*

He saw movement on the ramparts and raised his spyglass to confirm that the English were finally waving the white flag.

He turned to the commanders behind him.

— Everyone is to lower their weapons, he said.

— Should we destroy them? said one of them.

— No, said Toussaint. They are proud of their ships. Let them go to their ships.

NOW

I'm close in the story now to where I was when everything fell down. A few days away. I saw Marguerite at that shoot-out by the sea only a month before I ended up in here, before *here* turned into a coffin.

I feel like if I tell my story to you till the point when I came to hospital, then that will be the point when I break through into the light. It sounds dumb, I know, but that's what I'm doing. I'm digging and I'm telling you this shit, and I'm throwing the stuff I'm digging behind me, just like I'm throwing my story behind me.

It's dirt, my story. I don't need it anymore.

I no longer notice the pain in my hands, either. To begin with, the pieces of concrete were slick with my blood, and now I suppose I must've developed calluses, cos it barely hurts anymore. I don't know if I've moved, really, or how long I've been digging. It feels like hours, but it might be longer.

An hour ago, maybe, I heard someone calling again. This time in English.

— . . . anyone down there?

I don't like hearing the word *down*. I was on the fifth floor. If I'm down from where the people are digging, then things are pretty bad. I call back, but as usual no moun replies. Either I'm dead, or my voice is bouncing off the concrete.

— I can't come there, said Stéphanie.

She wasn't in the car with us, she was on the other end of the phone – Biggie liked to talk on speakerphone when he was driving. He was cruising around the slum, and he was trying to get Stéphanie to come and pick up Mickey, this soldier who was wounded, only she didn't want to come into the Site anymore.

— It's not safe for me, she continued. I'm staying in my hotel.

Biggie grinned.

— Steph, he said. Steph, chérie, ma copine chou-chou. Chill. Everyone knows you – I tell all my soldiers about you. They know I love you, they know not to hurt you. Écoute – quand je serai riche t'auras une belle maison. T'auras tout ce que tu voudras car je t'aime, tu sais?

— Yes, said Stéphanie. I know you love me, I know you'll buy me a big house – you're always telling me that. But it's not so simple, Biggie. They shot at us when we were distributing fucking food! Tu comprends ça? It's crazy. I can't come to the Site anymore.

— Please, said Biggie. I got a soldier been shot in the foot. I need you to take him to hospital.

246

— In the foot?

— Yeah, in the foot.

Stéphanie sighed down the phone. She's the only person I know who can sigh on a phone and get the right effect. That sigh, it's one of the things I really remember about her.

— Someone from Boston shot him, I take it? she asked.

— No, said Biggie. I shot him.

Silence for a moment.

— You shot him? Why?

— He was disrespecting me.

This was true. The guy – he called himself Mickey – was saying how if it was Route 9 who had shot people up and killed Boston soldiers, then Boston would have hit back already. He was implying that Biggie was weak, that he wasn't dealing with his shit. This kind of thing is always happening – Biggie says that when you're a leader, people always got to challenge you. That's part of being a leader, I get that.

But Stéphanie laughed, a hollow laugh.

— Jesus, she said. You gangsters with your respect.

— I'm not a gangster, said Biggie. People come here, they call me a gangster, but they don't know shit about the Site. No moun want to help with the education here, no moun want to give out food – apart from us. People here got anyen to eat, anyen to drink, but they got guns. What you expect gonna happen?

— Shut up, Biggie, said Stéphanie. I'm not some documentary maker for you to recite your poetic bullshit to. I *do* know the Site. You're a gangster. You sell drugs and you kill people.

— Yeah? said Biggie. Good. Yeah, I'm a gangster. G-star in the motherfucking *hood*. This is what I'm saying to Mickey – too right I'll take Boston down.

Biggie started rapping then:

— Can't get them with a gun, get them with machetes. Chop their asses up, fuck them up with baseball bats.

— If he disrespected you, said Stéphanie, why do you want him to go to hospital?

Biggie looked at me and shook his head, like, how can this bitch be so stupid?

— He's my soldier, man, my frère chou-chou. I love him. I just had to teach him some respect.

Stéphanie sighed again.

— I'll see what I can do, she said. But listen to me, Biggie. I like you, you get that? I want you to be OK. I don't want you to die.

— I don't want to die, either.

— Then listen. I was in a bar last night. Lots of aid workers go there and some MINUSTAH soldiers were there, too. They say they're going to hit the gangs in the Site, hit them hard. Some journalist got photos of the shoot-out the other day. MINUSTAH have to look like they care.

— *Pfft*, said Biggie. If they spent as much on hospitals and drinking water as they do on tanks, maybe we'd believe them.

I stared at him. Sometimes he didn't sound like he was in

248

an American ghetto. Sometimes he said things that weren't completely stupid.

— I agree, Biggie. You know I do, said Stéphanie. But listen, these guys are serious. They're going to come after you soon. They want to capture some gangsters, show some piles of confiscated guns on TV.

I could hear real worry in her voice, real concern, but Biggie made that dismissive noise again.

— MINUSTAH haven't done shit in the Site since they killed Dread Wilmè, he said. All they do is sit at their checkpoints. They even let us through when we go out to sell drugs if we pay them.

— I'm just warning you, said Stéphanie. That's all.

There was a click – she hung up.

— Girls, man, said Biggie and he did that turny finger thing next to his head. Sa ansent, that's why she worry so much. She thinks I ain't gonna care for her. I keep telling her I'll be a rich rapper one day. That record company gonna snap my shit up. I'll be like Wyclef.

Now I was staring at Biggie.

— She's *pregnant?* I asked.

— Sure, he said. My sperm are super sperm. Super soldiers.

I already told you Biggie had a three-year-old with his baby manman Valerie. Making Stéphanie pregnant, it was incredible. How he thought he was gonna raise the kid, I don't know. And what did he think she was gonna do? Did he think she'd move into the Site, play house with him? I couldn't believe he had been so stupid – like, hadn't he heard of condoms or some shit?

249

— She's French, I said. She works for the UN. What's gonna happen?

— I told you. I'll be a high roller one day, shot caller, full bank, motherfucker.

I gave up. I leaned back in my seat. There was fresh sea air coming in through the open window, and I had my hand wrapped around a sawn-off shotgun. I felt good. I had a lungful of weed, too – Biggie had just handed his blunt to me. But even though I felt sweet, I still had my sister in my mind. Me, I wanted a war. But you wanted Biggie to do something, you didn't just tell him. That was how Mickey got a bullet in his foot.

— Boston came too close this time, Shorty. They shouldn't have done that, shouldn't have messed with our community work like that.

— Word, I said. We need to hit them back hard, man.

I was thinking about Marguerite, though I didn't tell Biggie that. But that's what I wanted – I wanted to hit Boston so I could draw out my sister, grab her from the Boston fuckers, and bring her back to live with me. Shit, maybe I could find her a dog, or something, maybe the dog Tintin nearly ran over. She could look after it, feed it. Then we'd get her into the school, help her to be a doctor one day. She always said she'd get out of the Site. I wanted to help her get out more than anything in the world.

— Yeah, said Biggie. But first we're going to see the houngan. I want more spells. More protection. I want the lwa of war.

— The lwa of war? I said.

— Yeah. Ogou Badagry. Niggers got to respect that mother-fucker. You right – Boston come into our territory, we got to hit them back hard. That houngan gave me Dread's bones to wear, but now we need some deeper vodou: black maji. You get me?

— There's going to be a war? I said.

I was thinking about Marguerite. I was thinking how if I go into Boston territory on my own, I'm dead. But if we all go to war, then maybe I have a chance to find her, bring her back.

— Cool, I said.

The houngan, he lived in this van down a side street. It wasn't on the map I drew, so I guess Biggie didn't want people know-ing where the guy lived. The van didn't have wheels. One side of it was propped up on magazines, the other side on bricks. The windows were broken, but there were curtains in them. They had flowers on. I thought it was a pretty weird set-up for a houngan, but I didn't say anything.

Biggie knocked on the door. I'd never seen him knock on a door. Usually, he just opened up and walked in, or he stopped outside with his music blaring and he expected you to come out to him. An old man opened it. I saw that he wasn't the same houngan who did Dread's funeral; maybe that houngan died, or something. This one had got dirty shorts on, no top. His body was scrawny and there was gray hair all over it. His stomach hung over his shorts. It was like

251

it wanted to hide his crotch. There were heavy bags under his eyes and big red veins on his nose, and his eyes were bloodshot.

— You got whiskey? he said. You got kleren?

Biggie shook his head.

— I'll get one of the shorties to bring you some, he said. Anyway, it's not Baron Samedi I want.

The houngan smiled at me. Actually, it was more of a leer. I saw his crooked teeth, the gaps where some of them had fallen out. There was a smell of rot and alcohol from him. He was old. Like, forty, at least.

— It's not Baron Samedi he wants, the houngan said, so he doesn't bring whiskey. Little asshole.

I couldn't believe it. Biggie, he once shot someone in the foot for saying his hair looked stupid with cornrows. Now the houngan was calling him an asshole.

I pulled my Glock.

— You watch what you're saying, houngan man, I said. You disrespect Biggie, you get a full metal jacket in the eye.

Biggie put a hand on my gun, made me lower it.

— Chill, he said to me.

Then, cool as brushed steel, he turned to the houngan.

— I told you, Biggie said. I'll get you some. You gonna let us in, or what?

— Depends what you want, said the houngan. You want maji? You want charms to put on the crossroad to protect your territory?

— I want Ogou Badagry, said Biggie.

The houngan's eyes went big and wide. Biggie took out this bundle of notes, like, two months of drug money. He handed it to the houngan.

— We're going to war, he said. We need serious maji.

— You need a shrink, said the houngan.

But he opened the door and he let us in.

Inside, it was a tip. There were magazines everywhere and a few books, too. There were dirty clothes, a few cups, and plates lying in the mess. On the sides of the van were shelves that looked like they were made out of bits of corrugated iron and wood the houngan had found in the street. There were jars on them, with powders and stuff. Veves were drawn on the floor. There was a rattle in the shape of a skull, drums. I could smell sweat and whiskey and rotting food. It was like how you'd imagine a houngan's place, if you knew the houngan was a tramp, or mental.

The houngan gestured at a mound in the dirt that might have been a couch. Biggie didn't hesitate, just sat down. I started to sit down, too, but I must have made a face or something, cos the houngan laughed and gave me a push, so I got down on my ass on the shirts and magazines and stuff. I caught my breath and I tried to slow down my heartbeat.

The houngan took a proper look at me.

— You got a pwen, he said. I can feel it.

I put my hand to my pocket, to the smooth pebble that Dread gave me.

— Yeah, I said.

— Good, said the houngan. That shit will protect you. Someone must like you, kid.

Biggie smiled.

— My soldiers got to be protected, he said.

The houngan laughed.

— None of them as protected as you, my man.

He pointed to a jar on the shelf opposite me. It was nearly empty, but there was a bit of gray powder left at the bottom.

— That's Dread Wilmè, he said. What's left of him. The rest is on Biggie here, keeping him safe from bullets. You want I should put the dust on you, too? There ain't no gun will kill you, then.

— That's Dread Wilmè? I said.

It was, like, the stupidest thing I ever said, cos he just told me it was, but it was all I could think of.

— Yeah. All I do is I call Baron Samedi and he rides me, and he takes the ashes and sprinkles them on you. That way he'll recognize you when you're about to be killed. When he sees you all covered in that dust, he knows not to take you. He leaves you alone, for sure. Dread Wilmè is sacred, man.

The houngan leaned forward. His breath was like something physical in the van.

— All you gotta do is bring me some whiskey, he said. And some money, maybe.

— He doesn't need it, said Biggie. Shorty be blessed already. Dread saved his life – died right on top of him. Truth?

— Truth, I said.

— He's *that* kid? said the houngan. Shit.

254

He held out his hand, and I shook it.

— You're a legend in this part of the Site, he said. Is it true that Dread had a thousand holes in him when he died?

— I guess, I said. That's what my manman says.

— And the dude still lifted a tank off of Shorty here, said Biggie.

It's weird, the way everyone knows the story, not just me and my manman. I never get used to it.

— Stone-cold gangster, man, said Biggie.

— You Marassa, too? said the houngan. I heard Aristide took you both from your manman his ownself.

— No, I said. My sister is gone. I'm just me. I'm nothing.

The houngan nodded. He went over to the shelf – it didn't take him long, it was only one step to the other side of the truck – and he touched the jar. Then he kicked some stuff out the way, cleared a space on the floor.

— You're ready for this? he said to Biggie. This could be intense. Ogou is . . . Ogou is fierce. You've been smoking weed, playing with Baron Samedi and Dread's bones. But this shit is heroin.

— Heroin is my shit, man, said Biggie. I been dealing with heroin since back in the day. Boston came into our territory. We got to wipe them out.

The houngan nodded again. He got out some chalk and started drawing a veve on the metal floor of the van. It was delicate, quick, and I didn't expect that this wreck of a guy could draw like that. Then he poured some kind of powder on the floor, and he took up the drum and started to dance.

As he danced he sang:

— Attibon Legba, ouvri bayè pou moin!
Ago!
Ou wè, Attibon Legba, ouvri bayè pou moin, ouvri bayè!
M'apè rentrè quand ma tournè,
Ma salut lwa yo.

Manman dragged us to a load of ceremonies, so I knew what he was doing. He was calling Legba to open the gate between our world and the world of the lwa. Legba doesn't open the gate, nothing comes through.

The houngan beat and beat on the drum, singing that little song over and over again. I started to get a bit freaked out. Usually, when this kind of thing went on, the houngan switched over pretty quickly to some other lwa. Usually, there wasn't this electricity in the air – I could feel it crackling in my ears, running like shivers on my skin. The smell of the houngan was gone. Now the inside of the van smelled like gunpowder and sex and flowers. It was like the walls were closing in on me, and I turned to Biggie and he looked like he just saw a ghost.

Suddenly, the houngan stopped. There was silence, but it was like the silence you get before thunder, or before a dog barks. Then his head snapped round to look at me, and his eyes weren't his eyes anymore, but were like gates that have been opened, and there was emptiness on the other side of them, and it made your head hurt, like when you think about how big infinity is.

— What do you want? he asked, and it wasn't his voice – it was something that echoed.

The houngan, or whatever it was, wasn't looking at Biggie, he was looking at me, but it was Biggie who answered.

— We want Ogou Badagry, he said. We want to go to war. We need his help.

— I am the crossroad, said the houngan who was Papa Legba. You are at a crossroad. So you get me.

— Yes, said Biggie. But can you bring us Ogou Badagry? We need war in our met tet, we need to be strong . . .

He tailed off, cos the houngan had turned to look at him, and Biggie got a load of those eyes.

— No, said Legba.

— No?

— No.

He touched Biggie's head and Biggie shivered.

— You are full, Legba said. You have a dead man inside you.

Then he touched my head.

— And you are empty. You were Marassa, now you are nothing. You are half a person, but you won't be for long. The ceremony has already been completed. It was completed many years ago. Ogou Badagry is not for you.

— But our enemies, said Biggie. We need to destroy our enemies.

— This one knows how, Legba said, touching me again. This one can destroy anything, if he wants. He can build things, too, but it's up to him what he does.

I felt like I might pass out, but I dug my nails into my palms. Papa Legba is the crossroad, I thought. He can find anything, and give anything. He can return things that are lost.

— Will I get my sister back? I said to the houngan who was Papa Legba.

— What the fuck are you talking about? said Biggie. What the fuck is this?

The houngan looked at me.

— I don't know what you're talking about, he said. I don't deal with that door.

— What door? I said.

The houngan shook his head.

— I don't . . . This is all . . .

The houngan's voice was back to normal now; it didn't echo anymore. It was like a dub mix had stopped and we were back to the normal song. He slumped to his knees and the old eyes fluttered open, the bloodshot ones, not the ones that were blankness forever.

— What happened? the houngan said to us.

— I don't know, said Biggie. You were Legba, I think. He said that I was full. He said Shorty was half a person. You know what that means?

The houngan looked at me and he frowned.

— No, he said. But it doesn't sound good.

He turned as if we were done.

— Hey, asshole, said Biggie. I'm not paying for that. Give me the money back.

The houngan shook his head.

— I did what you wanted, he said. Not my fault the lwa didn't help you.

— I didn't want bullshit talk, said Biggie. I wanted protection. Aggression.

The houngan shrugged.

— Take it up with the lwa, he said.

— No, said Biggie. You take it up with the lwa.

He took out his Glock.

— Wait, said the houngan. You need me.

— No, I don't. You already gave me Dread's maji. Anyway, you called me an asshole. It's a matter of principle, you get that?

He emptied the Glock into the houngan, and the guy got thrown back so far he knocked down all those shelves, including the one with Dread in it, and it smashed as it fell on him. The powder went all over him, but it was too late for him. He was dead.

— You can destroy anything? said Biggie to me. Better come up with something quick, then.

The weird thing was I did think of something.

After we went to the houngan, everything sped up. Ever since Legba touched me it was, like, I don't know, it was like there was a door that was open in my head, and all kinds of stuff came through. I went out on patrol, and I helped Biggie put charms on the roads that led into Solèy 19, and I helped him sort out some guys who'd been short on their payments, and all the time it was like I was in this completely different place, where there were a lot more trees and shadows.

I'd also been having this weird dream about a castle and a carriage. It gave me an idea. I had it all worked out.

— Listen, Biggie, I said one night. I've got a plan for how we can take out Boston.

— What? said Biggie. Like, all of them?

— Yeah, I said. All of them.

We did it at night. Biggie wasn't so happy about giving up his whip, but I told him:

— If we pull this off, you can have as many cars as you want. We'll own the whole Site if we take Boston out. Think about it. You want to sell half the heroin in the Site, or all of it?

He gave us the car.

I told you I was the Mechanic, right? Show me a broken engine and I would fix it, no matter if the engine was in a car or a chainsaw.

So, I got this servo mounted to a gun in the back. I had a remote control in my hand, like the ones you get with a toy car. That was the hardest thing to find – we had to cruise pretty much a whole day through the Site, asking people. Kids don't get toys in the Site, but eventually we found some kid who had brought his from the country when his parents moved to Port-au-Prince to get better jobs – and ain't that a joke, like they say in the songs? We paid him 50 dollars for it. So now I'd got the servo out the toy car, you get me? And it was hooked up to this AK in the back of the whip. Packed into the trunk and the footwells was a load of dynamite, grenades, and rockets. I couldn't believe all this stuff when Biggie showed it to me. He said it was from Aristide, from when he wanted the gangs to secure the country for him, but Biggie said he never knew what to do with that shit, so he just left it in a shack.

— That stuff is dangerous, he said.

— Yeah, I know, I said. That's the point.

So, whip, servo, gun, explosives. The rest was just ghost-riding.

Some of the guys, they didn't like it. They said that Biggie shouldn't be listening to me, that I've had crazy shit in my head ever since we went to see the houngan.

Lil' Wayne said right to Biggie's face:

— Boko ba w pwen, li pa di w domi nan kafou.

It's an expression everyone uses, and it's kind of perfect for that moment and for Biggie, I guess, cos it means, *even if the houngan gave you a protective spell, there's no need to lie down at a crossroad.* Meaning, we were going to get ourselves killed.

Biggie, he just looked long and cold at Lil' Wayne.

— We're still alive after this, you come and tell me that again, he said.

So that was it. We talked about it for a bit, and then we were just doing it. We got the car ready, the explosives, the guns, and we did it.

We were at the end of the street that leads to Boston

territory. We knew that the Boston leaders were sleeping there tonight, cos we put some shorties on the case. Shorties look the same, running around, playing games. Boston crew can't tell a Solèy 10 shorty from a Solèy 19 shorty.

I was hoping Marguerite was there, too, and I was hoping I didn't kill her. I was feeling sick. My whole stomach was tight, like a bag packed with weed. I know I've killed people, and you probably think I'm an evil person, but the truth is I only did it to find Marguerite. I only joined Route 9 cos they're the other power; they're the only ones who could help me destroy Boston and get her back.

So this, right here, this was the moment I had waited nearly half my life for. This was the moment when I might be reunited with my twin.

Biggie raised a hand to say go.

I leaned down and started the engine. I jammed the brick on the gas pedal, just so.

Tintin pushed past me and adjusted the steering wheel a little.

— Better, he said.

The car rolled forward into the night. It crossed a line that none of us had ever crossed, and then it was in Boston, just like it was nothing at all, even though to us it was in another world. It cruised straight, ghost-riding, smooth like silk.

It passed the shack where the Boston chimères were sleeping, and I gripped the remote in my hand. I pressed the lever forward, and the servo engaged, and the AK in the car fired.

Ghost-ride drive-by.

All hell broke loose.

Guys started spilling out of the shacks and they were unloading at the car. I saw that one of them was limping, blood pouring from his leg. People were screaming. I thought, shit, I did this. Then I lifted up my gun, cos some of them had seen us and they were starting to fire at us. Biggie went down on one knee, his Tec-9 spitting fire.

For a long moment, I was just frozen. I'd never seen or heard so many bullets. The whole street was locked in a full metal jacket; the air was brass casings and steel-tipped; it was on fire. It was fucking crazy. I tried to call out, but bullets are faster than words, and I was just standing there in the middle of all that metal death.

I thought, I'm going to die.

I thought, this was a bad idea.

Then I saw her. Marguerite.

She was running out of a shack, screaming with fear. She had no gun in her hand, and that was good, I thought – that way Tintin or Biggie or Mickey wouldn't shoot her. Mickey was limping bad, but he was there anyway.

I started to move toward her, but not too close. I had to catch her with my eyes, otherwise this was –

She turned, looked at me. She was heading to the chimères who were shooting at us and the car, but she stopped.

— Run! I screamed. Run! Away from the car!

She stared at me.

— RUN!

Some of the Bostons turned to me and started shooting, and I threw myself to the ground. I thought, shit, they see it now, they see the trick. But they didn't move.

She moved, though – I saw her run in the opposite direction, further into Boston.

I thought, oh thank you, oh thank you, oh thank you.

Most of the Bostons, they were shooting the car. That was good. That was what they were meant to do, cos if they kept shooting it, then –

BOOM.

It was the middle of the night, but suddenly it turned to daytime, and there was a sun burning in the street. Stuff flew in all directions – pieces of car, a seat went over a shack. There was a sound in my ears like that electric tingling you get when you put your head under the water of the sea – the sound of the fish moving, I guess. I put my finger to the side of my head. I felt hot sticky blood on my cheek; it seemed it was coming from my ear. Where the car had been was just black scorches. One of the shacks fell down completely, a crash of sparks and corrugated iron. The air was filled with the smell of burning.

I realized I was doing nothing, so I raised my gun and fired into the storm. I didn't think it mattered, though, cos there couldn't be anyone still alive there.

I hoped that Marguerite had got far enough away.

There was dust and smoke everywhere now, and some of the shacks were burning. I walked forward, holding my gun in front of me. A man on fire came stumbling toward me and I shot him without thinking. A moment later, a bullet hit my arm and I screamed, but I kept walking. It was hard to hold the gun in my hand. I held it anyway. I was only half-conscious of people running here and there, of bullets flying. Most of the bullets were ours, I think. The Boston crew wasn't a crew anymore.

I was through the smoke and in clear air when I found her. She was huddling against a broken bike, watching the flames. She was so beautiful and so vulnerable. She was the only thing pure and uncorrupted in this whole slum.

— Marguerite, I said. Marguerite, it's OK.

I held out my half of the necklace.

— See? I said. See, I still have it. Where's yours?

I was looking at her neck to see if she was wearing her necklace.

She stared at me, fear and horror on her face.

— What are you talking about? she said. Who's Marguerite?

THEN

— All France comes to Haiti, said Toussaint. France has been deceived, and she comes to take revenge and enslave the blacks once again.

— You do not know that, said Jean-Christophe. It may be that they come in –

— In peace? In hope of friendship? No.

Toussaint was examining a new French fleet through his spyglass as he spoke. Some fifty vessels were anchored in the bay of Cape Town, their cannon trained on the town, their decks teeming with soldiers. The town itself, on the flanks of the hill, had seen a resurgence, he noted, after its burning not so long ago. More was the pity – it would be unprepared to withstand another fire so soon.

All morning they had watched the maneuvers of the French ships. At first, Toussaint had taken their movements for hesitation, but Jean-Christophe explained how the ships had to tack against the wind, and employ other such maritime tactics, in order to get into position and land.

However they viewed it, there were many men with guns on board. They intended to invade.

— If Bonaparte wanted peace, he would not have sent this fleet against us, Toussaint said. I fear he means to take the country by force.

He had thought the island rid of the French, but now a new commander had taken over the Republic, a man named Bonaparte, martial by inclination, a genius on the battlefield, according to rumors. It seemed that Bonaparte wished to reclaim Haiti.

— The new French ambassador, Leclerc, says he brings you gifts, said Jean-Christophe.

Toussaint laughed. These French seemed to think that the free blacks had no notion of classical antiquity. Did they believe he had never heard of Troy, of the giant horse given as a gift to the Trojans, its wooden belly full of enemy soldiers? He had used this stratagem himself, or tantamount to such, when he took Guildive from the English.

— Leclerc lies, he said.

When the news of the fleet's arrival had reached him, Toussaint had immediately ordered the withdrawal of his key advisors, and most of the army, to Dondon. The French could only be sending ships for one reason.

He had sent Jean-Christophe to take charge of Cape Town, with just enough troops to discourage the French from landing, even if they couldn't hold them long when they did. Leclerc had landed in a small rowing boat, reminding Toussaint of the previous time the French had tried this chicanery. He had asked Jean-Christophe for permission to land the ships, saying that he bore a proclamation from Bonaparte declaring Haiti free, and offering troops to help maintain the peace, as well as rich gifts as a mark of their friendship.

On receiving the envoy, Jean-Christophe did exactly what Toussaint had told him to. He told Leclerc that Toussaint had retired to the interior, that he could not allow the ships to land, and that the soldiers defending Cape Town had been instructed to defend their liberty with their lives.

Leclerc had not been pleased. He had arranged for his proclamation to be published covertly, and many of the whites had been impressed by its assurance of their continued liberty. They had beset Jean-Christophe, supplicating him, urging him to allow the French to land, to accept their help and friendship.

They would have sent a single envoy if they meant friendship, Toussaint knew. They would not have sent an army, they would not have sent a fleet.

He knew they must go to war again, and now it looked as if the French had grown tired of waiting and were going to land. Already, he heard shots being fired, distant detonations down there in the bay.

Such are the gifts they bring, he thought.

In truth, Toussaint had a very good idea of what France wanted. He had spies in Paris, too, and he knew what was said there. Some months before, he had published a Constitution of Haiti, naming himself as Governor-General for a term of three years. He had thought this politic, and done humbly enough. There were many who had pressed him to take up office as king or dictator in all but name. Even the whites had supported him, having been pleased when he restored to them a portion of their former lands. He was respected by all: by the soldiers, who appreciated his fairness and even, to his surprise, his harsh justice; by the whites; by the mulats. In his view, the constitution should not have been controversial. He had been careful to strip it of recriminations and demands. He had acknowledged the audacity of their rebellion, writing, *we dared to be free when we were not free.*

One item, perhaps, might have given offense. He had included a clause on freedom of trade, but surely that could not explain this new French invasion? It could not possibly be the case, could it, that profit should override the republican principle of the freedom of man?

He had not been importunate. Neither had he insulted the consul's person, Toussaint felt certain. He had written to Bonaparte himself several months ago, addressing him with all his pomp and titles, and enclosing a copy of the Haitian Constitution. The man was merely a king by another name, it seemed to Toussaint, but he was prepared to accord him his dues.

Toussaint's son, Isaac, who was now studying in Paris, had informed him of Bonaparte's apparent response on receipt of Toussaint's constitution. It was said that the consul had thrown down the paper and declared:

— France is outraged by this presumption. Toussaint is a revolted slave who must be punished.

Toussaint himself thought that a rather unlikely claim. After all, what had he done apart from declare the freedom of the slaves, which France herself had subsequently confirmed? His constitution made it clear that Haiti would remain under French suzerainty, excepting only its freedom to trade, and its freedom from slavery.

He had heard another story that was whispered in the salons of Paris, and this one struck his ears as far more likely.

According to this version, Bonaparte had barely even inspected the constitution. What had interested him more was a ledger that his master of accounts had prepared for him.

This ledger showed two columns:

The profit from Haiti's plantations, assuming slavery.

The profit from those same plantations, assuming a free populace.

Toussaint remembered these two figures as related to him by Brandicourt.

Nine hundred million francs, he thought. *That's what our lives cost. That's the reward for which the brave Republic of France, the champion of liberty, throws away our freedom.*

The game of diplomacy had ended. The French were disembarking and invading. Toussaint had been fighting them and then the English for years. He was weary to think that the battle must recommence, that more of his men must die. But still, *still*, he would not give up the country that his people had spilled their blood for.

The previous day, Jean-Christophe had brought him a letter from Leclerc, and it clearly showed the thorny path that lay ahead.

I learn with indignation, Citizen-General, that you refuse to receive the French squadron and army which I command.

France has made peace with England, and her government sends to Haiti forces able to subdue rebels, if rebels are to be found in Haiti. As to you, Citizen-General, I avow that it would give me pain to reckon you amongst rebels. I warn you that if this very day you do not put into my possession the forts Picolet, Belair, and all the batteries of the coast, tomorrow at dawn fifteen thousand men shall be disembarked. Four thousand at this moment are landing at Fort Liberté, eight thousand at Port Républican. You will find my proclamation joined to this communication; it expresses the intentions of the French government, but, remember, despite the esteem your conduct in the colony has inspired in me, I hold you responsible for whatever may take place.

LECLERC
The General-in-Chief of the Army of Haiti,
and Captain-General of the colony

Toussaint had laughed, even as he wept. Rebels? There were no rebels in Haiti. A few soldiers, maybe, who found the life of fighting hard to give up and had become bandits, but no more than that. Haiti was peaceful for the first time in years, and this Leclerc thought an army of thousands the best means of keeping it that way? He was outraged, too, with how the man styled himself: General-in-Chief of the Army of Haiti – as if he had ever stepped foot on her beautiful land.

It was clever, however, this issue of the rebels. Inventing these

271

rebels made it possible to claim Toussaint and his men amongst them. Some of the whites might even be convinced – obedience to France was a hard lesson for them to forget. Toussaint would not be surprised if this letter, like Bonaparte's proclamation before it, was making its way secretly around Cape Town.

He had Leclerc's letter in his hand as he looked down on the ships in the bay. Irritated and weary, he struck a match and held it to the paper. It curled, blackened, and then burned. Not until after the flame had bitten his hand did he drop the letter to the ground.

He turned, disgusted, and mounted his horse.

— Tell them to burn it, he said.

Jean-Christophe frowned.

— Burn what? The town?

— Everything. Tell them to burn everything – the whole coast. Let the French land amidst fire and destruction; let them have a taste here of the hell that awaits them for this crime. We will repair to the mountains.

— Everything? said Jean-Christophe.

— Everything, he replied. Burn it all.

A month later, Toussaint was at Dondon.

He still didn't have his son with him, and this grieved him. Isaac remained in Paris, where he had been sent soon after Toussaint gained control of Haiti as a gesture of goodwill and trust on his part toward France. He was, in effect, a hostage, and still the French came to reclaim the country.

He did have some peace, though, and he was pleased to spend this time at Dondon, sitting in the evenings, listening to the crickets, enjoying simple food, drinking wine, and talking with his closest advisors, the freed slaves who had been with him from the beginning. It reminded him a little of the life they had had at the plantations before all the bloodshed had begun, although of course then they had not been free.

Toussaint sat always in the same chair by the open flap of his tent. He could have slept in any plantation house in the interior, but he preferred the tent – it showed the troops that he did not believe himself better than they. Hanging at the tent's entrance was his long-coat; he hung it there to remind himself, and others, of who they were dealing with. It was burned at the hem, torn, and penetrated in several places by musket balls – the legacy of his ride from the north to Dondon after supervising the burning of the ports to slow the French. He had inadvertently come up on Leclerc's rear guard, and those brave French soldiers had fired on him – him, the governor-general! – and almost taken his life. His horse had been killed beneath him. And yet, as hole-ridden as he subsequently found his long-coat, not a single ball had insulted his flesh.

That was not my destiny, he thought.

Once he had ordered the burning of the coastline, there had been little for him to do but wait. He and his troops ate well from the crops and stores in the interior. But the French, he knew, would starve sooner or later. He had left them nothing but ashes. So he bided his time, receiving intelligence daily from his spies and his generals, learning of the civil unrest in Gonlaive, of the riots in Cape Town, of the hangings in Port-au-Prince.

Let them stay, he thought. *They'll kill themselves eventually and we can reclaim the coast.*

It was still his aim to avoid direct confrontation if possible. Jean-Christophe urged him to double his bodyguard, though, to station armed and trusted men around him at all times, to warn all the soldiers of his army to be on their guard. He suspected that the French would use some stratagem, some canular, to take him unawares and either kill or imprison him. Toussaint always dismissed this with irritation. The French might want their slaves back, but they were men of honor nevertheless. They would not stoop to such tactics.

— Besides, he told Jean-Christophe, for a man to sacrifice his life for his country when she finds herself in peril is a sacred duty, but for a man to arouse his country to save his life is inglorious. I am not Haiti. Should I die, we will still have our freedom, so long as we're prepared to keep fighting for it.

It seemed to him that if the first war for Haiti was a war of weapons, then this second was a war of letters. He read and wrote several a day. So he was not surprised when Jean-Christophe peered through the flap and told him:

— There's someone here who has a letter for you.

Toussaint stood and tied the tent flap full open. Then he stared at the man who stood there.

— Isaac, he said. My son.

He was amazed by how much the boy had grown. It was a commonplace thing, the growing of children, but it thrilled him and filled him with pride that he had produced this handsome man who stood before him! He was the Ogre; his son was a prince.

— I am so glad to see you, Isaac, he continued.

He stepped forward and embraced him, felt the broadness of his shoulders. Strong, too, as well as handsome! His pride seemed something alive that might burst out of him.

Isaac smiled, extricated himself from the embrace, then kissed him in the French fashion. Toussaint narrowed his eyes. The gesture had seemed pointed; was it meant as an instruction on how people greeted one another in civilized countries?

— Papa, he said. It is good to see you, too. You look tired.

— It's this country, Toussaint said. People keep trying to take it from us.

— So I understand, said Isaac. Well, I'm here to help now.

Toussaint sent for wine and food, then bade Isaac sit. He could not credit that his son was here, in the uplands of Haiti. He had believed him still in Paris, at his studies. He could not credit how much Isaac had grown up, either, and what a man he seemed.

I suppose he is a man, he thought. *In age, at least.*

Leadership had not found Toussaint until his fifties. Who knew at what age his son would be required to take up the mantle of responsibility?

Isaac explained that Bonaparte had requested that he sail to Haiti to try to end the stalemate between Leclerc and

275

Toussaint, and to reunite the island.

— I would love for the island to be reunited, said Toussaint. But Leclerc insists on landing troops on our shores and killing our soldiers. I interpret that as an act of war, and believe I would be a great fool not to.

Isaac smiled.

— You have never been a fool, Father, he said. Leclerc appears to have . . . overstepped his bounds. The consul is displeased with his service, and he has been recalled to Paris.

— Are you sure? asked Toussaint.

He had not heard this, but then, news from the coast was infrequent and slow to arrive. The unrest in the country had given rise to bandits, who robbed and killed many of those brave enough to dare the tracks.

— I'm sure, said Isaac. He has been replaced by a man named Brunet. I treated with him in Cape Town. He says that you have been grossly calumniated by Leclerc, that his predecessor spread many vile lies about you, and that he himself has nothing but the greatest respect for you, as the liberator of your country and elected leader of your people.

— And the troops? Toussaint asked. Will Brunet withdraw the troops?

— He says he will, Father. He asks only that you commit some of yours to the maintenance of safety in the towns and on the roads. He says that the bandits must be stopped for the peace and prosperity of the country. The civil conflict, too.

Isaac produced a letter from this Brunet. Toussaint unfolded it and read it.

To Toussaint, styled l'Ouverture,

I fear, Citizen-General, that you have been unfairly maligned by Captain-General Leclerc, who caused unfounded rumors to be spread around the towns of your reputed work to destabilize this country. I do not share Leclerc's views, I must assure you, since I am utterly persuaded that your sentiments tend only to bring back order in the district which you inhabit. As such I have ordered the withdrawal of all French troops from the island, and this evacuation has already commenced. I am prepared, also, to accept you as Governor-General, and officially invest in you the power to rule Haiti on behalf of France.

In the spirit of cooperation and friendship, however, I would ask you kindly that you render me aid in order to restore communication with Cape Town, which was yesterday interrupted for the second time this month, since three persons have been murdered by a band of fifty brigands between Ennery and Coupe-à-Pintade. Send toward those places faithful men to preserve the peace, whom you will pay well; I will be accountable for the outlay.

There are also, my dear General, arrangements which we ought to make in concert, which it is impossible to treat of by letter, but which an hour's conference would resolve. Had I not today been overwhelmed with business, I would myself have brought this letter and trusted myself to the good offices of your troops, knowing the honorable conduct you require of them.

Occupied as I am, though, I must beg you to come to my residence. You will not find there all the pleasures which I would wish to welcome you with, but you will find the frankness of an honorable man who desires nothing but the happiness of the colony and your own happiness. Never, General, will you find a more sincere friend than myself. With confidence in me and my officers, you will enjoy tranquillity.

As a final gage of my honor, I append to this letter a most precious article – your son. Only consider how France might have used your son as a hostage against you, instead of returning him, and you will have a measure of my sincerity. When you visit me you may bring him with you or not, as it pleases you. I assure you that the two of you will be reunited in either case.

I cordially salute you,
BRUNET

Toussaint turned to his son.

— Do you trust this man? he asked.

Isaac nodded.

— I knew him in Paris, he said. He is a man of honor.

Toussaint smiled.

— Then when we have supped and spent a night here in the mountains, we will saddle our horses. It seems Haiti may have found peace at last.

NOW

There's a crack of light. I don't think I'm imagining it. It's up ahead of me and it looks like a shining river on a map. It's tiny, or it's far away.

Sweat is pouring down me, which worries me. I don't think I can afford to lose any more water than I already have.

There are no more voices, and at present I'm not shouting. I'm still too far from the crack of light for that. Besides, I don't want to wear out my voice.

I think I broke one of my fingers. It's painful to touch it, and when I explored it with my other hand I found it hanging strangely. So I'm digging mostly with my left hand now. A minute ago, I had to brace my knees against the side and push with my back to try to move a metal bar that was lying across my path. I didn't move it much, but enough to crawl another meter.

As hope lights up ahead of me, a line for me to follow, I remember when all my hope was taken away.

I remember that I crouched next to Marguerite, or whoever

she was, for only one moment before the world exploded with noise again.

First, there was a rumbling bass noise, and I turned and saw a tank bursting through the wreckage of the exploded car. It was like a hip-hop video, but much louder and more real. Then there was a loud noise very close.

Thwup, thwup, thwup, thwup.

I recognized it from the night when Dread Wilmè died. It was a helicopter. I saw it hovering above the shack we were crouching by. From somewhere behind the tank, men in black uniforms and black helmets poured into the street, the whole thing like a nightmare, covered everywhere in smoke.

There was a rattle of machine-gun fire. I pushed Marguerite to the ground and lay on top of her.

I saw Biggie turn to the soldiers and raise his gun. A tear-gas canister sailed over his head, coughing out gray smoke, and he covered his eyes as he fired. I don't know if he hit anything, but lots of things hit him. I saw him shaking as the bullets tore through him, and I saw that Manman was not exaggerating when she told her story of Dread Wilmè, cos I could see the floodlights and the smoke through Biggie's body, through the holes in his chest, they were that big.

I thought about Dread's bone powder that Biggie had sprinkled on himself, to make himself proof against bullets. It didn't look like it was working.

The helicopter was firing down, too, and I saw Mickey thrown against a wall by the big rounds, his head nearly torn off. Tintin, though, ducked into an alleyway, quick as a snake, and I saw him disappear. I hoped he was running, not dead.

For many minutes, or hours, I didn't know what was happening. Everyone was shooting, and everything was crashing noise and smoke. I was aware of Marguerite below me, whimpering. I felt a pain in my arm and thought I'd been hit, then I remembered that I got shot earlier. It was starting to hurt. I found I couldn't see anymore and then I realized I was crying, though I didn't know if it was from tear gas, or what.

Impossibly, I heard Stéphanie's voice through the gunfire, and she was waving her hands; I could just make her out. The shooting stopped, like she was conducting it, timing its music.

— No! she said. He's not armed! Hold fire.

I saw her through, like, blurred glass. She was in front of the guns, telling MINUSTAH not to shoot. I saw that she was crying, too. I wondered if that was cos of Biggie. He was lying in the street near where she was standing, and he was leaking blood all over the world.

I looked down cos I thought I was armed. But she was right – I'd lost my gun sometime. I didn't remember dropping it, but I guess I did.

— What are you doing here? one of the soldiers shouted at Stéphanie in English. This is a goddamn military operation.

— I'm UN, she said. It's my right to be here. These are people you're shooting.

— Frigging hippies, said the soldier.

Stéphanie was coming closer and closer. Soon, she was

standing right over me. I could see the tears on her cheeks and the redness around her beautiful blue eyes. She saw the bullet hole in my arm and she pursed her lips. Then there were men in black all around us. One of them pulled me roughly to my feet.

— Take him to Canapé-Vert, said Stéphanie.

— He's a gangster, said the man in English. We're not taking him anywhere.

— He's wounded. If you leave him here he might die. Take him to Canapé-Vert, or do you want me to put in a call to Human Rights Watch?

The guy grumbled. He pulled my arms behind my back and I screamed. He ignored my pain, put handcuffs on me.

— Don't try anything, he said. You're lucky we're not just leaving you here to die.

I agreed with him – I didn't understand why I was alive, either, when everyone else was dead. It seemed stupid.

I looked back at Marguerite as they dragged me away.

— Don't you remember me? I asked.

I needed her to be Marguerite, otherwise I had blown up that car and all those people for no reason.

— Don't you remember playing horsey on my back?

She looked at me like I was insane.

— I don't know who you are, she said.

— But you didn't shoot me! At the docks! You must have remembered me.

I was shouting by now. She was being drawn away from me, even though she wasn't moving.

— I didn't shoot you cos you're a kid, she said. Now I wish I'd killed you.

I lowered my eyes. I felt as if someone had ripped out my insides.

— Who's that? said Stéphanie. Who's that girl?

— I thought she was my sister, I said.

There was this pain in my chest and I could feel that my heart was broken. I always thought it was bullshit when people said that, but now I saw that it was a real thing, like there were bits of glass in there, like my heart was a lightbulb and someone had come along and smashed it, and its fragments were inside my chest.

As we passed Biggie, a coughing noise came from him. He wasn't dead yet. I stared at him in horror. So did the MINUSTAH soldier who was pulling me along. Stéphanie went down on her knees and put her hands on Biggie's face.

He said something to her in a hollow whisper. It was a voice like the wind – quiet, and with no consonants in it. I couldn't hear – I was too far away. I saw Stéphanie's mouth move as she said something back. I didn't want to hear it. I wouldn't have listened even if there wasn't ocean noise echoing in my ears, like the interior of a conch shell, from all the guns and explosions. It was private.

Then Biggie saw me. He was lying in so much blood it was like he was floating on a red sea, like he was something more than a man. I thought then of Dread Wilmè and how Manman said that he stayed alive long enough to save me from the guns and the tank and to give me the pwen. Maybe she hadn't exaggerated, and Dread's bones on Biggie's skin really had created some vodou maji, and that was why Biggie still wasn't dead, even with all these holes in him. He stirred, and the soldier dragging me stopped, amazed. I saw the expression on the soldier's face and I thought, yeah, you'll be glad to go back to Europe – this is enough vodou shit for one lifetime.

— It was always you, Biggie said to me, and his voice was soft with wonder. It was always you.

I stared at him in that pool of blood and a frisson went through me, cos I felt like I was in my manman's story, like I was looking at Dread Wilmè, and I half-expected to see my ownself, ten years old, lying unconscious there. I thought of the stone in my pocket when I saw how many holes there were in Biggie, cos I was thinking maybe it was only the pwen that had kept me safe, that had got me just one bullet.

— Look at you, he said. I knew you was protected.

I couldn't believe that he was speaking at all.

— Yeah, I said.

— Man, said Biggie. You completely clean; all you got is a hole in your arm. It's like the bullets don't see you . . . Shit, I'm sorry, Shorty.

I didn't like him calling me that. I wanted to tell him my name, my real name, to make him say it right, but I didn't think I should be arguing with a dying man, so I just said:

— Sorry for what?

He closed his eyes.

— What for, Biggie? I said. What you sorry for?

He grimaced. He was so pale it was like the color was draining out of him with the blood.

— Your papa, he said. It wasn't Boston . . . It was me. I was there. Before I had . . . my own crew.

I felt my knees go weak and I wondered if that was cos I was in shock, or cos the world was falling away beneath me. But no, it was later that the world fell down. Stéphanie was looking at me, too. She had her hands supporting Biggie's face and the two of them were gazing up at me, all bloody, like they were in one of those Catholic paintings on the sides of churches.

— But . . . you said . . .

— I lied, said Biggie. I thought . . . hating Boston would make you a good soldier. The truth is, it was Dread who told us to kill your papa . . . Your papa hated Aristide, and Dread knew that, so . . .

Biggie continued to speak, but I wasn't listening.

In my head, a film started.

Flash. Papa and Manman arguing about Aristide.

Flash. That gun Manman suddenly had in her hand, I realized that perhaps it was Papa's gun all along, that maybe he had been working against Aristide, against his hired guns like Dread Wilmè. Maybe he was working against them even when he came and hauled us out of that basement, when we were being the Marassa. To me, it had always seemed like he was pissed cos Manman was turning us into freaks, but maybe it was cos we were raising money for Lavalas.

Flash. Papa falling, the machetes coming down like great shining birds, pecking violently, feeding on blood.

Flash. The gangsters screeching and whooping as they cut him to piti-piti pieces. I looked beyond the balaclava of one man and all of a sudden he was Biggie, and there was a hatred burning in his eyes as he killed my papa.

I opened my mouth, but nothing came out.

Listen.

It's getting too hot in here, the concrete above me is grinding, and I'm seriously afraid I've entered hell. I don't know how much time I have to tell my story, but there's something I want to make clear. I want to tell you something about Biggie. You hate him now, I think. You probably believe him to be a monster, but I want you to understand that he was just a boy, really. Like me.

I want to tell you something about Biggie, and this is it.

All of this happened on a day long before I saw my sister, or thought I did, long before Biggie told me it was him who chopped Papa into pieces.

On that day there was also an earthquake. I say also, even though I'm not sure that this is what has happened to me, but what else causes such a great sudden noise and the hospital to collapse on itself? Unless we've been bombed, and I see no reason why terrorists would bomb Haiti; it's already fucked up.

Anyway, yes, on that day there was a little tremor. We all felt it. We were riding in a pickup truck with the body of a Route 9 gangster; his name was Chico. It was Chico's funeral, and people were lining the streets, crying, cheering, chanting rebel songs. I doubt many of them knew who Chico was, but we always did good funerals in Route 9, in Solèy 19. It all went back to Dread Wilmè, when his body was carried through the slum and thousands of people came out onto the streets and followed it to the sea, and MINUSTAH stayed out of the Site altogether, they were so afraid that day.

So, the truck shook a bit when the ground trembled. Everyone looked panicked, but Biggie laughed.

— It's a small one, he said. It's nothing.

Haiti is on a fault line, you should understand that. It's like the whole country is cursed; we're on a crack in the world, and everything in Haiti is cracked, too. We're a broken country.

Chico was looking up at us. He was in an open coffin, and he had his best Adidas T-shirt on and a Def Jam baseball cap. Somehow his eyes had opened when the earthquake shook the pickup. Biggie reached down and closed them again. As we passed the people outside their shacks, they looked down at the mud in respect. Of course, looking down at the mud is normal in the Site.

Just then, there was a *bang*, and another, and we ducked when we realized that someone was shooting. We were close to Boston here, and Chico had died in a fight with them.

— Guns! said Biggie. Get them!

I pulled out my Glock 9; it was stuck in the back of my jeans. I thumbed off the safety and looked around, crouching. The pickup had stopped. I could hear a machine gun going off, and I saw Tintin throw himself against the side of the pickup, head down. Max was not so fast – he was lifting up his shotgun when a bullet hit him in the leg, spraying blood. He screamed and fell into Chico's coffin.

Someone was shooting, and I saw people running in all directions. I scanned desperately to see who was firing at us, and then there was a *ping* next to me and I saw a hole open up in the side of the pickup, like a metal flower. I looked toward where the bullet must have come from, and I saw a shorty in jeans that were hanging below his butt. He raised his gun again, but I was quicker – I squeezed off several shots.

Biggie was shooting, too, beside me, so I don't know which of us got him, but he went down in the mud. Then Biggie was vaulting over the side of the pickup.

— With me, he said.

I saw that one of the Boston crew had dropped his gun and turned to run. Biggie was chasing after him. From where the guy had been standing, I figured he was the one who'd shot Max.

I sprinted behind, clutching my gun. I kept expecting to be hit, but it seemed like this guy was the last. Maybe Tintin had killed one of them, or maybe there were only two to begin with. It doesn't take many kids to do a lot of damage when the enemy is riding in a funeral car, not expecting for shit that you're going to start shooting them up.

Anger was acid in my throat. I liked Max and he'd taken a bullet in his leg just cos the Boston sons of bitches had taken us by surprise. Max was cool. He used to sing old reggae songs, and he was amazing at telling jokes and doing voices. He could do Stéphanie like she was standing in the room with us – her French accent, the way she'd sometimes use street slang to sound cooler than she was, the way she'd kind of simper and laugh at Biggie's jokes, even though usually you'd think she was too hard for that kind of thing.

For sure, he never did that impression in front of Biggie.

So, running after Biggie, I was thinking about how we were going to blow away this little Boston cocksucker, and how it was gonna be good. I heard pounding feet behind me and I saw that Tintin was running, too. I fired my gun into the air.

— Route 9! I shouted.

I didn't usually do that kind of thing, but Boston had ruined our funeral. That was a pussy move.

I turned down an alley after Biggie, and saw the Boston kid pressed against a wall at the end. He was half bent over, panting. Biggie was looking down at him, his favorite gun, his Tec-9, in his hand.

— You want to say anything before I kill you? he said.

The kid – he really was just a kid, no older than me – straightened up. He looked right at Biggie.

— I could've killed that guy, he said. The one who was with you on the back of the truck. I'm a good shot. I could've killed him, but I didn't – I just shot him in the leg.

— Yeah? said Biggie. I don't give a shit. You ambushed us, you die. That's how it works.

The kid nodded.

— Do me a favor, he said. My name is Frank. Tell my manman I love her. Tell her . . . I'm sorry for letting her down.

Biggie made this noise that could have been frustration. He hefted his gun in his hand.

— You aimed for the leg? he said.

— Yes, said the kid.

— OK, said Biggie.

He shot the kid in the thigh and the kid went down, screaming.

— Come on, said Biggie to me and Tintin. Don't shoot him. This kid lives. He flipped open his phone. Stéphanie? We've got a man down. He needs to go to Canapé-Vert.

Me and Tintin, we looked at each other, like, what the fuck? The kid, Frank, was crying now, quietly, kind of whimpering. But I could tell he was crying partly cos he was happy.

Tintin shrugged.

— I guess Biggie's in a good mood, he said.

Another time, I went to see Biggie. I could hear him on the phone as I followed the alley down to where he was sleeping at that time. I don't know why, but I started to walk real quiet, and I was glad afterward that I did. I glanced round the corner and I saw Biggie sitting on this low brick wall that was just outside the shack. He was holding his cell phone against his ear with his shoulder, and I saw that there were tears pouring down his cheeks.

— But, Manman, he said.

I'd never heard him sound so vulnerable. I suddenly realized he was a boy, too – he was maybe five years older than me.

I heard a woman's voice from the other end of the line, but it was too quiet; I couldn't tell what she was saying.

— When are you coming home? Biggie continued. I miss you.

I knew Biggie's manman worked in Miami, where everyone drives Cadillac Escalades and there are hot bitches in miniskirts. Miami always sounded like heaven to me from the way the rappers talked about it in their songs. Biggie's manman was a cleaner, or an au pair, or something. Sometimes she sent money, and Biggie would buy more heroin with it, or give it to someone as a bribe.

— No, he said into the phone. You said it would only be for a year.

I heard her say something back, only it was too quiet to make out. I stood very, very still.

— Yes, yes, said Biggie. Of course I'm going to school. No, I don't get into trouble. Yes, I have anpil friends. One of my friends is coming round now, actually, so I've gotta go. Yes, he's nice. Young, a real shorty, but a good kid.

He's talking about me, I realized, amazed.

— OK, Manman, he said. But call me next week, OK?

Biggie had his gun in his other hand and he was turning it over, turning it over, again and again. He wiped his eyes with the back of the hand that was holding the phone, to get rid of the tears.

— I just want you to come home, he said.

Then he looked blankly at the phone in his hand. It was obvious she had hung up. Biggie let out a lungful of his air, all anger and heartbreak, then breathed in a lungful of the Site air, which was all heat and stink of sewage, and which didn't give a fuck about him. His face went hard, like he had taken the Site inside his ownself, made his ownself part of its indifference.

— Fuck, he said.

I stood there for another five minutes, maybe more. Then I walked into the yard and Biggie came out the house, and his face was hard.

— Biatch, he said. Step into my crib. Let's talk business. I want more money out of those mofos with the laundromat.

THEN

Toussaint tied his horse to a stake and watched his son do the same. They had come to the Georges plantation, where Brunet had made his camp. This plantation, unlike many others, had been well looked after, and fat ears of corn swayed in the breeze.

Brunet came out of the house to meet them, his wife beside him pretty under a parasol. Brunet had an honest countenance, the face lined a little by age, but otherwise handsome. Instead of a mustache he wore a close-cropped beard.

— Governor-General, he said. What a pleasure it is to meet you. I'm a long-standing admirer of what you have achieved in this country. Securing freedom for the slaves! It's a feat that will resound through the ages.

— Freedom wasn't my idea, said Toussaint. In fact, we have you French to thank for that. I only helped to spread the idea here.

Brunet gave a little bow.

— Well said, he pronounced. You are as humble as you are noble.

— Oh, I'm not noble, said Toussaint. The slaves are free, granted, but we're still low-born in the eyes of the whites. Besides, I thought your revolution had done away with nobility.

Brunet smiled. Toussaint was glad to see it – it showed the man was not an idiot.

— The Revolution did, said Brunet, but Bonaparte seems determined to bring nobility back.

Toussaint laughed out loud. He liked a man who was willing to criticize his consul – that suggested he was able to think for himself. He had known Brunet for all of two minutes and already he preferred him to that pompous prig Leclerc.

— Isaac I've met before, of course, said Brunet. In Paris.

— Indeed, said Isaac. You are well met, sir. I trust you're finding Haiti to your liking?

— Well, said Brunet, I found it, which is all credit to my ship's navigator. As to whether it's to my liking, I believe I shall take a view on that once the brigands and thieves are dealt with. I prefer a law-abiding country, I must say – that's so much better for trade.

— On that we concur then, said Toussaint. I'm sure that with the cooperation of my armies we can render Haiti safe for everyone, and provide a fertile ground for society.

Brunet nodded.

— As am I, he said.

He introduced his wife, who smiled demurely when

Toussaint kissed her on the hand and did not shrink at all from contact with his negro lips. He appreciated this gesture, as not all well-bred white ladies behaved so.

— Now, please, do enter, said Brunet. We'll have some refreshments.

Toussaint went first, Isaac behind him. The interior was cool and dim, the light filtered by gauze curtains. A glass and brass chandelier hung above a leather-topped desk, several comfortable armchairs, a chaise longue, and a beautifully polished floor. The room was tastefully decorated in the colonial tradition, but was markedly different from many Toussaint had seen in that it hadn't been defaced, burned, or looted. The master here must have been good to his slaves to see his property respected in this way.

Madame Brunet excused herself, saying she felt that politics were best left to men. Toussaint didn't necessarily agree, but he nodded politely and bowed as she left the room.

They chatted idly for some minutes, sizing one another up, then Brunet made a slight noise of irritation.

— The servants are taking their time with the wine I ordered, he said. I'll just check on it.

He stepped from the room.

A moment later the door opened and a dozen men entered, armed with pistols and swords. They trained the guns on Toussaint. For a moment – just a moment – he didn't understand, then a heaviness settled on his heart.

I wonder if they think me some kind of black magician, he thought, *that I should require so many men to restrain me.*

Isaac turned to him in bewilderment.

— Father . . . he stammered. What are they doing?

— What do you think they're doing? said Toussaint.

Paris had provided his son with an excellent academic education, but in many ways it had taught him nothing. Toussaint looked into his son's eyes, where he saw something of himself and was glad. He pushed Isaac behind him and drew his saber to face the twelve men.

Yes, perhaps *this* was his destiny.

The door opened again and Brunet stood there, a sad look on his face.

— Put away the sword, Governor, he said. We're not here to kill you, but to arrest you for treason. You won't be harmed. I promise you that, nor your son.

Toussaint laughed.

— You promise?

Brunet had just enough grace to look ashamed.

— I apologize for the ruse, he said. It was the only way to resolve the situation without bloodshed.

— The situation being the inconvenience of my wishing Haiti to be free?

Brunet ignored that, instead gesturing to the sword in Toussaint's hand.

— Lower that, he ordered.

Sighing, Toussaint complied.

— Just one thing, said Toussaint, please, before you restrain me.

— Yes? said Brunet.

Toussaint moved his hand toward his trousers and the soldiers aimed their guns at him, eyes narrow, fingers white on triggers.

— Don't shoot, he said. Don't shoot.

Toussaint held one hand up in front of him as if it could stop a bullet if one came, and reached very slowly into his pocket. He drew out the pwen and handed it to Isaac, his movements as exaggerated as mime so that the soldiers would see he wasn't producing some hidden weapon.

— What's that? said Isaac, who had been educated in Paris, and who had never fought anyone in his life, nor been whipped, nor stood in a swamp as a houngan danced and beat his drum.

— A pwen. It contains the spirit of a lwa – a lwa of war, I believe. It belonged to Boukman and now it belongs to you. It . . . It's Haiti.

Toussaint found that there were tears in his eyes. Isaac looked at him like he was mad, but he took the stone.

Toussaint nodded to Brunet to indicate that he was ready.

The men rushed forward and tied his arms behind his back. They marched him from the house and into a carriage.

They're taking me to Cape Town, he thought.

But they didn't take him there. They proceeded straight to the coast and, separating him from Isaac, pushed him into a boat, then rowed him out to a frigate anchored offshore. A gentle breeze carried to him the scent of the land – spice and earth and sugar – but the scent grew fainter and fainter as it was drowned in salt. Then he could smell only the sea, which

297

was the smell of death to him because the sea was everything that lay beyond Haiti, and Haiti was life.

It would have been kinder to shoot me, he thought.

Night had fallen and, as he listened to the clapotis of the sea against the wood of the rowing boat, Toussaint was reminded of that night when he and Jean-Christophe had swum out to the French ships. *We should have burned them*.

As soon as he was hauled on board he heard the heavy metallic rattle of the anchor being pulled up, and he knew he had lost. Haiti was lost, and he would never see her again. He felt the motion of the ship and realized that he was leaving the island the same way his father had come to it – over the ocean. For the first time he understood why vodou believed the dead to rest under the sea, for the narrative of the world was one of exodus – from the womb, from Eden – and return. The slaves had come to Haiti by the sea, and it seemed that it was to the sea that they were destined to return.

He had been denied even a porthole, as he was locked in a cargo hold, and he wept to know that they had taken his country from him. Still, he refused to give up hope. He dried his tears and straightened his back to show that he had not been broken. In the darkness, he thought about death because he knew that was what awaited him. He knew that they could never truly take Haiti from him, because in death he would know those he had lost once again, would speak with them and hold them again. In killing him, the French would be returning him to his ancestors, to his wife, would in some sense be giving him what he wanted.

He thought about the Rapture, the moment when all the dead would rise up to heaven together. His father had taught him that this event would occur when Jesus returned to the earth, perhaps in ten years, perhaps in ten thousand. Then all death would be undone and all calamities reversed in a single stroke. It had always seemed a remarkable idea to Toussaint. He pictured the drowned walking up from the bottom of the sea, pirates and the navy alike, their skeletons barnacled and clothed in seaweed, to join the general drift up to heaven, as the gravity of the dead reversed itself. He saw graves open and spill their contents upward; he saw battlefields scatter into the air in a clatter of bones and armor.

But this version was wrong, he understood now. The dead did not have to wait for some unknown day for their reunions. Bois Caiman and the stone had taught Toussaint that the version presented in vodou was closer to the truth, that people were always traveling to death, always accompanying Baron Samedi and la Sirene to the land under the sea to meet their missed ones there. Death was a constant welcoming, with those already dead always waiting, and a perpetual reunion. Because what, otherwise, could come after? Once the Rapture is done, what then? Then there would be nothing but stillness, and the world abhors stillness.

No, he thought. *There is no stillness, not now, not ever. There is another version. A true version.*

Death will continue. There will be no triumphant ending with souls ascending through the sky, no waiting for a reunion that might only happen after ten thousand years. There will be a steady and endless stream of the dead, filling the land under the sea that can never be filled.

But this is not sad.

This is beautiful.

The beauty of this is that when you die there will always be someone waiting, there will always be those you have lost, standing there, the curve of their back and the stance of their feet so familiar. There will always be someone there, saying:

— We have waited so long. It is so good to see you. Come here.

Come here.

NOW

I have to tell you the rest quickly now, cos it's necessary that I die soon. I don't want to, but the time has come, I sense it. I was trying to reach the light, so I was hauling on a block – at least, I think it was a block – and something came free. There was a great creaking noise and then it fell down on me, crushing me. I think my leg's broken. It doesn't matter, really. I'll starve or die of thirst soon anyway.

Manman was right. I was born in darkness, and I will die in darkness. I can't even see the crack of light anymore, cos it was blocked by the thing that fell down.

Now you know why I want to throw my story behind me, like rubble. Now you know why I don't want it anymore. I'm a killer and I shot so many times I made a goal in the end, and I got what was coming to me. I deserve all this, I realize that. Still, the feeling I had when I knew that Biggie was one of the men who killed Papa, when I realized it was Route 9 all along, that was like something tearing inside me, like I was giving birth to something, but the only thing that can come out of me is misery and darkness.

Tintin came to visit me in the hospital, I told you that. I didn't explain anything. I just listened to him talk his stupid hip-hop talk and then I pretended to be asleep, so he would leave. He brought me a CD walkman and some CDs. One of them was Biggie rapping about air strikes and Tec-9s, and one was of Biggie Smalls saying he was ready to die, and I thought, yeah, I know the feeling. In the end, I can't bring myself to hate Biggie, not exactly – he's a chimère, what did I expect? – but I don't want to listen to his music, either, so when Tintin was gone I shoved the CDs away from me.

Tintin will end up leading Route 9, I bet. Biggie's dead, and so is Mickey. Tintin will say that he was a hero that night in Boston; he'll talk it up so he didn't run away. I know this. I don't care, though. Let him have his precious Route 9. It'll still end in a hail of bullets, like the rap songs say.

Stéphanie came to visit me, too. She sat down on the edge of my bed, though I didn't want her to. She had been crying; I could see the redness around her eyes.

— They don't want to give Biggie a funeral, she said. They think it would become a pretext for violence in the Site. After what they did, with their guns!

She started to cry. I felt like I should put an arm around her or something, but I didn't. She might have wanted to help the Site at the beginning, but she got seduced by Biggie and his

302

gangster lifestyle, and all that went out the window. She may have been UN, but she wasn't much more than a girl, twenty-five at the oldest. Some people like that, they're drawn to the power of guns, even if they say they only want to save people.

— Why did they do that? I asked her. MINUSTAH. Why did they kill him and the others?

— They think they're helping, she said. They think they're helping to keep the Site free of crime.

— If they want to do that, they should pay for some schools, create jobs. Then people wouldn't want drugs.

Shit, I thought. I sound like Biggie.

— I agree, said Stéphanie. I tell them that, but they don't listen to me. Sometimes when you have a gun in your hand it starts to do your thinking for you.

I knew what she meant. Sometimes when I was holding a gun it was like the gun wanted to kill people, not me. Never me.

That was a lie I just told you. I'm sorry. I don't know why I'd lie. You know perfectly well that I've wanted to kill people in my time, and that I've done it, too.

Stéphanie didn't stay for long. We didn't have a lot to talk about. I asked her what she'd do with her baby. I said I knew from Biggie that she was ansent, and I could see it, too, from the way she held her hand on her belly, even if it wasn't showing yet.

— I'm going back to France, she said. To Lille. I don't want my baby growing up here.

I told her that was a good idea. I told her I wouldn't want

303

my baby to grow up here, either, if I had one. She smiled at that. Soon after, she left. She said she'd visit again.

She didn't.

I hope she got out alive. I hope the earthquake didn't bury her and Biggie's baby. Since I'm already confessing, though, I might as well tell you that part of me wouldn't mind if his baby was never born. I understand Biggie and I don't hate him, but that doesn't mean I forgive him.

Finally, my manman came to visit.

She sat down in the plastic chair beside my bed and she cried. Then she asked me what had happened. I told her everything I've told you – I told her the whole story. The only part I left out was that it was Dread who ordered Papa's death, cos I didn't think she could stand to know that. At the end she wasn't crying, but I think that was only cos she had no tears left to cry. Then she stood up from her chair and she leaned over me.

— I did this, she said. I blamed you when you joined Biggie and his gang, but I was the one who did it.

— No, you didn't, Manman, I said. It was me. I should have listened to you.

She sobbed.

— No, it was listening to me that got you into this mess, she said. You should never have listened to me.

— Why, Manman?

She sat back down and she looked away from me, at the wall. Then there was, like, a click in my mind, and I could see

304

why in the grief of her eyes. I could see what she was about to tell me and I wished I could stop time, like it stopped when I was down by the sea, looking at Marguerite, or the girl who seemed to be Marguerite. But time just kept on going; I could hear it being cut into pieces by the clock on the wall. I couldn't make it stop.

Manman rubbed at her eyes and she looked over to the corner of the room. This fly was there, buzzing and buzzing against the window, not realizing it was glass it was trying to get through and that it was trapped.

I felt like that fly.

No. I wished I could *be* that fly; at least it would die soon, and its imprisonment would be over. I remember the sun was bright against the window, making it look like a painting of a blaze, an opening into hell.

— Marguerite – began Manman.

— No, I said. No.

I didn't want her to tell me. I knew what she was going to say and I didn't want to hear it. I tried to put my hands on my ears, but Manman wouldn't stop and she pulled them away.

— They killed her that night, my manman said. Marguerite. I lied to you about it. When I went out into the street after they'd all gone . . . I didn't see her at first, it was so dark. When I saw . . . something broke inside my mind. I told you she was alive cos I wanted you to have hope. It was something I didn't have anymore, but I wanted you to have it.

I had known it already, but when Manman said it,

something broke inside me and I stopped being me, stopped being a person.

I tried to breathe, but it seemed like all the air in the room had gone, and I was in a void. Good, I thought. At least then I'll die.

But I didn't die.

My heart kept up an offbeat rhythm in my chest, kept making its stupid music. At last, with a raw sound, air flooded back into my lungs.

— But . . . the girl . . . she didn't shoot me, down by the sea.

— Someone else, said Manman. Someone who didn't want to kill you. There are people like that, you know – even in the Site.

I stared at her. She had broken my heart, and part of me wanted to break hers. Part of me wanted to tell her:

— Manman, did you know that it was Dread who killed Papa? Did you know that when you moved to Solèy 19, you moved into the house of your husband's killer and named it your own?

But I didn't tell her. I didn't really want to hurt her, even now. Let her think that Papa died cos we lived in no man's land, not cos Aristide and his cronies found him a nuisance. Let her go on believing the world was a place where random bad things happened, not a place where people – boys – did terrible things just cos they could.

Manman reached into her pocket, and before she even took out her hand I knew what would be in it. I knew what she was trying to give me, and I knew that if I took it, it would be like I was absolving her, so when she tried to hand me Marguerite's half of the necklace, I closed my fist against it, refused to take it, and crossed my arms over my chest.

— You should take it, said Manman. You could put the pieces of the heart back together.

— No, I can't, I said. She's dead. You took the necklace – you keep it.

— I'm sorry, said Manman. I'm so sorry.

I closed my eyes.

— Leave, please, I said.

Sometime after that, everything fell down.

THEN

When Toussaint first arrived, his cell had a window and through it he could see the River Doubs and the Besançon road. He could see mountains with snow on them, something he had never seen in Haiti. It was a sight that filled his heart with fear – that, and the cliffs and precipices of this godforsaken land in the alpine region of France.

Initially, despite being imprisoned, Toussaint was treated with respect. He was permitted paper and a pen; he was encouraged to write, in fact. He should have been suspicious about that, but he retained the foolish conviction that he would be allowed a trial. He conversed with the director of the prison, a civilized man, and received from him books and plays to read, as well as news of the outside world. Once, this man, Bresse, brought him a certain play by Alphonse de Lamartine that had been published and performed in Paris. It dramatized Toussaint's life, telling the story of his struggle in rhyming monologue without regard for truth or even likelihood.

He read the play, shivering at his high window, with

amusement and amazement. Hardly a word was true. In it, he was a Greek god, fierce in countenance and in battle, an avatar of furious vengeance, determined to wreak murder on the slavers. He was uneducated and single of purpose. There was no mention of his supervision of agriculture, his efforts to ensure his people were always fed, or of his sudden acquisition of the ability to read and write and make maps. One of the play's more outlandish fictions was that he had buried a fortune in the mountains of the interior, a cache of gold, silver, and jewelry taken from the plantation owners, when Toussaint had always taken pains to restore the slavers' possessions to them. He considered writing to the playwright to inform him of his mistakes, but he did not.

Instead, he wrote numerous letters to Bonaparte, pleading his case, arguing that all he had done he had done for Haiti, that his constitution had been intended to secure her safety, that he and the country remained faithful servants of France, but not slaves.

These letters went unanswered.

After some two months' imprisonment, he received a visit from Bonaparte's aide-de-camp, a man named Cafarelli. When the envoy was shown in, hope blossomed in Toussaint's chest like a rare flower.

— Toussaint l'Ouverture, said the man, I come from Bonaparte with an offer.

Toussaint smiled, something he had not done in a long time. Perhaps he would see his son again, after all.

— Tell me, he said.

— The emperor wishes me to convey to you that, should you –

— The emperor? said Toussaint in disbelief.

Cafarelli colored slightly. He was small of stature, with thin whiskers in the place of a mustache. He seemed a little like a rat that had grown enormous on scraps of prison food, put on a doublet and hose, and come to pay a visit to the prison's most famous inmate.

— The . . . ah . . . consul is so styled now, Monsieur l'Ouverture.

Toussaint laughed. The blacks had freed themselves after French philosophers argued that all men had a right to liberty, after the French rose up against their king. Now the French had replaced a king with an emperor.

— Apologies, he said, stifling his laughter. I have interrupted your offer.

— Yes. The emperor wishes me to convey –

— You've done that part.

— Yes. If you reveal to me the location of your buried treasure in Haiti, he will restore to you your freedom and pardon your crimes.

— My crimes?

— You rebelled against France.

— No, said Toussaint. I rebelled against slavery. Never against France.

The aide-de-camp shrugged.

— Do you deny that you declared a constitution without permission? That you named yourself Governor-General without ratification from the con— the emperor?

310

— No, but it was merely a constitution, and my term was merely three years, and the terms expressly forbade me from standing again. You should have seen what the Haitians wanted to give me. They'd have made me a king had I not resisted. I gave them freedom, I gave them peace, and they would have made me a dictator in return. Your emperor should thank me for my forbearance and strength of character in my insistence on democracy and my desire to maintain links of trade and amity with France. I even made Haiti a dependency! I could have severed all ties had I wished.

— You deny that you enriched yourself at France's cost?

— Of course I do, Toussaint said. There is no treasure. You have been misinformed. He gestured to the slanderous play-sheets on the desk. Has Bonaparte been attending the theater too often?

— He's too busy for that, said Cafarelli.

Toussaint rolled his eyes. The man had no humor. Still, he had based his judgment of Brunet on such fleeting impressions, and that man had deceived him utterly.

— I've been instructed to ascertain the location of the treasure, said Cafarelli. Give it up to us, and you will go free.

Toussaint put his face in his hands.

— Then I will die here, he said in a low voice. There is no treasure.

Cafarelli placed a hand on his shoulder; he was not wholly unsympathetic.

— You only have to hand it over, he said.

Toussaint wept then.

There was no treasure. Anything that had been taken from the slavers had been distributed amongst his men, had been used to shore up the foundations of the country, to prepare for her freedom. But a playwright said he had buried riches and, believing him, Bonaparte wished to seize them. Toussaint recalled his wry amusement at the inventions of the man who had written his life for the stage. Now he would strangle him gladly.

Days later, Cafarelli came again.

— Do you continue to be obstinate? he asked.

— I continue to maintain that I have no buried treasure, if that is what you mean, said Toussaint. Ask my men, if you wish.

— Oh, we intend to, said Cafarelli.

Toussaint cursed his runaway tongue. He would not have his men suffer for this madness.

— I have been instructed to obtain from you a written response to Bonaparte, said Cafarelli, swearing that you possess no treasure. Tell the guard when you have finished and I will deliver your letter to the emperor.

Toussaint waved a hand irritably.

— Very well, he said.

General and Emperor,

You will permit me, Emperor, to say to you, with all the respect and submission which I owe you, that the French government has been completely deceived in regard to

Toussaint l'Ouverture, one of its most zealous and coura-
geous servants in Haiti. All I have done, I have done in the
name of the blacks and in the name of Haiti, not to offend
France or your exalted person. Indeed, when the English were
finally repulsed and our constitution was declared, I made
Haiti a subject and dependency of France, something I need
not have done! I sacrificed my blood, and a part of what I
possessed, to serve my country, and in spite of my efforts, all
my labors have been in vain.

I possess no treasure. I have no wealth, no silver plate
buried in the earth of Haiti. I have only my freedom, which I
achieved through the offices of my esteemed prior master,
Bayou de Libertas, and which the French state was pleased
to confirm. I labored long to acquire honor and glory from the
government, and to gain the esteem of my fellow citizens, and
I am now, for my reward, crowned with thorns and the most
marked ingratitude.

First, Emperor, it is unfortunate for me that I am not known
to you. If you had been thoroughly acquainted with me whilst
I was in Haiti, you would have done me more justice; you
would have known that my heart is good. I am not learned,
I am ignorant; I could not read ere my fifty-fourth year on
this earth. But my father and my friends showed me the road
of virtue and honor, and I am very strong in my conscience in
that matter. I did not lead my men for my own personal glory,
but for the glory of freedom, which was an idea we learned
from France and her own Revolution. If I had not been

devoted to Haiti, I should not have been here – that is a truth! I am wretched, miserable, a victim of all my services.

I ask you for my freedom that I may labor, that I may gain my sustenance and support my unhappy family. I call on your greatness, on your genius, to pronounce a just judgment on my destiny. Let your heart be softened and touched by my position and my misfortunes.

I salute you, with profound respect,
TOUSSAINT L'OUVERTURE

In addition to the letter, he sent with Cafarelli an account of his life, which he hastily composed in the hope that it would cause Bonaparte to look more favorably upon him. He prefaced it with a request for a fair trial and expressed hope that this account might inform the legal process, might be given to judge and jury as testimony of his honor. He omitted the ceremony at Bois Caiman, which, he feared, could tend to make him appear savage and unformed. He said instead that his ability to read, although coming late in life, was conventionally won. He wrote of a French mercenary whom he had paid to teach him, smiling as he wrote at the felicity of his invention, for words were a kind of weapon, and so he had commissioned from this mercenary precisely what he would normally sell. So taken was he with the idea that he almost came to believe it true, and he could even see in his mind's eye the many hours he had spent with the French sell-sword.

He commended both these things to Cafarelli's care, then he waited.

And he waited.

For weeks, no reply came. Months, even. Then, with no warning, things changed. The director of the prison was sent away, and a man named Colomier left in charge. This man took from Toussaint his writing equipment, his desk, his bed, and, finally, his cell. Colomier took away his view of the mountains, confining him to an underground cell, tiny, without windows of any kind. Toussaint found himself languishing in a dungeon, the walls slimy with damp and mold.

All of a sudden, he was in darkness. Food stopped coming, and water. He licked the moisture from the cold stone walls, but he knew it would not sustain him many days.

In this darkness he could no longer distinguish between his dreams and reality, and he tried to tell his story to an invisible audience, an audience that never spoke back, in an attempt to preserve his sanity.

He understood what was happening here – or thought he did, because there *was* a possibility that he had gone mad, that paranoia had seized him.

Yet . . .

No, he was sure he understood. *This* was his trial, *this* his judgment. He had been sentenced to death.

A slow death.

Since the director of the prison had been sent away, he

could not be held accountable afterward. This Colomier, who had replaced him, was young and inexperienced; he would say, no doubt, that Toussaint had attacked him, or offered resistance in some way, and in self-defense he had consigned him to the darkness. That would be the story. Toussaint's death would be marked on the prison's records as caused by general malaise, not deliberate starvation.

Yes, Toussaint knew how these things worked. He was an inconvenience, so Toussaint would be left to die. His testifying before a court was inconceivable since he would only say that he had done nothing wrong, and that could not be risked; no slight to French honor would be borne. If he died in prison, however, they could continue to paint him a criminal, to make up calumnies about him, to talk their silly talk of treasure, as if he were a pirate. And they would quietly bring slavery back to Haiti and undo all his achievements.

Toussaint lay in the darkness.

He did not know how long he had been in this place, or even whether to measure it in days or weeks or hours. He knew from his time with his army that a man could last little more than three days without water, three weeks without food. He had continued to nourish himself with water from the walls, but with no food forthcoming he soon lost the strength to do so.

He was no longer himself, either, it seemed to him.

One instant, he was in the prison cell, in darkness, and the next he was standing on a street lined with rickety edifices made of strange, gray material and metal, and there were signs everywhere that he didn't recognize. He saw another of those rolling metal carriages with wheels as it exploded in a ball of flame, like at the ammunition store in Guildive, and guns were going off everywhere – but this was not Guildive. He saw young men in strange dress and soldiers in black uniform, carrying shining guns that looked smooth and alien.

At one point, he was floating above a ruined country, looking down on buildings that had been transformed to rubble, and circling with him in the air were great machines with blades spinning on top of them.

At another point, he was a man with peculiar hair that fell past his neck in thick ropes, and he was standing in a muddy street, a strange flying machine above, as men with masked helmets fired bullets into him and through him, the pain unbelievable. He was dying, but he was crawling toward a boy who was lying in the mud, and he knew that he had to stop the vehicle that was about to crush the boy.

At yet another point, he was in a place only subtly different from his cell, and here there was a weight pressing down on him, and he could smell blood and decay. He was a boy, a young boy who was never going to see the light again.

He understood that somehow, in some sense, he was this boy and this man simultaneously.

After the incident at Bois Caiman, Toussaint had spoken to Boukman of the impossible things he had seen and asked whether he was going insane. Boukman had replied:

— We can be possessed by the lwa of our ancestors, the Gede spirits, so who is to say that we cannot be possessed by the lwa of our descendants?

If that were true, thought Toussaint, then he truly had accomplished nothing, for his descendant was also trapped in darkness, was also dying, his flesh was also slowly enervated by deprivation. He had staked his life to give his people freedom, but his people still were not free.

He even questioned if the dead would be reunited, as he had come to believe on the ship leaving Haiti, or if everything would stay broken and never be made whole. He tried to picture his father's face, Boukman's. He could not. There was only a hint of a recollection, a memory as impossible to grasp as a reflection on moving water. All that was left of them were a few features, a story or two, the odd thing he remembered them saying. He was not even sure if these memories would accord with those of others who had known them, or if, in remembering, he was warping the dead, changing their shape as the sea or the earth do, stripping their bones.

I am in darkness, in a small space, and my mind is a small dark place, too, he thought. *We are all trapped in a cave, and that cave is ourselves. The shape of its walls moves like water; this barrier disturbs what little light gets in and makes everything we see unique to us.*

The Boukman Toussaint saw and remembered was not the

Boukman anyone else saw, and for this reason Boukman was destroyed not once, but twice: a death in the world and a death in the memory. He was pulled apart and changed by a hundred different minds, all perceiving the world differently.

How could a person be reborn, be so mauled and twisted by distinct minds? How could murder be undone? And how could it possibly be that one day Toussaint would walk into a cool cavern underneath the sea and Boukman would be waiting for him, saying, it has been too long?

He thought of the trick Boukman had performed at Bois Caiman, of the zombi who was dug up and interrogated about his experiences in death. Toussaint smiled. There were no zombis, only the chicanery of theater. No one who was buried would rise again, coughing on the loam of the earth in which they were interred.

No, he would die in darkness and would go on into darkness, too. There would be no reunion, and nothing would be made whole. There would be no Rapture – he had known that before – but now he saw that there would be no return, either.

There was only exodus.

Toussaint closed his eyes, or thought he did. He could not be certain in this darkness whether his eyes were open or not.

He was weary. It seemed to him that it would be easy to slip over from this dark place into some other reality, and that death would not be long in coming for him, in taking him away.

He was right.

*

And yet . . .

And yet . . .

And yet it seemed that death was not the end, after all.

Toussaint was taken aback, soon after dying, to find himself drifting up above his body, hovering in the air of the cell, and looking down on himself.

There was no pain anymore, no anger. When he looked down he saw with a dispassion he had never been capable of in life how emaciated he had become, how the French had turned his face into a death mask, almost fleshless, the cheeks hollow, dark shadows below the eyes. He saw his bones pressing at his skin from within as if eager to break out, to be free.

Although it was dark, he could see the cell walls. Lichen clung, sickly green, to the stone. They bore scratches, some the raking parallel lines made by fingernails, some illegible words, written by illiterates, perhaps, or ordinary people who couldn't see in the dark.

Strangely, although his fury and disappointment had left him along with the feelings of cold and starvation, although he seemed to have left the sensations of the flesh behind him, he felt drawn to that husk of a body below. He felt that he would like to drift down again, to sink into it, to comfort it. It seemed a sad and lonely thing, an empty vessel that he ought to fill. He strained toward it, yet nothing happened.

Then it was as if something caught him, some updraft like those thermals that suspend birds in the sky, and he was pulled upward.

His body faded below, and then he was inside Fort de Joux,

looking at the stone from inside, and for just an impossibly small iota of time he knew what it was to *be* stone, to breathe and flow so slowly that a century passed in a heartbeat. Then he was in the light again, drifting through the iron bars of the cells above, a rusty taste in his mouth, before bursting through the roof and lofting his being into the alpine air.

He gazed down at the castle that had held him, so small now, an eyrie perched in the mountains. Below lay a valley which began as a rocky ravine, angled down through pine trees, and ended as soft green pasture. The road to the prison twisted and turned through it. He smiled, for it was the essential quality of a valley that it must have an issue, that it must come to an end and spill out into fertile lowlands. A valley, he reflected, was an escapable thing by its very definition. It was difficult to find your way out of a cave. But a valley, ah, a valley. You could walk out of a valley, out of the dark place, away from the awful sharp towering of the mountains, and into the world.

As Toussaint floated, a light rain began to fall. Droplets passed through him, became, for brief instants, one with him. He felt the freshness and the eternality of the water, and when he saw the white rivulets of the waterfall, tumbling from the cliff to his east, he understood that all water was the same, how no drop was different from any other.

He had no body, so he did not feel joy precisely – he *was* joy, just as he was water, and stone. He was the air and the air was free and that was joy. He managed by an inflection of his thought to float down, over the prison, toward the grassy lowlands. He was above the birds; a crow circled, cawing, underneath him. The sun was high and bright in the sky; the trees and grass yearned toward it.

Toussaint understood that he was dead. He did. But he understood, too, that they couldn't hold him anymore; they couldn't keep him in that place where there was no light. He was finally and completely free.

No . . .

No . . .

No, because then he was pulled again. He was no longer flying, but being carried by something invisible yet powerful. He rose up, up, up. The valley became smaller and smaller, until it wasn't a valley, but a single cleft in a stone, filled with moss. Then he was in a vast whiteness, like a thick fog.

He rose through it, broke through it into a clean blue sky, and the clouds he had come through were a great white carpet below him, stretching all the way to the horizon, where he could see stars. Stars – in the daytime!

With a rush, the clouds began to roll beneath him; the sun above turned through the sky. There was no precise sensation of speed; he had no skin to register the pressure of air, no nose and no throat to feel the rushing push of the wind as he moved, but he knew that he was going very fast, just as he knew he was traveling around the world.

I'm going home, he thought.

He broke through the clouds again and saw the green island laid out underneath, vivid against the blue of the sea. It was dusk – he saw the sun setting over the water to the west, saw lights glowing from the land, so many lights.

Toussaint descended with growing wonder, staring down at the strange country he was falling into, seeing the sprawling cities that had swallowed the forest, the great buildings that had replaced the plantations. A colossal machine with the wings of a bird flew underneath him with a roar, turning him in the wake of its eddies. He fell past it – or fell through it, perhaps.

The cities were too big; it was impossible. So many people could not live in one city! They would go mad; it was a kind of prison. Thousands and thousands of lights glowed in the gathering dark, and as he accelerated through the air he saw that each light was not a home, as he had thought, but only one of many windows in each building. The lights burned everywhere; the people in the Haiti below him seemed unable to bear darkness. Even the flying machine, banking as it approached the ground, flickered with red and white lights. Between the cities, even, stretched tendrils of light, as if the cities themselves required connection, required touch, like people, and so were putting out filaments of bright engagement, as if they had been turned, by the habitation of so many people, into living beings themselves.

All this, he noticed in a heartbeat. Then he was closer, and he saw that this was a broken land. It had seemed so beautiful from above, sparkly and many-pointed with light, but now he saw that most of the buildings were collapsed or collapsing, and everywhere was rubble. Trees and walls lay flat on the ground, flying machines circled, as if fascinated by the damage.

What happened to it? he thought. *What?*

As he neared the tops of the buildings, the ruination became even more clear – he could see where people had erected villages of tents amongst the debris of the city. From its location on the island he could tell that it was Port-au-Prince, but it was not the Port-au-Prince he knew. It sprawled, it contained multitudes – and it was shattered.

And yet . . .

And yet . . .

And yet, rushing through the air, Toussaint saw black people everywhere, walking the streets, talking, sitting in groups around fires. He saw only a handful of whites, and he understood that this great city – this immensity of lights – was a city of blacks, and he was shown that in this shining future his people were free.

A roof rose quickly to meet him. It belonged to a great square building with thousands of windows, many of which had shattered as the building had slumped to the ground, as if too exhausted to remain standing. He tried to cushion his fall; the hard plane of the roof was coming faster, faster, faster, and then . . .

Then he was inside dense material – it wasn't stone because he couldn't feel it living – and there was twisted metal, too, and glass. He was inside this nightmare only briefly before he landed with a crashing impact.

He waited, but nothing changed.

His journey had ended; his exodus was over.

He *had* returned.

But to where?

He was in a small place, he sensed, something like his cell in the French prison.

He was aware of someone whimpering in the dark, and he was not at all sure that it wasn't himself.

He was inside the broken building, he knew that. But that was all he knew.

He put his hand in front of his face. He could see nothing. He was stunned by the heft and weight of his arm, by the familiar conspiracy of muscle and tendon and joint that raised his hand before him. He ran his tongue around the inside of his mouth, felt the foreign hardness of the tooth firmly planted in his gum, the one the gun shell had knocked out.

My tooth grew back?

He opened his mouth to scream, and that was when the pain struck him: the sensation was of a brick slamming down onto his leg, of a fire in his arm. He probed with his fingers and felt the stone-like material that trapped him. He was in a body once again, though not his own, apparently.

He was a prisoner once again.

He was trapped in an impenetrable ruin, with something heavy bearing down on his leg. He didn't know what had happened to this world, but he could see that it would never be the same again. He was not in a valley, he realized with horror; he had never been in a valley.

He was in a cave, and there was no way out.

ALWAYS

We are in the darkness.

We are always in the darkness.

We understand what Boukman said in Bois Caiman; we understand it for the first time. Behind the mountain is another mountain; behind the fire is another fire; behind all of this is another thing, another mass, and it does not correspond to the contours of this world; it is everything that is here in the world, but it is so much more, too.

We have a mouth – we can feel it in our face, an opening into us that can let the spirit out – but when we use it, when we speak, there is no one to listen. The voices that come to us, drifting through the darkness beyond our prison, they might as well be the voices of the dead.

Far beyond our walls, far beyond the bounds that hold us, there are people who want to help. There are always people who want to help, but they are too far away, and we are too silent. Though we have control of our own body, can animate our limbs to touch the boundaries of our reality, we are

326

powerless to break through our reality, powerless to go out into the light, where the masters live.

We are a slave.

We are a slave to this space, to the inevitable decay of trapped things. We can feed ourselves, but there is no food; we can work with our hands and with our minds, but there is nothing on which to work; we have eyes, but there is nothing to see.

There is no future and no past.

We are in the darkness.

We are one.

NOW

I have an idea.

There's nothing else I can do, so this is my only idea.

It's the last thing left.

I remember how Manman said that back in the day, instead of offering sweets, they used to kill two chickens for the Marassa and give the lwa the blood, proper old school. I can feel the blood from my arm, thick and kind of trickling.

I figure it's worth a try.

I don't know how to make the veve of Marassa. Even if I did, it's too dark and I don't have shit to write with. But I put my fingers in my wound and I bite a scream that wants to come out. I take some blood and I smear it on the rubble in front of me.

My voice, it's rough and dry; it's like a cog on a bike that hasn't been oiled. But I sing as best I can:

— Marassa Simbi,
Mwen engage dans pays-a,

Marassa Guinin, Marassa la Côte,
Mwen engage dans pays-a!

I sing it over and over, even after I think my voice will dry
up altogether, refuse to move anymore, like cogs do sometimes. It doesn't.

But nothing happens, either.

Some time passes, and nothing continues to happen.

I realize that I'm ready now, that all my options are gone. I'm
waiting for the end – or we are, I should say. It seems there's
someone else here, someone older, but someone I know.
Someone I've been, or who has been me. Someone from my
dreams. I know that doesn't make sense, but I'm dying; I
don't have to make sense.

I've told you my story now, so perhaps you can leave me
in peace.

I wonder if maybe I should have taken that half of the
necklace from Manman and put it with mine. I wonder if I
should have forgiven her. No, that's a lie. I know I should have
forgiven her. She's my manman, and I sent her away full of
shame and guilt. For all I know she's dead now, and I'll never
be able to say sorry.

I close my eyes, try to picture my manman's face. It's not
happening. I manage to remember an eyebrow, a certain
smile. But the image of her is like a TV screen where the
aerial has gone crazy. Not only have I lost her in the darkness,

but I've also lost the memory of her. She's destroyed completely; I got nothing left but an eyebrow and a smile, some things she said, the memory of the warmth of her hug.

She's gone, and I'll never see her again, not even in my mind, cos my mind is a dark place and images get lost in it, distorted.

I say it to myself over and over, I'll never see her again. But not with my mouth cos my mouth is too dry, with my mind only.

I begin to cry.

I wonder, if I die, and she's dead, will I see her then? Will I see Marguerite, too, and Papa?

And I answer myself, no. There's nothing after death.

I know cos I've been in the darkness all this time, which is as close to death as you can get, and I've seen no moun, apart from when I was Toussaint and I saw all those people of his – Boukman and Isaac and Brandicourt. But that wasn't real; that was my mind breaking, like my leg, crushed by concrete and darkness.

I keep my eyes closed.

I begin to die.

There's a ripping, tearing noise, very loud and close. I think, this is maybe the end, maybe death is finally come. I'm glad. My arm and my back hurt, my mouth is again as large as the world, and there's someone here in the darkness I need to meet, who I need to be one with.

Through the pain of my thirsty mouth I say:

— Thank you.

Then there are anpil shouts and screams. I think some of them are in English, but most are Kreyòl. At least one sounds like a woman's voice. I wonder if this is the land under the sea where the dead go, and if I'm gonna meet my sister there.

But suddenly I smell something other than my sweat and blood. I can smell the outside, I can smell the real sea, far off.

I open my eyes.

I see people looking down at me, with wide smiles on their faces. There's the sharp jaw of some kind of digger above me; it looks like a dinosaur looming above me, and I'm afraid of its teeth.

Someone's crawling over the concrete toward me. Then hands are on me, lifting me up, touching me as if for luck.

Something unties itself inside me and floats loose. At the same time, something takes root inside me, or someone, I should say, cos I feel . . . I don't know, but I feel that it's the person who was in the dark with me, the person who was dying with me in the dark. I know deep down who it is, but I can't say it even to my ownself, cos it's insane.

I can read, I think. And I have feelings and a soul in my chest, and I can talk and laugh and cry just like a real person, and I'm capable of doing good things. I've fucked up in the past, oh yes, I know I have, but, Manman, I'll try to make you proud.

I wonder again if Manman is still alive. I'd like to see her; I'd like to tell her I'm sorry, that I forgive her. Cos I understand, I really do. I understand why she did what she did, why she

331

told me Marguerite was alive – it was to spare me that pain. She knew what Marguerite was to me, that she was one half of myself.

I'd like to accept from Manman the half of the necklace that she took from Marguerite, so I can wear both halves together, so she can see that I'm whole now, no longer half a person. I'd like to be hugged by her, to know that she will always be there, no matter what I've done. I'd like to know that she forgives me, too, as I forgive her.

But this isn't gonna happen.

Manman is gone. She must be gone. I saw the way everything was destroyed.

Some of the rescuers, or whoever they are, they're trying to talk to me. I can't speak, though, not yet. I'm aware of people moving the stuff that's weighing me down, then hands catch me under the armpits and lift me up, and I'm over someone's shoulder and I'm being jolted as they carry me through the rubble. It's still dark here, we're still inside, or at least we're still under all the stuff that fell and broke.

— Wait, says one of the blancs in French.

— What?

— There are a lot of people out there. They've been holding vigils for days. If we don't prepare them, there'll be a riot. They'll see one boy and think there are more.

— Hmmm, says the first voice.

I'm set down on the rubble, still in the hospital, and I see the man who was holding me start to go out into the light.

Suddenly, I lose my shit. I don't mean to, it just happens. I feel something snap inside me. I want to go with him, you see. I don't want to be left behind in the darkness anymore. I start to scream and cry. My face is all wet. It's seriously embarrassing.

So, the guy turns around and comes back to me. He bends down close. He says:

— Rete trankil, p'tit, rete trankil.

Maybe it's cos he's telling me to calm down in Kreyòl, maybe it's cos he's been kind enough to use my own language, or maybe it's the way he bent down so gently, so sympathetic, I don't know, but the important thing is I stop screaming. I manage to nod at him, like, OK, you go and come back for me.

— Bon, he says. Bon.

Then he really does go into the light, and he leaves me here. I want to follow him so bad. There's, like, a glow of white around him, like the fuzz around the sun. When he properly leaves the inside and goes outside it's like he just disappears, burns away into light. It makes me think of Marguerite, the way her frizzy hair merged into the daylight, the way you couldn't see where she ended and the hot blur of the sun began.

From the stunning whiteness into which he's vanished, I hear the blanc say:

— We've dug out one boy.

He puts a stress on *one*. I hear a couple of people make sharp sounds of happiness, but anpil more people cry and wail. I guess a lot of them are there waiting for people who aren't boys – people who're still under the rubble.

— He's a teenage boy, about fifteen. We're bringing him out. We've found no other survivors.

More crying now.

When the blanc comes back and picks me up again and walks us forward, I see the people who've started to rush into the building, the ones that the police and the blancs haven't been able to hold back. Some are whooping with joy and some are crying. I see Haitians crouching with their hands over their mouths, tears running down their cheeks.

— Is anyone else alive in there? one of them asks. Did you hear anyone?

— No, I say. There's no one.

There was, though.

There was someone else, but he's me now.

The man carrying me stops to get his breath. We're still inside, just. I'm gazing around me cos everywhere is twisted iron and shattered concrete, and I realize we're in the lobby of the hospital when I see the broken glass from the front windows all over the tiled floor. There are anpil blancs here, too, in red helmets; I think maybe they're firemen. I can just see through the hole where the doors were, and I perceive that the whole city has fallen down, that there's only rubble out there, only trash. As I look round I see that I *did* float above the hospital, that the country really has been ruined, that everything I saw is true.

I feel tears coming down my cheeks. Manman, she can't be alive, surely? But I'm alive. I'm alive, and I know I'll look for her and maybe I'll find her. I let my hand open and my

334

half of the necklace falls to the ground; I don't need it to be complete anymore, and so I leave it there among the other broken things.

It's strange. I do this, and an image appears in my head. It's the mural on the next street, the one on the morgue, of the girl being raised up to heaven, an angel's hands under her. Only now, the face of the girl is Marguerite's, the girl is Marguerite. There's the sharp hotness of tears at the corners of my eyes, cos that's what I want: I want her to be taken, to be held, to be embraced.

One of the blancs says:

— You're very lucky, you know.

And I think, no, I'm not. Everything that matters to me is dead. Even this country is dead.

These blancs, they look very proud, though, so I try to smile, cos I know how much they love to help, how much they're always helping, how they can't just mind their own zafè and keep off our island. Look where their help got us; look at the mess we're in . . .

But no, I can't hate them, cos there's a woman in front of me: she's shining a torch in my eyes, she's using a bottle to drip water into my mouth – it tastes like everything good in the world – mangoes, bananas – and she has this T-shirt on, it says, *Médecins Sans Frontières*. This woman, she's got blonde hair and blue eyes, fine blonde down on her ears. She's the woman who took the baby from Marguerite all those years ago. She's been here ever since, or she came back, I don't know. But I don't think she recognizes me. I understand, I don't blame her for it, cos I'm covered in dust and dirt; I'm a dead person dug up and brought out into the light. So I just say to her what I wanted to say all those years ago.

I say:

— Your hair is amazing.

I say:

— Your ears are the most beautiful thing I've ever seen.

And she looks at me, like, what the fuck?

Then I hear this noise; it's a noise I know so well, a voice I know so well. And I'm pushing past this woman, even though I love her, even though I love everyone here. Seriously, it's like my whole heart is this shining ball of love in my chest, beating like the sun, a hammer that builds and doesn't destroy.

And then . . .

And then . . .

And then I'm moving somehow, limping, following that voice. She must have heard when the blanc said that they dug out a boy; she must have been one of the people waiting, one of the people holding a vigil. I'm stumbling through the broken glass to the ragged hole and finally I'm in the open air and it fills my lungs and there's a blue sky above and we're in the light now, burning our eyes, tears streaming down our face, and I look over the road and . . .

. . .

. . . My breath stops in my chest, cos there's my manman, screaming and screaming. But they're not bad screams; they're screams of joy. Then she's running toward me and she grabs me, she swings me up, and she's hugging me and hugging me.

And it's OK, it's good, it's OK to touch me, cos I'm not Marguerite, I'm not Tintin; I have skin covering my body. I don't have holes in me anymore. I'm whole and I have a soul entire inside me. I've lived and died so many times for this country, and there's nothing that can get in and hurt me.

And I say:

— Manman. Manman, I love you. I kept shooting and I made a goal, but I'm not gonna shoot no more.

And she's saying words all the time, too. Words like, love, my boy, love, words of fierceness, words of joy, love, love, love.

I think, yes, I was a zombi all along. I should not have been afraid to be a zombi, though, cos . . .

Yes, I died, over and over.

But now I've been reborn.

Yes . . .

Yes . . .

Yes . . .

I was in darkness, but now I am in light.

AUTHOR'S NOTE

This is a work of fiction. While I researched this book, I am a novelist, not an expert on Haiti, and any errors are mine alone. I occasionally simplified and adjusted the facts to fit into the shape of the story. I suspect, however, that anyone reading *In Darkness* will be curious as to how much in it is true and how much is made up. The simple answer is that I believe that the book is true in essence. If you were hoping that some of the more unpleasant things you have just read were made up, then I apologize.

I did not invent the character of Toussaint l'Ouverture, and I have been faithful to his story, at least in spirit and in essentials. It was necessary to smooth out the history to some extent. For example, in this book I have ignored the issue of the Spanish side of the island (the modern-day Dominican Republic), with which Toussaint had a complicated relationship. However, the important things are true. Toussaint really did lead a slave rebellion at the age of fifty-four, defeating a major colonial power and freeing his people, even if only temporarily. He was a simple, uneducated man who achieved one of the greatest and least acknowledged military victories of all time. His character was, as far as we know, calm, wise, inspirational. He was betrayed in the way presented in this story, and he really did die in a French dungeon.

The ceremony at Bois Caiman did happen, though not much is known about it, and I have embellished the details for my own purposes. In reality, it was most likely an invocation of Erzili Danto, one of the most important of the lwa, to support the rebellion.

Shorty never lived, nor did his family. But Route 9 and Boston – and the war between them – are real, as is nearly every detail of life in Site Solèy. It is one of the poorest, most violent slums in existence, even more so now in the wake of the 2010 earthquake. It has frequently been named as the most dangerous place on earth. People really did, and do, eat pies made of mud, such is their desperation. Babies really were, and are, left to die on piles of trash. For years, the slum was virtually cut off by roadblocks and, especially during the bloody period in the first decade of the new century, the police and attachés were accused many times of shooting unarmed civilians during demonstrations and home invasions. Many residents simply disappeared, never to be seen again.

Dread Wilmè was a real person. He lived and died in much the way I have described: hailed as a hero by his supporters, who claimed that he provided security, education, and rudimentary health care in a place where the government

340

provided none; vilified by the government as a gangster and a murderer. The truth, as always, is probably somewhere in between. Fierce controversy surrounds his killing to this day, and in particular surrounds the question of how many civilians were killed during the operation. His funeral was a lavish affair, attended by thousands and marked by speeches. As far as I know, it unfolded more or less as described, with Dread being pushed out to sea on a burning boat.

Finally, no work of fiction is an island, even a book that is set on one. I would like to thank Caradoc King, Louise Lamont, Elinor Cooper, David Fickling, Sarah Odedina, and Madeleine Stevens for all their help in constructing this story.

And I would like to thank you, too, for reading it.

Nick Lake
Oxford, 2011

For more information about Nick Lake and his astonishing novel, including an author interview and a reading guide, visit **www.in-darkness.org**